MW00685892

Winner of the 2013
Kenneth Patchen Award
for Innovative Fiction

OPPRESSION FOR THE HEAVEN OF IT

MOORE BOWEN

Journal of Experimental Fiction 51

JEF Books/Depth Charge Publishing
Geneva, Illinois

Copyright © 2013 by Moore Bowen
All rights reserved

Cover and interior art by Moonway

Kenneth Patchen Award Widget
designed by Michael J. Seidlinger

ISBN 1-884097-51-0
ISBN-13 978-1-884097-51-5
ISSN 1084-547X

JEF Books/Depth Charge Publishing
The foremost in innovative fiction
http://experimentalfiction.com

OPPRESSION FOR THE HEAVEN OF IT

MOORE BOWEN

Dedication

To my children and grandchildren for bringing joy and for keeping us focused on the future.

And to all those with serious and chronic mental illnesses and their families who struggle all their lives to find adequate care and to cope with the effects of stigma.

Contents

Prologue   3

I. *Innocence and Experience*   8

II. The Great Flipped Blip   55

III. Psyche and Corrections   163

IV. The Presence of the Past   223

V. He Wore this World like a Loose Garment   251

Epilogue   265

Acknowledgements   268

About the Author   269

Prologue

I see him everywhere I go. Suddenly without him being on my mind at all, I will see him in the back of a head at a concert, in a gesture across a room, in a particular build and walk ahead of me on the street. Moonway is short, about 5' 4." His frame is stocky, and sparsely fleshed with a large head and broad shoulders. He has blonde wavy hair half way to his shoulders and a reddish blonde beard which he twirls between thumb and index finger when he is in a thoughtful mood. He has thick curly blonde lashes. He is near sighted and wears wire frame glasses over pale blue eyes. As an infant, those eyes gave him a knowing and worldly wise look. His pupils are dilated from thorazine.

When high on pot, his talk is peppered thickly with vivid, private, and highly symbolic images as well as familiar cultural ones. Good is Christ and self-sacrificial blood. Evil is the familiar horned Satan. He is taking a voyage on a ship, he says. He is charting his own course and steering his own ship; and, because he is an inexperienced navigator and captain on rough and stormy seas, the voyage is chaotic. He is still afloat.

I wrote the above in my journal in August, 1976. Diagnosed with paranoid schizophrenia in April of that year, my son, Moonway Michael, has been disabled ever since, but he still maintains an identity of himself as the artist and writer he was becoming when first diagnosed. In spite of barriers imposed by the disease, Moonway still works as hard at these activities as most people work on jobs or careers and harder than many. Like most people, he yearns to have his work recognized, understood, and respected.

Writing is also one of the things I do. Among other

rewards, it is therapeutic. It often gives me a sense of constructing coherence, harmony, even a kind of beauty, out of chaos and distress. In writing, I can lose myself in a most pleasant way, even when writing about myself. Is this what T. S. Eliot meant when he said writing is "an escape from personality?" Additionally, in writing I can communicate important contents of my inner life that I find impossible to talk about in much depth, often that I am not even aware of until I have written it.

Thinking about all this, I asked Moonway if he would like to collaborate with me on a book about his schizophrenia. He at first said <u>no</u> but then changed his mind after a few days and threw himself into the project.

We taped conversations throughout the year of 2001. I researched old letters and journals I had saved and some of the mountainous medical and legal records that have accumulated, and I started composing this book. We began this in the dead of winter. Ordinarily a bad time for Moonway, this winter proved to be an especially hard time for him. He was "decompensating," psychiatric jargon for "relapse," in a way that had his treatment team very worried about extreme social isolation, poor medication compliance, socially unacceptable hygiene, insomnia, disturbing neighbors with his noise. I worried that the writing project was stirring up too much emotion and causing the greater-than-ordinary winter distress. But his enjoyment was so obvious and so great that I could not slow it down.

Schizophrenia is a disease that, by definition, produces disordered thinking, poor concentration, poor judgment, memory problems that result in problems taking medication and keeping appointments, and all the other difficulties that so many patients experience in complying with treatment. But, while working on this book, Moonway never missed a taping session, could focus for longer hours than I could, often won me over to his judgment when we disagreed as he did when I asked him, Why do you want the title to be *Oppression for the Heaven of It?*

Well, he said, the modern churches are being crucified as cults by the Orthodox Church and red terrorism. I think the modern church should flourish and come into its own: Moon, Karesh, Jones. Oppressing the orthodoxy and domestic reds. There's a lot of domestic reds that get their kicks crucifying Christian mental patients, you know? Martyring us. And the orthodox religion does the same thing. That's true, Mom. It thrills them. Richard up here at the Help Line, he does it. Crucifies me. Literally. On purpose. Word got around I got these CIA parts and wires in me. They produce counter conspiracies. They phone each other, link up with the CIA or FBI, U. S. marshals, police, psychiatry, APA, "American Psychiatric Association."

They conspire against me—not running these parts and wires I got all through me right. Or getting them run so they're snuffing me. Murdering me. The charge is attempted murder. Oppression for the Heaven of It. Oppressing back. Oppression and revenge. Crucifying back. Martyring back. No matter what color or sex.

Hmm. That is your idea of Heaven, but it's not mine. Tell me if you would accept my misreading of your title? *Passion for the Heaven of It?* or *Just for the Heaven of It?*"

How about we compromise? *Oppression and Passion for the Heaven of It.* OK?

It's getting a little bulky.

Well, whatever you want to call it. Do a service to your generation, calling it *Passion for the Heaven of It.* Wouldn't it? I wouldn't be crucifying religion or psychiatry that way either.

I was thinking about the passions involved in this book, the passions of mental illness in addition to revenge, terror, rage. Any that you enjoy about your schizophrenia?

No. Not at all. Tortures the mind. Comes from stereotyping and video typing in the profession and among the populace. It blinds the eyes when you get fascinated with hallucinations. So, no. I used to lay there and stare at the wood paneling until my eyes just hurt. I was so fascinated by contacting the dead through the paneling. LSD is more merciful than sober hallucinations if you want the truth. Nothing beats dope, Mom. Not God, not the church, not Satan. Anything better than being high on dope? My passion lately is money. M-o-n-e-y. Moola. Cashola. Payola. Money. Greenback.

Yeah, I think I understand. You don't have much money. You get high on Christ? And God? Or used to?

Prayer (I have taken the vows of chastity concerning money though). And when I hear from the damning God, protective of me, the all-damning Almighty saying he is going to damn Mark Sargent, Northridge Police Chief, to Hell unless he leaves me alone. When I hear from him, the cruel God, the dictator God. I like that. God will tell me to do something sometimes, change a sign, change a page, do some jotting or writing, and I do it. I know it is God, Mom. I'm positive. No apologies. But nothing tops dope. Christ and dope, folks.

I was about 14 or 15 when I started. I liked that Columbian Gold, I tell you, better than red. Dope don't do me much good, though, does it, Mom? No, it don't. Just dries my eyes out, makes me hallucinate. I keep looking for excuses to use, though. In AA. In the media. Grudges that won't clear up. That's why *Oppression for the Heaven of It*, right? Women and colored oppress, too, Mom, my mother, Belinda Adams, don't they?

Yes, Moonway. People who are oppressed often become oppressors if they get power. That's right.

But they're not as oppressive as the people that oppressed them.

Some aren't; some may become saints. Or comedians. But many victims become oppressors.

Especially that nigger Luther. Wasn't he a hot head?

Martin Luther King? Yes, he was passionate about his cause and justice. But I can't see him as an oppressor. He is one of my heroes. More like one of the saints, though not perfect. None of us are. I wish you wouldn't call him a nigger.

My heroes are Janis Joplin, Charles Manson, Adolph Hitler, Karl Marx. Psychiatry in Resistance Corporation, PIRCing people, Mom.

This talk has certainly given me a better understanding of your passions about the title. I think I can work with your version.

I

Innocence and Experience

I must have died and been brought back to life, Mom.
Went to Hell. Went to Heaven.
Went to the Universe.

1. Asylumite Misfits since the Beginning of Time

Moonway's abiding concerns are central identity questions: Who am I? Where do I come from? Where am I going? What is my purpose and place in the universe, and how do I fit in? What is reality and how do I know it? These are the human questions we all ask in our separate ways as we contemplate ourselves and others, birth and death, nature and the stars. Schizophrenia most often strikes at a time of critical transition into adulthood, a time when many relationship issues with family, sex, and society are fermenting. Moonway's talk is riddled with references to these still-unresolved issues: extreme confusion about family ancestry, family trauma, who he really is, who his real family is, and what has been done to him. He challenges me and my perceptions of reality with questions about these issues.

I met with Moonway for a taping session at his apartment. Just as his case manager, Eleanor, had told me on the phone, the kitchen was filthy and stinking—garbage overflowing its bin and littering the floor, sour smell from empty gallon milk jugs scattered over the counter top, dirty dishes piled in the sink. I said, I better do some cleaning before we start taping.

No, Mom, leave that for the cleaning lady.

The cleaning lady was here last week, and Eleanor said you didn't let her in. It would make Eleanor feel better if I cleaned it up some.

Could we tape while you're cleaning?

So I turned on the tape recorder and started to clean a space in the sink.

What's on your mind, today, Moonway?

Well, I'd like to pay attention to the relatives on your side of the family while maintaining maximum support for Dad. Are we a family of asylumite misfits? People that have been ushered out by stereotypes and videotypes for psychiatric documentation since the beginning of time?

We have a lot of illnesses in our family. Did I tell you about Aunt June, Daddy's sister? She had schizophrenia.

You didn't mention the schizo part.

Here, I stopped the tape to check the reception. I was making too much noise at the sink, so I said, Let's go into the living room for taping, and I'll clean later. There, tobacco smoke overpowered all other smells.

So, Moonway, we were talking about Aunt June. Except for brief periods, she lived most of her life on the family farm, with Mama and Daddy after they got married. Mama told me about her: "I liked June. She was good to me even though she treated me like a little kid. I didn't like that. I figured I was all grown up at thirteen when I married James. But she was so nice I didn't mind it much. She was a good seamstress and she made me pretty dresses. It's funny, she never made a dress for herself. She would patch up James's old overalls and cut off the legs so they would be shorter. She mostly lived in his old clothes. I never could understand. She had beautiful hair. She always worked at the potato harvest in the fall and earned fairly good money. We never knew what she did with it because she never bought anything for herself."

What June did with her money remains a mystery to this day. There was speculation that we could find it if we knew where to look. There might even have been some attempt to remove some of the stair steps and see if she might have slipped it in under them. I have wondered if she might have tried to help pay Daddy's medical expenses from Scarlet Fever without ever telling anyone.

Daddy was so sick the doctor didn't understand how he could live, high fevers for weeks and deep abscesses. One in his hip left him crippled with a short leg. He couldn't walk at all for several years. Mama said he would get his brother to come down and lift him to the floor, and he would struggle and struggle just to turn over. Finally he did learn to walk with a crutch, to garden, to hunt, and to cut wood.

I asked Aunt Phyllis what it was that motivated him to learn to walk when it was so difficult for him that he wouldn't try for a long time. She said, "He got your mother pregnant. He wasn't too crippled for that."

June stayed through all that and was a big help. She stayed until a couple of years after your Aunt Myra was born.

She helped take care of Myra and paid a lot of attention to her. Then she got very sick. I never heard anyone call it <u>schizophrenia</u>, but I believe it was. Mama said she tried to chew up the bed sheets. Finally, at Daddy's insistence, her sisters, Phyllis and Barbara, came up to take her away. Although Daddy told them they had to watch her carefully, they didn't want to believe she was mentally ill, and, at some point, they put her in a second story bedroom to sleep. She opened the window and jumped out.

Suicide or just to go out?

I don't know.

Probably just to go out? What did they do, lock her in her room or something?

I don't know those details. She spent the last years of her life—maybe eight to ten years—paralyzed in a psychiatric hospital. It might have been the one that is now State Mental Health Institute, SMHI, where you were.

Though she was gone by the time I was born, and I didn't know her, her sickness was a shadow, among others, over our childhood. Myra felt abandoned. She has felt great sadness all her life about Aunt June. Mama too. And maybe Daddy, but he never showed sadness. He would just get mad, rage and yell at anyone around—mostly Mama and us kids—or the machines. And he sometimes beat the animals. In his rages, he was insane. Maybe everyone in the throes of an uncontrollable rage is insane. So we call mental illness <u>madness</u>.

Mom, I think we're German right? On the Adams' side. That's just my theory. But I think we've been hounded by the allies, a lot of German, Japanese, and Italian kids since WWII and the Proxy wars. Spied on, snooped on, blacklisted. You don't believe me, do you?

I don't believe that happened.

They're trying to cover it up by calling it child abuse. I don't know what's happening to the infants beyond my generation in that aspect. They must be going through Hell. Heil Hitler. Ha. None of it happened to you guys, probably. I bet that's it, the missing link. That didn't happen to you guys. It's happening to us.

I wrote to Senator Page, documenting it. Kind of gross to tell you. And she's putting it under wraps and key, not getting it out there. There's a big hush on it. I documented all the Nazi hungers that went on. I sent letters to her. All the suffering that goes on in those mental institutions.

I could tell you a story about the Nazis, Moonway. Maybe it's related in some social way to your belief about Nazis. One of my favorite people from my early, early childhood was the Congregational minister who used to come to Greenville and do church services and bible school in the little school house. I was about 4 years old. He carried me around on his shoulders. There wasn't much affection in my family, they didn't believe in it back then, and I was enthralled to be getting that kind of attention. Looking at the world from up there, I felt protected and paradoxically powerful. He was run out of town, 1942, middle of the war. I heard from gossip that it was because he was German or of German descent, and they accused him of being Nazi or a sympathizer.

I also heard stories about a local chapter of the KKK to which some of our distant relatives belonged, and my father always said they should have let Hitler exterminate the communists. That and other sorts of bigotry were often voiced in the family and in the area. I remember first becoming aware of it as bigotry in the early fifties when I was a freshman in high school, and Senator Joseph McCarthy was a hero to many in the area, Daddy included. I had a history teacher who was fired when I was a freshman for bringing a copy of the *Daily Worker* into the classroom. I had gotten to know and like him. He and his wife befriended me. That turned me into a radical liberal at thirteen.

Moonway, the culture you were born into was not recovered from the national paranoia created during the wars, both hot and cold of the century. By the time you came along, there were all the issues of racism and civil protest of the sixties including KKK and Neo-Nazi activity that you must have seen on TV. We still haven't recovered. Is all this the relevant social environment that provides symbolism for mental illness for our generation? For you?

I'm pleading the Kansas City Cable defense here. ACLU. This is just a legal entry. Maybe we should bring some lawyer's names in here, Mom. It pays to have lawyers on your side. There were three uncles on your side that were in the military and three uncles on Dad's side that were in the military, right?

All four of my brothers were in the military. None in combat.

Yeah. Four on Dad's side too. Eight. I'm a real Napoleon, ain't I? Real Lieutenant General. Ha, ha.

They pretty much all went to the military in that generation. Especially rural men, when they finished or quit high school. It was like a rite of passage in the fifties in our area.

Was Grampy Adams in the military, Mama?

No. He must have been the right age for the First World War. I'm not sure why he didn't go, but I have a vague memory or hunch that it had to do with farming and having his aging parents and a sister to care for. He was needed on the farm. He was crippled and too old for the second war.

Just a minute, Mom. All lawyers, all, and all advocates, all, and *Madness Network News*, all—I'm pre-pleading the 5th amendment. Mom, was Hitler still-born like you say in one of your poems during the barn fire, "He came still-born?"

Hitler was not still-born. He lived through his birth and childhood and probable adult insanity to become an emblem of evil with the holocaust. If he had been treated with Thorazine, Haldol, or Clozaril, would the Holocaust have been prevented? Or would someone else have assumed the leadership of that terrible time? That is a futile question but one that makes me think about how to treat the cultural insanity that goes undiagnosed and untreated. My poem "Fire" was inspired in part by one of my brothers who was still-born.

Fire

I wash her belly, shriveled

13

by disease, mapped by old stretch marks,
marks of a brother I never saw,

nameless and graveless too
for all I knew. White jags
in the skin catch the light

and glisten with water, like
lightning. It strikes
often there where we grew up.

There are scars: a collection
of blown radio tubes, a hole
in the freezer lid, a dent

in the iron stake a cow was chained to.
She was seven months gone
when it hit the barn. I heard

from stories. Father woke
at the crack, saw the exploding
glow, struggled to rise.

Fogged with sleep, he forgot
he couldn't walk, remembered,
cursed. Mother—alert before he spoke

to his cause—was already
out of bed, hurrying, balloon-
bellied and barefoot. No long talk

there. A music of curses and grunts
and action. Keeping time
with crackling flames and screaming

horses, she reached the barn
and pulled the bar back and saw
the pair, neighing and prancing,

lit by the flame, flame dancing
in their eyes. She stared,
struck, and struck again

inside out, my unknown brother
dancing. She grabbed a halter.
She loved to dance. Grace-

ful, she haltered and led.
She went back for the mate
and led her out, but they always return,

and there were cows, pigs, chickens.
She went back. She led until
neighbors came to drag her

away. They all returned
to the flames. He came, still-
born. I trace the scars.

He died?
Yes. He was born dead.
What was his name?
I don't think any of my four lost brothers were named.
All of them were born before me. I don't even know how or
where they were buried.
Was Hitler a psychiatric experiment? Should
psychiatry assume responsibility for him?
I believe he conducted psychiatric experiments as part
of his racial purity plans, but I would have to research it to
know the details. We are, in a way, all experiments, aren't
we? Psychological as well as physical. Nature is the great
experimenter, and nature is impersonal, doesn't assume
human-like responsibility for anything. Freud was a
contemporary of Hitler, and that period was a very active one
for psychiatry, perhaps the birth of it as a discipline. I don't
know that I am responding to what you asked because I don't
really understand your question about Hitler.

15

Loaded, hunh? Ha, ha.

Are you asking loaded questions?

They're not loaded. You ask lots of loaded questions. It's curiosity and things I suspect. What was your perspective on my childhood? Were there Nazi hunters involved, Mom?

No.

German hunters?

No, no hunters, except my father and brothers and neighbors who hunted deer.

Probably just bounty hunters, hunh? That deer meat we had last week is tasty.

No, no bounty hunters. The deer meat is all gone except for some mincemeat I made. Hitler and World War II made a profound impact on everyone who lived through it. On the Morris side of the family, Uncle Paul went to Germany. He and Aunt Annie, Mama's siblings, both had bipolar disorder. Her sister, my Aunt Margaret, would say, "Now Annie we're going into that store, and don't you go dancing in the aisles and singing and praising the Lord." Her brother Uncle Dan was the most successful at subduing her. He would take her aside once in a while to have a talk with her in private. She would often be fairly calm for days after one of his talks. Once she packed up and went home.

The more manicy she became, the more her rage would come out, and she would start denouncing in loud tones all the objects of her prejudice: homosexuality and other sexual "abnormalities" were favorite targets. She was very judgmental, would sometimes say cruel things about and to people. She loved to gossip and often told embarrassing personal secrets. I finally confronted her about this when she was telling one to a ten-year old in the family, the one about catching her sister, Aunt Barbara, making out in the barn with a married uncle on the other side of the family. I asked her to stop repeating that gossip to kids. She was apologetic to me, but in her talk to others I became "that woman" who inhibited her freedom. She was hurt by limits people put on her self-expression. I don't like it when people do that to me, either.

She could be fun with her zany energy, dancing and playing her mouth organ, but any attention just inspired greater manic activity, and she would eventually lose her audience, or people would laugh at her instead of with her. By the end of the summer, she would begin to burn out and go home to Connecticut where she crashed into depression through the winter.

I have only seen her a few times in her depressed moods when she is very quiet and withdrawn, doesn't talk to anyone, seems like it is a big effort even to try to smile or to acknowledge a greeting. In these times, she seems very sad, like she is aware of the whole of human tragedy and is grieving over it. But maybe she is just mourning her own personal losses.

When her house burned down, and she lost everything, she moved with her severely alcoholic son into a motel across the street. Now, she eats at the MacDonald's nearby, and worries her family by the poor conditions she lives in. Some relatives and Adult Protective Services have tried to intervene. But mother and son refuse to budge from this location.

Uncle Paul, Aunt Jenny's brother, was diagnosed and began treatment in his middle age. He, too, came up to the farm house to stay in the early years of his sickness. They both seemed to want to return home, like they were looking for salvation there. Daddy had died by then, and the farm place where Mama still lived at that time was the closest thing to their childhood home they had left. Paul spent several years there off and on. He didn't do as well as Annie at taking care of himself. And he was far less social and public in his manic times. Instead he paced the rooms and halls of the house all night, muttering to himself. Or he went out in the middle of the night in the dead of winter to tramp around the woods roads above home and cut wood for the stove.

Then he would get depressed and crash on the sofa dozing with the TV on. His daughter came to get him one of these times when he was not taking care of himself at all. She said he had worn out two sofas at her house before he came up to the farm. One winter he didn't keep the fire going, and the pipes all froze up.

I was afraid of him when he was manicy and afraid for

him when he was depressed. Eventually at the family's intervention, mainly your Aunt Myra and me, he checked himself into the VA hospital and became a permanent ward of their care. When not hospitalized, he lived in group homes or halfway houses the rest of his life. Long term, he seemed to be happier with that arrangement. I want to think he liked the security of being cared for. But at the time I didn't feel that way.

I visited Uncle Paul at the VA Hospital one afternoon in December 1975, this huge building—there were two of them—filled with men muttering to themselves, shuffling repetitively, hands and faces gesturing to an unseen audience, and attendants and nurses hard to find and few. Due to overcrowding, Paul's bed was in the corridor. He was confined to his ward. He looked about 90. His eyes, even when looking directly at me were far away and vacant. He told me before I took the steps necessary to have him taken back to the hospital that it was awful there. It was worse than awful. And I wouldn't do anything to get him out; I didn't want to be responsible.

He didn't get well, but he did improve enough to spend many of his remaining years in a group home. Remember when we took him down there? You rode down with me, and he talked all the way.

Yeah, I remember. I liked talking to him. War veteran, wasn't he?

Yes. I think he was in combat. There is another story there, too, that may be relevant to his later problems with depression. When he left for Germany, he was recently married, no kids. When he came back four or five years later, she had four babies, supposedly fathered by her step father. Paul said, "I wanted to kill him." Instead, he apparently did the best he could to provide for the kids. I think he didn't get seriously ill until after they were all mostly adults. Who can tell how much the rage and grief of that time affected his brain? Post Traumatic Stress they call it now. He died several years ago, over 75.

Did he smoke cigarettes?

Yeah.

I'll live long then, won't I? I'm taking another suicidal puff to truce with the Indians right now. Pact with the tobacco lords. Ha, ha.

I don't know if he could have lived as long as he did if he hadn't gone to the hospital when he did where he got regular meals, medical and mental-health care.

Well, I'm out for good, now. I'm staying out in freedom. I don't want to check in to those places any more or be put in them. They're not fun, Mom.

I know, Moonway, you did not like your experience with them. Both my parents were teetotalers, but there is alcoholism in the family, too, that contributes its stresses. When I was about two, my grandfather, the father of Paul and Annie and Mama, was killed by a train on the railroad track, likely passed out from alcohol according to neighbors' stories, but Mama always said it must have been sunstroke. The sisters liked to speculate about what was in the bag someone saw him carrying that day. Mama said it was probably candy for the kids. Neighbors said it was likely booze. And Uncle Dan's wife told me that he knew it was alcohol.

Aunt Barbara abused alcohol and died with liver cancer. I got to know her when she came from her home in Idaho to live one year with us. She was quite a character, liked male attention as much as booze, too much, and got into trouble with it, was jailed for "alienation of affection" over that man Aunt Jenny caught her with, later lost her first husband and custody of her only child because of it. I liked her a lot. Others in the family on Mama's side have had trouble with alcohol abuse.

Yes, Moonway, we probably are a family of asylumite misfits since the beginning of time.

But not only in our family. There were others in Greenville. A distant relative a few miles down the road from the family farm, has had problems all her life, off and on, but remained able to take care of herself most of the time, with occasional help from electroshock treatments. In her eighties now and living by herself, she recently had surgery, and the social worker tried to set her up with Meals on Wheels, but she wouldn't make out the paper work. I don't know how she took care of her children, but she still takes care of herself, not necessarily to the satisfaction of those who try to care for her. She manages her money, goes to church, has some social life. Seems like she causes more distress to the people trying to care for her than to herself.

And there was a woman lived across the road, no relation at all as far as I know, had to be taken away to SMHI way back in the forties. I believe she had schizophrenia, too. Your Aunt Myra told me a story she remembered: Mama was standing at the window one time talking to the farm workers when they came up for water at the pump. Maria screamed from her upstairs window, "You stop talking about me." She ran down her stairs, out her door, across the road and into our house; and she attacked Mama. Daddy tried to reason with her, but it was no good. He finally dragged her out the door by the hair of her head. Crippled as he was, it must have been difficult for him. The police came afterward and talked to him about the incident. Were they trying to find out if his action was justified, or if she was safe to live in her house? Eventually, they took her away, and she never returned, likely institutionalized for life.

Mama, don't you think I'm making a lot of progress in the last twenty years. Haven't been violent since '82 or '81.

Yes, I do, Moonway. Especially these last years since you were last at The Medical Center for Federal Prisoners in Missouri, MCFP you call it. You seem to be mellowing out, too, for longer periods, not so intensely angry. Do you feel happier?

Yeah. Except I wish the CIA would unseal my nostrils and emotions.

I think you are better with your emotions in many ways. Expressing affection and caring, managing your anger better.

I think I remember watching them take Maria away in an ambulance. But, after hearing about it so often, I'm not sure if it's memory or imagination. I was very young when this happened, the age of her youngest son. He was disabled by mental illness all his life, probably major depression, and perhaps retardation too.

All of that going on in the little hamlet I grew up in, Moonway, before you were even born.

Do you think that is a consequence of this raw environment here and the cold? We all have it, don't we?

I don't know that anybody knows for sure what all the causes of these illnesses are, but the environment must certainly play a role: poverty, trauma, accumulated stresses, unresolved emotional issues and relationship problems, tensions between social expectations and individual desires. At the NAMI convention (National Alliance for the Mentally Ill), Eric Kandel talked about how learning and trauma and all experience alter the structure and chemistry of the brain. Also genetics. I wonder, too, about the role of those mysterious faculties, personality and character, though it seems now politically incorrect to implicate them as causes of mental illness. No one has succeeded in finding a way to study them in a rigorous scientific way. Yet we all know, don't we, that character is a tremendously important feature of our psychology?

There were many physical illnesses in the family, too, that contribute to mental distress and likely to mental disease. Aunt Phyllis said June had a kidney disease that caused her mental illness. You were sick for a long time with nephritis when you were small. Daddy was crippled by scarlet fever. When they married, Mama was just under fourteen, less than a year out of the TB sanitarium where she had lived for three years. Her mother died not long after coming out of that same sanitarium against doctor's advice; she had TB and throat cancer, came home, she said, to take care of her family. But she died and left them to fend for themselves, two older brothers and four siblings younger than Mama.

My grandmother's illness was a major factor in Mama marrying Daddy. Before she died, my grandparents wanted to see one of their daughters settled in a good marriage. In coming so often to our farm house, it's almost like Annie and Paul were trying to live the promise that their parents hoped to give them when they gave Mama to Daddy in 1929. Daddy's sister, Aunt Phyllis said, "They sold her, that 13-year old girl, to a 38-year old man."

Reality, like literature, is full of ironies about people trying to control fate. My grandparents were hoping for help with caring for the family. But during Daddy's illness he lost all his financial assets. And Mama went through more life threatening diseases during her marriage: polio, cancer, injuries and illness from too-frequent childbearing, ten pregnancies in all before she had her fallopian tubes cut. Surely all that feeds into PTSD, probably produces it.

Mama, too, sometimes demonstrated a fragile hold on reality. When she heard about a dramatic event that caught her interest, she would frequently take ownership of it and repeat the story as though it happened to her. She also plagiarized. While selling strawberries that Daddy grew, she met a poet who befriended her and came to visit her occasionally for a few years. Mama started showing her copies of poems she said she was writing. She passed them around to friends and relatives. When she showed them to me, I believed she did write them; they were written in her hand in pencil. But I also had a funny feeling about them, so I didn't feel comfortable giving her the praise and encouragement she clearly wanted, and maybe needed.

Then, when I was cleaning at the farmhouse after Daddy died, I found a stash of poems clipped from *The Newburgh Daily News*. Many of them were the ones she was showing as her own. By then I had a great love and respect for literature and for the effort required to create it. For years I pondered over the right thing to do with her about those poems. I never confronted her directly about them. I didn't think the time was right when I found them, so soon after Daddy's death, and then there never did seem to be a good time. I never felt right not doing it, but I never got the sense that it would be good to do it either.

I may have gotten to know Mama better by that moral dilemma than I ever could have otherwise. Because I wanted to understand her, I started listening to her more. I actually became less judgmental and, I hope, more compassionate. And I began then to tell her when stories she told did not match my memory of the events she told about. I would say, "Mama, I don't remember it that way. I remember it this way." She would always say, "Oh I probably don't remember that right."

But I don't remember things accurately, either. I am very insecure about my ability to know reality, to remember what really happened in the past. And when I am disappointed, I often discover how out of touch with reality my wishes are and how much they control my mind and make me crazy sometimes.

Falling in love is definitely a state of insanity, you know? I have been crazy in love a couple of times in my life, positively delusional. And I have been crazy mad at being betrayed in love. Maybe we all have a tenuous hold on reality.

Mental disease and delusion are in the human family, Moonway, a fact of the human condition. But that is not all, is it? Nor is delusion necessarily an evil. From this distance, I remember a time of living in a delusion of a long future of loving and being loved as one of the happiest and most productive times of my life. Now, I am glad I had that time.

Also, there is much joy in reality in spite of all the deception and suffering. My role model for living in reality, Aunt Phyllis, never married and a nurse in her long professional life, was both witness of, and attendant to, all manner of human suffering. She talked often of things she had seen and helped with; I have some of her stories on tape. But she lived to be ninety-five years old, still taking pleasure in making quilts and picking wild strawberries to make preserves which she gave away. I believe one cannot live to be that old and stay that healthy without finding life full of value in spite of the suffering, even in an odd way, maybe, because of it.

Mama suffered through all her diseases, through abuse as well in her second marriage, and through her tenuous hold on reality. But she always loved to dance. She believed that after she died she would be literally dancing in a heaven on earth paved with streets of gold. All her life she danced as often as she could. After she got sick with her final cancer, she declared she wanted to die on the dance floor, and she almost did, going out dancing up to ten days before she died. She was well-prepared for the Heaven she believed in. For Mama, it was a place of unlimited earthly delight without suffering, a luxuriously rich place. Was her belief a delusion? What is a delusion but a belief we hold without substantial evidence from reality? Don't we all hold such beliefs? I like to think she was dancing in her morphine-fogged mind right up to the moment she died at age eighty-three.

Daddy, raging through so much of his life, quietly cultivated peonies and roses with tender care. When Mama was gone once to visit her sister in Florida, he hitchhiked the five miles to town to pick up letters from her. Then he would limp up the hill to our house in Greenville, the only times he ever spontaneously visited me in my married life. We would talk while I made lunch for us. You were a baby then; he bounced you on his knee and declared you a thorough-bred, the most affection I ever saw him show anyone. After lunch, I would drive him home.

He built that whole house up there in Greenville?

Yes. He designed it to replace the little house he grew up in, and he hired people to help him build it. That was before he married Mama. But already, he had visions of a prosperous farm and family life. Is it any wonder he was enraged by the ironic turn of events?

I think it's time to quit this tape for now. I'm too tired to clean after all that, will have to do it later.

Moonway, although all individuals are unique, in its broad psychological patterns, our family is not unique. Our sufferings are a cameo portrait of the human condition since the beginning of time—family feuds, war, environmental destruction, economic greed, dishonesty and corruption in all our institutions.

Both the sufferings and the joys can be a foundation for compassion and connection with others. It depends on what we do with them, how we interpret them, the meaning we make of them. Feed the hungry. Shelter the homeless. Paint a picture. Sing and dance. Write a book.

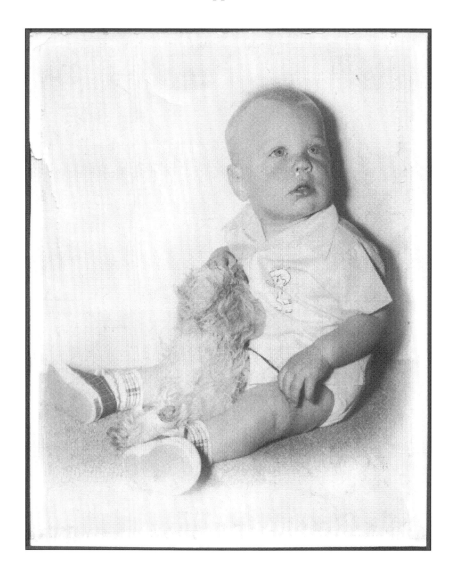

2. Gold Piping

Moonway was a sweet little boy, easy for people to love. Born September 18, 1956 after a short and very intense labor, he looked like a gnome. He was a big baby, eight pounds, thirteen ounces, and his head was squeezed into a

Moore Bowen

cone. His eyes were a startling and startled light blue. He had strawberry birthmarks on his nose and forehead that disappeared by the time he was about one. He blinked, stared at me, blinked some more, looked around.

I was eighteen, still childish myself in many respects; I had married nine months and two weeks before, and this was a pregnancy I planned practically from the time I agreed to marry. Giving birth is among the most profound emotional experiences of my life. High from ether and from the surge of hormones that comes with giving birth, and giddy with relief that the pain was over, I fell in love instantly. The accumulative effects of unresolved disappointments, traumas, and sorrows fall away at such times. It was a much more intense joy than falling in love with Richard which was accompanied by so many doubts and fears and, way before my commitment to live in reality, unrealistic expectations.

Moonway's first years gave me a great deal of pleasure in mothering. I loved cuddling, feeding, bathing, reading stories and poems, teaching, and learning from him about unbounded enthusiasm. A baby or toddler knows how to live in the moment and to experience everything passionately. I was astounded by everything he did. He talked young and became a story teller by the time he was two and a half. By the time he was four, he was a master of the language, I thought, and an artist, too. I've used one of the stories he told in my own writing. Is that plagiarism?

One hot day he talked all afternoon about building a giant bathtub to keep cool in. It had a fountain at the faucet end endlessly running clean water. He drew verbal pictures of an elaborate network of gold piping arching the tub. Like I imagine most children are, mine all wondered about the world in ways that reawakened a long-buried awe in me. One bright moonlit night, he asked his grandfather Martin Michael, "Grampy, if we had enough ladders and nailed them all together, could we climb to the moon?" He became a delightful companion.

Mothering him made me believe that mothering was my purpose in life, and I decided when he was only nine months old, to have another baby. I promptly became pregnant, and Martin was born when Moonway was eighteen months old. Their early relationship with each other was full of affection. I have memories of them playing in the back yard, arms frequently around each other. Moonway captured his father's heart, too, and Richard frequently took him hauling lumber before he was out of diapers, taking the entire care of him, sometimes for overnight. Moonway took great delight in pulling the chain to honk the truck's horn.

About the worst thing I can remember before his nephritis is the time he crawled behind the hot wood stove, and I was afraid he would burn himself. I was pregnant at the time for Martin and couldn't reach in far enough to get him. I grabbed the straw-bristled broom, the handiest thing I could find and tried to scoop him out with it. The bristles brushed down across his face and left scratches. I felt like an abusive mother.

I suppose there were other incidents like this, and I know I often felt exhausted and insecure about mothering. But mostly what I remember in detail are happy incidents of Moonway's infancy.

He often worries about his inability to remember these years in detail.

Mom, I bet I would remember more of my childhood if I moved back to Greenville. Probably that would fill me in. I bet Martin and Sis remember more. Sis because she lives there and Martin because he keeps going up there.

I don't know about Martin, but Shirley seems to remember way back, much further back than I do. She says she remembers having her diaper changed. I think most of us don't have much memory of the time before we were three or four. Memory seems to come with language, and then it is very selective and mixed up with wishes and passions, not very accurate.

I better do some cleaning in the kitchen. Eleanor says the housekeeper can't get here again this week. She is worried the housekeeper may give up on this job because it's too much for her.

Oh, Eleanor. She's a big fat nag. Don't worry about

her. She worries too much.

3. Did Armageddon Happen Already?

Just after I got pregnant for the third time, Moonway, four years old, became sick with Nephritis, a life threatening kidney disease. It started with a sore throat and a sudden high fever. Wanting to get him some attention fast, I called the closest doctor who had evening office hours. We took him there rather than waiting until the next day to consult our regular family doctor or driving the extra twenty miles to the emergency room. I can still see and hear that doctor—face red, voice halting and slow, breath smelling strongly of Listerine which covered the alcohol odor enough that I didn't pay attention to it at the time. He took Moonway's temperature and explained, "There's a bug going around. It's not serious." He gave us free samples of cold remedies.

Back then, I did not know the symptoms of strep throat nor the possible serious consequences of not treating it. We heard the gossip about this doctor's drinking, but I don't remember anyone ever questioning his competence as a doctor. Most people liked him. I was soon to discover that the information about strep throat was common medical knowledge at the time. He should have known. I should have known. The serious illness that followed could have been prevented by a throat culture and treatment with antibiotics. Moonway recovered from that sore throat, and I didn't think much more about it. We all looked forward to a new baby.

Several weeks later, standing on the couch naked after a bath, he looked bloated in the face and around his bottom. I took him to our regular family doctor. He quickly diagnosed Nephritis, the kidney inflammation commonly called Bright's Disease; Emily Dickinson died from it. He was hospitalized for a week or so and treated with medication, and he seemed to recover in a relatively short time.

I'm not sure I remember the exact timing of the relapses that followed, but I think it was several months later when I saw he was again swelling. When he was hospitalized this time, our family doctor consulted with the one pediatrician in the area. This hospitalization was longer and more difficult to treat. The medication became stronger, but eventually, Moonway seemed to recover again and came home with steroid medication to continue taking daily and a sodium-restricted diet. The pediatrician became his primary-care doctor.

One of the side effects of the medication was bloating. I became chronically concerned with his weight and diet, and it was difficult to tell if the bloating was from Nephritis or from the medicine. So it was a relief to take him to see his doctor every week with a urine sample. Simultaneously, it was a burden because of the distance to travel and finding care for Martin, but I don't seem to remember feeling the burden at the time.

We were told that Chicken Pox would be dangerous, maybe fatal, if he got it while on steroids. Not quite five years old, he started school in August of that year, but only went three weeks when he did get Chicken Pox. He was much sicker than most children with the disease, but he survived. However, the doctor decided he should not to go back to school because the threat of communicable diseases was too great. His immune system was being undermined by the medication as well as by the repeating attacks of Nephritis which caused him to lose albumin through his urine.

The new baby was born in mid-September. We named her Sheila, but Moonway started calling her Shirley right away, likely because of a little girl friend he had found in his three weeks in Kindergarten. The name has stuck to this day. I remember Shirley's infancy as a happy time for all of us. We had something of a four-month respite from the worst worries about Moonway's sickness in our attention to her. Both Moonway and Martin cuddled and kissed her and talked to her a great deal. We kept hoping he was getting better, and likely that hope sustained us.

Then he got sick for the third time. Each time he was hospitalized, the disease was getting progressively worse. During all these attacks, he was uncomfortable from the swelling, but not in physical pain from the disease that any of us could see. However, the whole experience was psychologically very painful, and I could see that early on.

He hated being left in the hospital, and I hated leaving him there. At that time there was no provision for parents to stay overnight with sick children as there is now. Not only did I have to leave him, I had to leave Martin, three years old at the time of the first acute attack, for long days when I went to visit him, and with this third episode, I had a new baby to leave. My milk dried up, and I had to stop nursing her because of all the time I was spending at the hospital. It was painful for all of us. The prevailing wisdom of the time in our area was to bear up under such psychological pain, which largely meant—from my perspective now—burying the feelings of terror and confusion. There were no social workers in the hospital then, no invitations from any professional source to talk about what we were going through emotionally.

Thankfully, we received many offers of help with transportation and child-care from various family members, a very great comfort in itself. And they did their best to avoid talk about feelings. That's how the culture worked at the time—denial and distraction.

Also, it was a comfort to witness the dedication of the pediatrician and the love Moonway inspired from nurses at the hospital. One nurse, limping from arthritis, must have been close to retirement age, brought from her home sodium-free cheese, sliced thinly because Moonway didn't like the chunky salt-free cheese from the hospital cafeteria. Others brought him gifts of stuffed toys. They were very kind and loving to him, paid extra attention to him in the midst of their busy days. I'm sure this played a role in him again recovering enough to come home.

After this episode, I believe he was free of the acute phase of the disease for nearly a year. We might almost have been lulled into a false sense of security if it hadn't been for the continued bloated appearance, especially in the face, the continuing concerns with diet, and the weekly urine tests for albumin that showed the disease was controlled but not cured. I got Kindergarten materials from the school and did some home schooling.

Sometime around his sixth birthday in September, Moonway got sick again with the final and worst of four acute episodes. Because his doctor did not expect him to live through this one, he suggested an experimental treatment, injecting albumen directly into his veins. His kidneys were shutting down by the time this treatment started; he was swelling more and more, and he had virtually ceased to pass urine. His scrotum was swelled up to the size of a large grapefruit.

His doctor gave Moonway the injections himself. He cried, screamed, thrashed, fought. The doctor's face would get wet with tension. I held him down. It was the only way to get the needle in.

For several days after the injections started, he continued to get worse. Twenty-five of his sixty-five pounds was excess fluid, and he passed no urine at all. He was getting very few fluids because of the danger of swelling, but he continued to swell.

On the fourth day, I woke out of a dream in which I saw his face, normal sized, healthy looking. That dream is vivid to this day. I rushed to the phone before I was fully awake to call the hospital. I said, Is Moonway better? Is he urinating?

The nurse said, No, he's very sick. You come in as early as you want and stay as late as you want.

I thought she was telling me he was dying. I hung up the phone, crying so hard that I wonder how I managed to make arrangements for Martin's and Shirley's care and get to the hospital. When I got there, his face looked just as I saw it in the dream. The nurse said the fluid had shifted; it was now settled in his back. Later that day he began to urinate, and he got better quite rapidly after that. Did my dream come from my wishful thinking, and it just coincided with the day he began to heal? He was in the hospital for six weeks that time, the longest and last time for Nephritis.

He had a tutor at home for a short time the year he was six. He learned quickly, stayed on grade level, and started school when he was seven in grade two. He continued to take medication until he was eight, and we continued to worry for years that the disease wasn't over, that it might come back. Eventually, some time after he stopped taking medication but before adolescence, the doctor said they could find no trace of the disease left.   I can still feel that thrill of joy when I remember it, but the scars remain with Moonway:

I measure my whole life by hospitals, Mom.   You know that, don't you?

What do you remember about your Nephritis?

Going to the hospital. I hated that. Do you remember anything, Mom? Did you volunteer for mental illness or get shock treatments or something.   Seems as though you'd remember some of this.

I remember a lot of that, but I do have a bad memory for many things. Maybe I should have gotten shock treatment or something.

No! Do you know if something happened to me from treatment, if I died or something and I was smuggled through a Denver hospital?

No. That didn't happen.

Because when I went to Denver, Colorado, I flashed back like I'd been there before—when I was up in a restaurant over a building. Mom, did Armageddon happen already? I think it's all over the earth. In the universe. In Heaven and Hell. Because of torturing me.

That hospital felt like torture to you, hunh?   Like Armageddon? You were barely four years old when you first became sick with Nephritis, only seven when you had the albumin treatments. Do you remember those injections?

Now that you mention it, I flash back a little. I been crowding that out all my life, never facing it. I'm glad I was brought back to life.

Come to think of it, in retrospect it felt like Armageddon to me, too, though I don't remember thinking of it as torture at the time. And yet, think of the endurance and whatever else it takes—faith?—that allowed us all to go about our daily lives in spite of feeling like we were pitted against forces over which we had no control. Think about how much you have survived.

Pain from the disease. And the medicine. Mostly my kidneys, stomach, groin. That hospital up here did a number on me. I was never the same after that. You must have noticed changes in my behavior, too?

Yes. There was a real marked change in your personality, I thought. You became withdrawn and fearful and preoccupied with the bizarre in your drawings, monsters and things like that, not the cookie-monster kind.

I been a doctor and a psychopath ever since then.

I was concerned enough about the changes in you that I asked your doctor about them. He said, "Oh, he's just growing up. Kids change." You were about eight then.

It was the hospital, Mom. Boy, that was horrible. Pain. Suffering. Fear. Isolation. I think my whole adulthood stems from that hospital. That's why I don't remember much of my childhood, probably. The experimental drugs they put in me, Mom—Doctors' fear of retaliation and law suits. The experiment was a success, but I'm not analyzing what worked and what didn't. And they're doing the same thing, now. Psyche's doing the same thing to me all these years. Eleanor says I gotta go to social group, for Christ's sake! I got a grim future unless I devolve myself from these institutions, a grim one. Unless New York City can make us young again with the thoughts intact, without pain. I don't know what to advise. They brought me back to life. Those experimental drugs, if they were drugs. If I did die and was brought back to life.

The steroids were drugs, but the experimental substance was albumin. It's a protein the body normally produces. I think it wasn't risky like the steroids in terms of side effects. It was experimental in the sense that they didn't know if it would work to make you better. Can you see that Eleanor is recommending what she thinks best for you?

No I can't. She don't know nothing. There were probably a lot of other experimental drugs they didn't tell you about. I think there were some cover ups because of their just fear of law suits. A lot of that goes on. Eleanor better fear 'em, too.

They told me everything. Remember Dr. Donaldson?

Yeah and Gregory, too. I think I was healthy long before the treatments stopped. Those treatments afterwards, the examinations, those didn't have to be. The aftermath treatments just complicated it.

You took medication until you were eight to prevent repeat attacks.

That was probably good. But the visits with the doctor and the trips to Presque Isle. That was all unnecessary. That was a big expense. Have you been reimbursed from Chrysler or Ford or anything?

You know what I'm grateful for?

Did you guys finance it?

You want to know what I'm grateful for"

What?

I'm grateful that we did it. We had medical insurance to pay for it. We didn't go without food or warmth or gas for the car. Family rallied around and helped with child care.

Well, you ain't got to pay for it. See Chrysler. See Ford. Get your money back. Shall we keep the research private or what? Go public with it? Profit off it? Ha, ha.

You have funny fantasies about money. I don't want to profit from it.

Well I want you reimbursed. You did it for me. I didn't like the pain though. I don't want anything painful. And I don't want any more blood taken out of me if it's going to pain me. I'd rather die than go through that again. At least in the grave, I'd . . . No, that might be more painful, hunh? Ha, ha. Let's pick apart the childhood Nephritis some more if you want to. They laughed at disease's cure.

But think of the endurance that allowed us all to go about our lives.

I must have died and been brought back to life, Mom. Went to Hell. Went to Heaven. Went to the universe. Did Uncle Johnny and I rocket jet. Was I smuggled into space? Did all that happen?

Not that I know of.

You sure? You're not shitting me? Jimmy Carter truth? That didn't happen?

It happened in your mind, didn't it?

Yeah. Those experimental drugs are something. It might have been the church's reaction against medicine, too. They might have had something to do with it.

But we endured. We came out on the other side.

We survived it! Divinely appointed. Divine Right of Kings.

Even though it was painful, we survived. You didn't die.

I did die, Mom. I went to Heaven. I went to Hell. I went to . . .

You are not dead now.

I did. That's the honest Jimmy Carter, AA truth. I went to Heaven. I went to Hell. I went to the universe. I went to the Pope in Rome.

Yes, in your mind. I see. That must have been quite an adventure.

It happened. I went to the other side, essentially. I visited the dead.

Come to think about it, that's where all experience happens for us, doesn't it? In our mind.

I visited Christ. I was crucified as a heretic by Christ in Heaven. Judgment days he's saving up, the son of a bitch. It might have been the white anti Christ, though, where Grammy was religious.

What was Heaven like for you.

It sucked, sucked monkey cock. Nazis rolling across Heaven with Limousines.

Wow!

That's what should happen to Christ, not because he's Hebrew. I've accepted the Hebrew Christ as my Messiah: Heil Hitler. Mom, how come I got to keep giving? Maybe I should if I want to stay free, get along. Times are changing, ain't they? It's going feminist and colored in the world, ain't it? We can't stop them. The Nazis can't. The Kaps can't. China has the bomb. I better get along with them. Get along with Eleanor. China has the bomb, you know? Where were we?

Nephritis and feeling tortured.

That's why I'm so paranoid, ain't it? The world's

35

against me in my mind. Everyone hates me. That's how I think and feel. I felt like a crucifixion you know, when I was a kid. You sure you were all just trying to help me? Can't remember a thing. That pretty much blotted out my childhood. I been getting flashes from Christ ever since that Nephritis, too. Mad at me, like. The white one. For cooperating with the Hebrew Christ. The true Christ. That death wasn't fun, Mom. But the grave might have been worse.

What was it like for you, the death you thought you experienced?

I did, Mom. I can't describe it. Ever since that Nephritis and I was healed, I've been having flashes from the white anti Christ that I better not cooperate with the true Hebrew Christ anymore, or something will happen to me. I realize now it's the white Anti Christ giving me flashes that I better not cooperate with the true Christ. The true Christ is the Hebrew, Nationalist, Zionist, Imperialist, you know? And he's my Lord. If I had a Lord.

I thought Christ was white when I went into the church, saw the white Christ. Had a vision. Placid, tranquil, glory, white Christ. Must have been the albino I met in the after life. Luther had his place. The afterlife. The after life. I didn't like those church drugs that came into us against medicine. I didn't like those at all. That might have been it.

Is it in my mind? I don't know what went on in that hospital room, to tell the truth. I don't remember. I just blotted it all out. Did all that happen? And Christ bloomed the world, made it stop thinking and remembering. I don't know, Mom. I don't want to lose my soul and spirit, though. Well, this might have all actually happened to the world. That's maybe where I get my sense of destiny from. Maybe I did meet Hitler and we made an agreement.

In that hospital?

In the after life. I did die, Mom. Was it the religious drugs that brought me back to life just so they could inquire?

You had pills. They were steroid . . .

Terror?

No. Steroid. And the albumin injections were . . .

Heil Hitler.

. . . an experimental treatment at the time. You were losing albumin through your urine, part of the disease process. Your body needs the protein and you were losing it. The white of an egg is albumin. When your body doesn't have enough . . .

What the body needs is a good drink of animal blood, Mom. Make sure it's pure, no micro organisms in it. But that's what the world needs.

Do you have any gratitude about surviving it?

Just glad to be brought back to life. Happy now. Content. Rosy. Safe. I like my money though. I do remember Dr. Donaldson. And all those toys.

You had a birthday in the hospital the last time you were there when you were six. All the hospital staff brought you gifts. Your bed was filled with toys.

I remember the little elephant. I gave it to Shirley.

4. When the Shit Hit the Fan

Mom, I remember things that I vowed I was going to remember from childhood that I do. Going fishing and swimming in Greenville Lake and at Grampy Michael's camp. Playing games with Martin and Shirley that I made up: Buggy, Fishy, Kitty-Go-Round. That vase Dad or you bought, crystal, conical like an upside down missile head. A little game I called *IT*—a silent, inner game I played by myself. Being *IT*. Grammy Adams' place. I always felt good there. Safe. Warm. Comfortable. Going to those big feather beds.

We stayed with Mama for six weeks after Daddy died, April 1963; you were seven, your first full year in school. I didn't think she should be alone through the coldest part of the winter. We helped with some house repair and painting the downstairs, first time in my memory it was painted. You and Martin went to school on the bus, remember?

But, Mom, have we been through a nuclear war against America in my childhood? Did I start it?

Nuclear war, the attacks on Hiroshima and Nagasaki, was part of World War II. The World Wars could each be considered an Armageddon in the 20th century. That was long before you were born. Do you remember training for nuclear war in elementary school?

I remember hiding under the desks. Did I start a nuclear war by my disobedience in childhood?

No.

Did Johnny and I rocket jet when I was a kid?

No.

Rocketed from Cape Canaveral, down here? When I was a kid. And they closed it down. You want that stuff buried. Or it didn't happen? I'll bury it if you want me to. This is an appeal to the 5th amendment.

That must be about the time we would have been watching the first space explorations on television. I was excited by those flights, and I watched all of the launches I could. Does your sense of rocketing from Cape Canaveral suggest you were making up stories and remembered them afterwards as happening. Or interpreting events as happening to you? Or did you reinterpret the events much later after you became ill with schizophrenia, after you had visited your Uncle John Michael in Florida a couple of times? Or all of the above?

I don't know. But something else I remember: Auntie Mame Myra told me about Kennedy needing to be killed. Boy the shit hit the fan when I repeated that in the Greenville Lake School. After we all heard about the Kennedy assassination, she said we needed that change. And I said that in my classroom, and I think that's when the shit hit the fan.

Really!

Auntie Mame Myra said it was a positive change. The assassination, I think. She said it in the car when we were riding along one time. And when I said it in school, that must have been when the shit hit the fan. I don't know which class it was. I must have been about seven. It's true, she said it.

Hmm. I know she didn't like Kennedy. He was the first president I voted for. It was an important act for me, coming from my right-wing Republican family to vote for Kennedy.

I bet she was a victim of those cro-magnon theories that must have circulated down there in Washington where she lived and worked. I don't remember the teacher, nor what happened specifically. But something changed in the world when I said that. I might have been stood in a corner.

Age seven was your first year in school, and you were getting shy and withdrawn by then. I don't remember that you were ever punished that way at home. Were you?

I don't remember much of any punishment from you, except with us getting caught smoking cigarettes, and then you let us go to the fair anyway after saying we couldn't.

You must have been older when that happened. You were about ten when we moved to Northridge and you and Martin both got paper routes soon after. Remember that teenager who harassed you and Martin on your paper routes?

No.

You were about ten or eleven. He was maybe thirteen or fourteen, older and bigger than you. You would come home and tell me that he was bullying you. At first, I thought you needed to learn to take care of yourself with bullies, and I tried to give you advice about how to. But then one day when you both came running home, breathless and frightened, I lost my temper, took off after him and found him, scolded him, told him how ashamed he ought to be, a big boy like him picking on little kids. I told him I better not hear anymore about it. He didn't pick on you after that. The next year I was doing student teaching, and he was in one of my classes, a model of good behavior. It's mostly true: if you can stand up to bullies, they mostly back down. But sometimes the power differences are just too great and children need help coping. Do you remember any of that?

No. I remember going up to the school where the old age home is now. And just treating Martin and Sis so horribly. We were all new to the area, feeling frightened, shy, insecure. I didn't need to aggravate that, Mom. I treated them bad in Greenville, too. Not as bad as I did when we got here though. Trying to make it up to yous. Best I can. I relate it to the shock of moving here to Northridge. Been chronically depressed ever since then. Mom, wasn't I shock treated in adolescence or childhood or places throughout my life that you know of? Be honest.

No.

Do you not recall me being shock treated because you were shock treated?

I was not shock treated, and you were never shock treated either.

I think Armageddon did happen already. Did I start a nuclear war? But that's not all. I remember being over here to Northridge Junior High and reading a little story I wrote about a skeleton in a closet that looked like John F. Kennedy. They didn't like what I was writing and drawing. That teacher at Northridge gave me an A for my story. Put me in front of the class and had me read it. It was about Venusians, residents of Venus, and a skeleton in the closet that looked like John F. Kennedy.

Oh, I wish I could remember that. John F. Kennedy must have been an important symbol to you. I must have seen that story?

You must have.

I remember a poem you wrote on a Mother's Day card you made me.

> All day long
> You wash and iron, cook and clean.
> Not once do you complain.
> Instead, you sing a song.
> The mirrors crack.
> The train goes off the track.
> But even though you can't sing,
> You're still a handy thing.

Your early childhood disobedience doesn't seem important in my memory, nor Martin's nor Shirley's. Things like Martin throwing Shirley's potty in the river. She never did learn to squat in the woods, and when we went camping, your dad always made her a potty out of a cardboard box. She was heartbroken when she saw it floating away. She cried and cried. And then Martin got scolded.

There were many good times, and I don't remember that your disobedience was anything out of the ordinary for children learning to live in a social world. We all chafe at social constraints and disobey, Moonway. Except for fighting between you and Martin in the car, I don't, in fact, remember much disobedience until the conflicts between your dad and I escalated when you were in Junior High. And then there were times you were mean to Martin and Shirley, and one time you and some of your friends set off a stink bomb in school. I had to go in to talk to the principle about the appropriate punishment for that. But, no, Moonway, your disobedience did not start a nuclear war. And your repeating of Auntie-Mame Myra's story didn't shatter the world for all of us. And you didn't start the war between me and your father either. That all had to do with changes in me and Richard and the relationship. And in the whole culture at the time. Transitions. Women's Liberation. Diverging paths in personal and cultural journeys. Tensions like you have with Eleanor or Victor are not unusual.

5. I Raised my Run-away Fist

One hot summer day, we were in the car at MacDonalds' parking lot, and Moonway was eating 2 cheeseburgers, fries, and a chocolate milkshake when he said, What was your perspective on the divorce, Mom?

That's a huge subject. What do you want to know?

Was it unbearable for you? Was Dad unbearable for you?

I wanted to live life my own way. He couldn't, or wouldn't, tolerate some of the things I wanted to do. One thing I wanted to do in college was play the role of the old whore in *Three-Penny Opera*. Funny, all these years later, I get to play that bit-art in the school I am teaching at. Not doing what I wanted got unbearable. In the early years of our marriage, I could hardly tell myself what I wanted, and I certainly couldn't tell him. Maybe if I could have, things would have been better. Or maybe the marriage would have ended sooner. Or maybe it never would have begun. Not much point in regrets about might-have-beens, hunh?

No. I understand, now. I didn't at the time. I blamed

you, mostly. Then, at times, I wanted to just run away from Dad and go down there and live with you. Hard to let go, though, hunh?

Yeah, I work at it.

Remember that Joan Baez tape? What did you ever do with it

It was a record I bought during that time in college. *Baptism: A Journey Through our Time.* I gave it to you way back in the seventies. When you gave it back, I think I threw it away because it was so scratched up.

I must have used it over and over again, all high and wrecked. Some things on that record made me so depressed, though, Mom. It was good for me in a way, gave me a feeling of suicidal power. I'm not suicidal anymore, though.

She was looking at some of the dark passions on that record, looking directly, not blinking: readings from Whitman, Blake, James Joyce, Rimbaud, Baudelaire *Les Fleurs du Mal*, Lorca, John Donne, and others, writers who were or would become some of my favorites. I am fascinated with the dark side, felt it strongly in the 60s when I bought that record. That kind of expression doesn't make me depressed, though it does sometimes reflect a depression in me. I found an interesting contemporary review by Bruce Eder of the album on the Internet.

> Baez by this time was immersed in various causes, concerning the Vietnam War, the human condition, and the general state of the world . . . . Baptism was Baez getting more serious than she already was . . . . In 1968, amid the strife spreading across the world, the album had a built-in urgency that made it work as a mixture of art and message . . . . 'All in Green Went My Love Riding' by E.E. Cummings, and the lullaby 'All the Pretty Little Horses' are beautiful, and . . . . also a singular reminder for '60s history buffs that not all of the antiwar movement's music, or the work coming out of the folk scene in 1968, was necessarily loud, harsh, or bitter.

That review suggests many of the moods and aspirations I felt compelled by in college. I thought many of them were mentally healthy. I still think so. And there was a joyous spirit to the age, a childlike wonder and hope about the possibilities for good and happiness in human life. Sometimes I feel nostalgic for the quality of passions expressed during that time. Maybe I'll get that album on CD.

Nowadays, women's got rights. They still need a lot of protection, though from reactionaries, don't they? Restraining orders or something.

We haven't finished that transition yet. There is still a lot of abuse going on, driven by power lust. It seems to be one of nature's primal drives. It always has been a source of tension, perhaps the major source of tension, in the war between the sexes. You can see it in the ancient Greek plays: Euripedes, *Medea*; Aristophenes, *Lysistrata*; Chaucer, with the character of Alys in "The Wife of Bath" and her tale.

That time you were in Greenville preaching with your church, I got into a bit of a debate with your minister about the issue. He came by and introduced himself. I told him I was glad to see you doing so well, and I thanked him for whatever role he played in it. But he had other things on his mind. He started preaching to me about the place of Christian women, about how a man should be the head of the house. It wasn't a loud debate, just quietly tense. I told him that I disagreed, that women deserved equal rights, and that marriage ought to be a partnership instead of a patriarchy. The whole issue was very much in the air of the time. I could no longer tolerate obeying, and your dad couldn't tolerate disobedience. I suspect he felt my changes and my disagreements as my abuse of him. It was a violation of the unspoken agreements between us and in the culture at large about the rightful role of women.

Mom, is that what it's all about? Love-hate?

Yes, I think so. Love-hate conflicts are about power, about who has control, personally and culturally. Look at the battles among Jews, Christians, and Muslims through the ages that are still going on. A family feud, quite literally, among the sons of Abraham. And the issue of power is central.

I'm glad you made your decision and went out on your own. We had some times in Middletown, didn't we? And we're having times, now. Intellectual times.

Much of the time, now, you and I seem better able to work out disagreements between us than your dad and I could, more accepting of the differences between us. Still, I wasn't with you as much as I should have been. I am very sorry about that, Moonway. Much as I would like to believe that such nurturing hazards don't play a role in mental illness, I believe they do. At the very least, they may trigger and aggravate a disease process waiting to happen. We will likely never know how much this experience contributed to your drug addiction and to your mental illness. You started doing drugs during that time?

That was cut though.

And LSD?

Pre-conversion and post conversion.

And you started running away from home right after the divorce, early adolescence?

He swallowed the last of his lunch and crumpled the bag.

I raised my run-away fist in all of those places and streets and institutions, then and later. In Florida as a teenager. Later in Florida again, Colorado

I was a freshman in High School the first time, ran away with Jeff and Joanna, two friends. We went to Sudbury in Canada. Capone and yippies met there. We had potato picking money, took the bus and hitchhiked. We were reported missing and got picked up by the police. Dad and Joanna's folks came and picked us up.

Another time we ran away, only got to Queen's Village before we got picked up. The police brought us home that time. They were figuring out our MO by then. I went alone once to Detroit. My longest runaway was to Florida. Maybe Dad was getting tired of reporting me by then, was hoping I'd go down and get hooked up with John and their family and stay a while, get straightened out. But at Daytona Beach, I hooked up with an escapee from the Charleston Correctional Facility. The police picked us up before we got far, returned me to John's. Just think, if I'd got to California, I'd be competing with Uriah Heep. Of course, I'd be dead if I'd succeeded in those runaways. I was trying to get away from circumstances I couldn't take, feelings about the divorce. I gotta smoke, Mom.

Is it painful to remember this?

It's just a struggle to remember it. Actually, Mom, it was FBI investigations. Psyche and corrections. They been shock treating us, experimenting on us, the whole family for years and years. That's what's caused all this. You don't believe that do you?

No, I don't, but I understand that you do. And I do understand that there are larger social forces at work that have a mighty impact on the course of personal events.

I got to smoke, got to get rid of this trash, too. We can talk through the car window.

He trashed his bag, and came back to light up.

You, me, Sis, Martin—boy, we all became a bunch of tramps, didn't we, Mom? I really started something with my running away, didn't I?

We could see my leaving the marriage and the area as my running away before you ran away. Did I start it?

I don't blame you, Mom. And I'd a never got all these art ideas and animation if I hadn't gone through what I did.

It isn't a bad thing for me to continue to examine my conscience about the matter. Even if someone came along and showed me with scientific evidence that you would have run away then and developed schizophrenia later no matter what else happened to you, I would still think it good to feel the twinges of conscience that force me to look at myself. Even if it was the right thing for me, it still was a very hurtful thing for all concerned to go through. I should feel sorry about that hurt. That's how we develop moral character.

But it's not the whole story. The whole social structure plays a role. The FBI and psyche and corrections have been important agents of those forces in your life. I do see that, even though I don't have your specific beliefs about what they did and when they did it. Before we get to that, we need to talk about your conversion. But another day. You need to get back home. Eleanor is coming at 2:00.

6. The Spirit Moves

The years that followed the divorce were very difficult ones. Things were so bitter between Richard and me that I felt I had to leave the area to give my children and me some respite. I took a teaching job in Middletown, ninety miles south of Northridge and Greenville. The move was a triple desertion of Moonway and Martin, leaving the marriage, losing custody, and then leaving the area. It was hard to be a good parent from 90 miles away. I tried. I bought a little house in Greenville to have a place to stay as often as I could get away from my teaching work and to have Moonway and Martin for visits.

However, my efforts did not work, at least in the short term, and one year after the divorce, we were back in court again to enforce the rights of the children to visit me. All three often felt divided loyalties, did not get enough help in dealing with them, and became confused and often depressed.

But Moonway's reaction was the most extreme and took most of the attention. Not only did he run away several times, experiment with drugs, and abuse Martin and Shirley at Richard's home when there was no one to adequately protect them, but he also refused to communicate with anyone or to accept any counseling help that I tried to get for him, and he was failing in school. So it was with mixed feelings that I greeted his conversion to a fundamentalist church when he was sixteen. My move to Middletown began the long correspondence between Moonway and me that continued whenever we lived apart, and he announced his conversion in a letter.

1972
Mom,

I've done it. For Good. I've decided to commit my life to God. The only truth left on earth. Christians are being slaughtered in China and Russia. Have you noticed the movies? Blood, Gore, Death. Thousands of perverse sex acts. Sodomy, homosexuals, lesbians. A prophecy in the bible being fulfilled which is the European Common Market. The Bible foretold that. The Jews, the original children of God, have been persecuted throughout history. I've read books, meditated, and done enough dope to make Abby Hoffman look sick. I've visited portions of the mind you will probably never experience. Never have I found the peace God has given me through the dedication, commitment, and blood of Jesus Christ. Another prophecy is that one man will rule all nations with a rod of iron. Compare that with the Iron Curtain and see what you've got. Have you noticed Nixon's friendliness with Mao. It will happen. First, one world government. Then one leader. The church is disappearing. Soon the Christians will arise from the face of the earth when Christ appears from the clouds. The spirit moves and Jesus is coming back.

I realize this letter might kind of zap you. But I really believe it. I better get ready for work. God loves you. I'm free.

Love,

47

Moore Bowen

Moonway

I was "zapped." With my feelings about the Christian fanatics in the family and my embarrassment when Mama converted when I was thirteen, I did not trust his church. Also, embracing so much of the sixties ideologies as I did, I didn't like the fundamentalist attitudes toward feminism, homosexuality, and racial "purity." In some letters from the time, I sensed Moonway's desire to convert me, and I resisted.

Oct. 12, 1973
Dear Mom,

Things have been a real scramble.

Yes, I did get the easel you sent for my birthday. It's really nice. Thanks a lot. Now if I can just find the time to do some painting.

I'm going through a deep spiritual change. I spend most of my spare time reading the Bible. It's really wonderful the way Jesus has transformed my life. I've read in some books doctrines which teach that love is just a state of mind . . . some kind of chemical reaction. If this were so Jesus could never have done what he did, died for you and me. Jesus once said, "Greater love hath no man than this, that a man lay down his life for his friends." That is what God did for us. In the person of Jesus Christ, God came to earth and placed himself in our hands and said, "Do with me what you will." They beat him, spat on him, scorned him, hated him, dragged him through the mud, and nailed him to a cross. I was doing the same things to him spiritually by sinning against him. When I was doing all those things which he had told me were wrong, I was saying to him, God, I'd rather do my thing. But my own thing was making me miserable. So when I stopped fighting the Lord and accepted him, he forgave my sin and rejoiced at my return, just as in the Parable of the Prodigal Son in St. Luke, 15:11-24. (Read it if you have a Bible). So now I have been launched into an entirely new life which extends into eternity. Heaven. Mom, this new life is for everyone who will take it. I'll be praying for you.

Though I resisted, he did seem transformed, and I was grateful.

> Dec 7, 1973
> Mom,
>   Excuse my short, messy letter. The middle finger of my right hand is out of order. I ran it through a printing press and had to have 3 stitches. Got my grades in the mail today. All little As. I've been doing a little drawing. Charcoal and ink. Things are really looking up. I'm making new friends every day. Real friends. Not imaginary friends, created by a bag of dope. And I in turn can be a friend because Jesus has put real love and concern for others inside me.
>   It looks like I'll be down during Christmas. Don't know when. I'll let you know. Gotta go, fingers getting cramped. Read these tracts. See you sometime.

A great relief that he had found something that was helping him far outweighed my disagreements with the doctrines of Moonway's faith. His behavior changed in all ways for the better. He stopped running away, stopped harassing Shirley and Martin, became an honor roll student, and did some impressive lay preaching for his church. Communication between us improved tremendously. After those years of him refusing all my offers of help, I was thrilled that he asked for my help enrolling in college.

Then in 1974, he fell in love with a woman already pregnant with someone else's baby, and even this was a source of pleasure for him and me.

> 1974
> Dear Mom,

Glad to get your letter. Danielle is doing good. I wanted to see you when you were up, but the baby dropped into the world a little early. She's a cute little girl named Sarah Joy.

I'm on spring vacation right now, but I don't think I can make it down. Got some forms for financial aid to fill out and a room to clean and I'm helping with the publicity of a movie coming up. I've included a flyer if you want to come. And mainly I got studies. Haven't got below a B this semester. It sure is great to be on a road that gives a more super intense meaning to every detail of one's experience.

I remember times back on the other road (You know the one with the pot holes in it). Often I would lay on my bed flying on acid or something trying to make up my mind on some considered action. Then after what seemed like innumerable centuries, I would come to the conclusion I was thirsty. So up I would get and step out through scorpions, lizards, sculls, etc. I would battle my way through a dense cloud of fear and thousands of thoughts of what calamity could overtake me, just walking to the sink.

After floating downstairs I would stop to look out a window, forgetting I was thirsty and then horrified that I was not completing an act I had set out to do. After a while the knowledge that I was after a drink of water would return. I would again set out for the faucet only to be sidetracked into a profoundly interesting crack in the wall, an illusionary, horrifying, fascination for me.

Sometimes I would get my drink. Often I would never make it. Always afraid of the evil that could happen.

But someone always watched me. And one day He offered me a drink. At first glance, I refused because the glass looked too clean and the water so pure. But He told me to just let Him touch me with His blood and I could drink forever.

<u>This water sure is good, Mom.</u>

I don't know what I'll do this summer. I want to work a lot on my art. I'll probably get a part time job, too. I'm also going to be involved in a lot of street meetings.

Love,
Moonway

That church and its symbols remain important to him to this day through a variety of disappointments with it and lapses in attendance.

Four years, Mom, I didn't use dope after I got in the church when I was sixteen. Four years. That did me good. But they sure are strict. I was disappointed after a while, but now, I'm glad they were so strict. Those four years of prayer and not watching TV didn't hurt me. Physically anyway. Emotionally, mentally, yeah. I went four years without drugs, no cigarettes, only two joints in four years. I've had a lot of sober time, you know, Mom. A lot of it. Clean and sober time.

And I fell in love with Danielle, but I was a virgin then, and she wasn't. I didn't know how to handle it. There were two or three good-looking girls in that church I could've married.

But I'd been using drugs and drinking even though I'd been in Christian circles. I bet there's orgies all over heaven, Mom. Sometimes I think the second coming has already happened.

There's orgies all over the earth isn't there? All through the animal kingdom.

I don't want to be involved in them. Disease.

There you go. Be careful.

I am. Never had any form of STD. God knows I couldn't take the pain or the problem. Maybe we should sort out some more of these external affairs such as the church. There's a charismatic cult I generated I don't want to go into because of Manson survival instincts. I don't want to go up there and die with those people. The underground said I should. Well, they didn't say that. They implied it though. I

51

know what they meant. Harmony Family Christian Center up on the Crown City Road. That's where I want to build my Grace Land you know, Mom. But they won't have it. Could build a real modern Protestant Monk community as well as live on it, but . . . . Maybe I should get the plans down for that. I already have over my radio, taking this thing right out of the cults.

I remember going there, feeling lonely all the time.

I didn't know you were lonely then, Moonway. I thought you were in company you liked, felt passionate about. Did you go because you were lonely?

No, I'm not masochistic. I didn't like the lonely feelings. Well . . .

I meant, Did you go there seeking company?

Company and God. Guilt mostly after I got into the church. Guilt complex a mile long if I didn't pray and read the bible.

I did find God in the church though. That one anyway. He's been looking out for me ever since, God has. Sometimes God alone. This happened down at the Light House one time. I was high on relatively good pot, and, uh, I went in there and they started talking to me, and I broke down and cried, and I felt so good. So lonely though. Conspicuous. I cried and screamed. They were praying in tongues, and I said, "Oh God, they got their own language." I saw a vision of the white anti Christ. Just Christ standing there with an approving, so-serene-and-nice-and-peaceful smile, Mom. No crown of thorns on his head, just that vision in the book of Revelations. I don't know if that came from my childhood, or the dope, or God himself, probably all three. Mostly God though, I think. I still am a member of the church. I like the attention. God. God and the attention. I'd kneel at the altar and pray, and I'd see purple rings descending down over me. Got a painting of it stashed away in there somewhere.

I was lonely at ULN , too. Remember, you got me in. Completed four and a half semesters. Dean's list twice.

Then another breakdown over a girl up there. Kathleen Sawyer. She had a boy friend. I found out too late, and I was still a virgin. I enjoyed my education. I liked the feeling of power and enlightenment, but I didn't have much of a social life in school. That's the nature of education, too, ain't it? Everything goes into studying.

My favorite course was art. It's still my favorite. Although they kicked me out of the art department. Because I was up there getting a free education, I think. Getting ahead of them probably. Seven, eight, nine years ago they kicked me out. I'm not sure. They told me I couldn't go back there. I remember my psychology, poetry, and political science courses, too. My favorite was poetry. Garrett Barnes taught it. I think my minor up there was art and poetry. And then it went to art and psyche. I should change it back to art and psyche, except that gets too dangerous, revolutionaries start digging around in the fallout. I like William Blake and Emily Dickinson. We didn't study Emily Dickinson though. That was a book you let me borrow one time. I don't know if I'll ever be able to get those books back to you that you lent me. I'd like to, but they're all in Dad's attic.

I forgot them.

Other things I remember about ULN . The stereotype and videotype from having Dean's list grades up there ain't bad. Took a lot of revolutionary activity to get noticed though. Lot of people call it negative. A lot of revolutionaries are doing a lot for social problems in this country. A lot of aversive negative stuff going on in society. Cigarette time. Cigar-wretch. I remember working out in college and bicycling 5 miles a day. If I'd 'a been eating right in college, I'd 'a been right in 7th heaven, Mom. Exercising, lifting weights, bicycling 5 miles a day.

You were doing good then, hunh, those first two years?

Yeah. No social life in college, though. I studied all the time. I wanted them As. And I'm glad I got them.

I, too, remember those years feeling pride for Moonway's success and a glad hope for his future. I had just started to keep journals in those years, and I often recorded details of interactions with Moonway in them. Reviewing them, I see that I hadn't entirely let go of my worry: "Spring

1975, every time I see a young man about 5' 4" with blonde hair, square shouldered, I feel a momentary impulse to call his name." This was less than a year before Moonway's first hospitalization at SMHI. Likely, he was already experiencing symptoms.

II
The Great Flipped Blip

I chase God with my diminishing life,
and find that I am pursuing a mad man.

7. Crazy, Insane Drug Mind

In April 1976, the minister of Moonway's church, Reverend White called me in Middletown to tell me Moonway was hospitalized at State Mental Health Institute, diagnosed with schizophrenia. He said Moonway had been in trouble for some months with street drugs. Evenings after teaching all day, I drove two or three times a week back and forth from Middletown to SMHI to visit him. To stay awake while driving, I would drink coffee and talk into my tape recorder about my visit with him, a pattern that was to repeat itself often in the coming years. Those recordings eventually became material for poems and other writing.

My Son, the Artist

Moonway sat at the table, unmoving
eyes focused on a spot above
and behind my left shoulder
and talked of the journey
he was taking. A long journey,

he said, on a ship he must pilot
alone through treacherous waters.
He said he was called to go,
he wanted to go, he might not come back.
He did not call me Mother.

As I did when he was small
in another hospital room,
frightened that he was dying,
I gave him water colors, ink,
and paper and told him to paint.

Moonway was discharged in a few weeks this first time. On May 8, I picked him up at SMHI and took him to Greenville with me for the weekend. Sullen and uncommunicative, he went off by himself to the Greenville Bar for the evening. I stayed awake trying to read until he came home after a few hours and went straight to bed without even saying goodnight. The next morning, as soon as he got up, he wanted to go home to his Dad's first thing.

I drove up to Greenville again on May 23 and took him to MacDonald's for a meal. He was talking more but also paranoid. He said, "The CIA is after me. Someone stole my billfold at the Police Station with writings in it and a letter from you."

I said, "You lost your billfold? "

"No, Mom. It was stolen, I know, and you should be concerned and look into it. They're after you, too."

In the early summer of 1976, Moonway, driving his dad's car, rolled it over. He was not seriously hurt physically, but his delusions intensified. He was admitted to SMHI and then transferred to County Mental Health Center. This accident proved to be so traumatic for him that he hasn't driven since, and he constantly monitors and instructs the driving of anyone he rides with. "Full stop here!" "Slow down." "Watch all ways."

My friend Marie, an LPN working with psychiatric patients at the time, was living in the area and visited Moonway at SMHI. After this second discharge, he went to Florida to visit his Uncle John Michael and family, and I wrote to him there.

> July 11, 1976
> Dear Moonway,
>
> Marie was here week before last. She left some books for you to read. If you are not planning to come home for a while I will send them when I get done reading them. Martin tells me that your dad discovered your pot plants you left at his house and wasn't pleased about them. Marie took the sprouts you left in my care and planted them in her garden. She says you can have half of whatever grows. In view of what I just wrote, you should probably destroy this letter if you don't want anyone reading it.

After visiting in Florida, Moonway hitchhiked to Colorado. He called once to ask me to send his money and his prescription for glasses. He said, I tried to make contact with a church out there, and I was bounced out because I was too loony and mouthy. I asked him where he was living. He said, In the streets and in a cave I found.

By August 31, Moonway was back in Lincoln, and he

came out to my house in Greenville for a few days before I went back to teaching in Middletown. I was awfully glad to see him. I thought he was better, and I felt good about him during that visit. My worries receded to dreams recorded in my journal.

> September 9. In a late afternoon nap, I dream that Moonway and I are going into the woods. Not much memory of the trip in except we seem to be on foot and following a grass-covered path, not much traveled.
>
> We are a long time coming out. The way is swampy and rough. We are riding bikes some of the time. Some of the time I am driving a car and he is in the back seat. I am leading and uncomfortable with it. I talk, he doesn't say much. While driving the car, I overtake and pass a big dump truck. A huge dead bear fills the entire dump. I say, The bear is singing about life and death. I tell Moonway frequently, This doesn't look like the way we came in. I don't know where we are. How do we get home? I fear we have taken a wrong turn. It is late afternoon, and we need to get out of the woods before dark. I hurry. I wake before we get out, haunted with the sense of being the leader and knowing I am lost.

On December 6, he was not doing well again, and I wrote to a friend about doing dream work in the midst of his third psychological crisis, dream work that did not pertain to him. I congratulated myself on being detached.

On December 19, Moonway attacked Richard with a small scalpel from my college-Biology dissecting kit and inflicted a surface wound. He left the house, went down to the nearest Dunkin Donuts and called the police to tell them what he had done. Richard's wound required stitches. Moonway was arrested for assault and put first in the Northridge City Jail. I visited him there, the only time in his legal history where I was required to talk to him behind bars. I held his hands through the bars and told him, I am on your side.

Afterward, I wondered what I meant and what it meant to him to have me say that. Later, he was transferred to the Woodland County Jail to await trial.

He wrote me from there, responding to a letter from me.

Mom,

I could use a sketchbook and one of those small pencil sharpeners. Your mail (book and letter) arrived with a letter from Jim Walker, my transactional therapist, while I was writing to make amends with Dad. About all I can tell you right now is to shut up and stop feeling guilty. And in no way do I want to stop you from loving me. Also I think you are too quick to make me out as the exploited genius. You are not the only one who can help me. I do not need help; I'm OK; you're OK. All you need now is Christ. Kind of a simplistic answer but it must serve for now since I've got to finish writing Dad and then write Jim. The only thing that would be damaging to me now is jail. It is the only thing that could hinder my "rehabilitation." I would flourish in the loony bin or CMHC , County Mental Health Center. But face it. The jails and prisons of this poor wretched country are run by a lot of insecure children in Men's uniforms. Some in this jail do not dare write the editor of *Newburgh Daily News* concerning their grievances for fear of recrimination from the guards who open all mail. Even I have doubts of this letter reaching you. I am quite certain it will, but the mere fact that there are doubts indicates to me that the court system is failing miserably.

Also (phew, lemme breathe) I want to apologize for the terrible noise that came from me about the "Pray for the Schools" bumper sticker on your car. It was quite subversive (in right way) of you. It also shows a slight deviation (at least in my head) from your proclaimed atheistic lifestyle and existentialist meaningless universe. (Pant Pant Pant)

Also, I forgive you for all and anything.
Love,
Moonway

When I visited him, I took him art materials and explained that Pray was the name of a candidate for State Senate. He gave me a self-portrait, split vertically, left side of his face disintegrating, left arm severed and bleeding, Jesus up in the corner, indistinct and tiny.

By late winter, he was again committed to SMHI. Visiting him there, I was very discouraged with the quality of care he was getting, or not getting, and with the attitudes of staff toward him. In a meeting, the director of his ward told me, "Moonway is a violent person."

One time I found him all groggy. He had a reaction to prolixin: muscle spasms, pain, a knot in the neck, difficulty breathing. He said staff at first accused him of faking it. Then, at the insistence of other patients, they finally called a nurse over and she gave him a shot. By the time I got there, he was feeling detached and relaxed. He hadn't had any supper, and we had coffee and Cheese Danish that I brought.

Some of the other patients came over and talked to me that night. One of them wanted some of the Danish, and Moonway gave him some. Another one came by to tell Moonway he had the same reaction to medicine. I thought both of them were more kind, respectful, and supportive than staff.

I was rereading R. D. Laing at the time, and I wanted to believe that insanity could be a curative process. I hoped each crisis could bring him closer to his rage, and then his fears. I hoped there was a bottom layer, and if he could get through that, he could be better afterward. I remembered times in my early twenties when I felt fear so strong, I felt ill—fear of chaos and meaninglessness, fear that no one is trustworthy, not even me, existential nausea. Was that what he felt when he said, "Mom, I am afraid I might flip out and not be able to come back."

In April, I had a recurrent dream in which I am sleeping. I hear something that should wake me, someone calling my name, an alarm, or something else. I try and try to wake up and can't. I struggle until I am exhausted and give up. Then I wake up.

Later that night, I dreamed he was swelling like he did when he was a little boy with nephritis. Nothing I do will stop it, but I keep trying, trying. His doctor says, He is dying, will very soon be dead. I argue, You don't know everything. I half wake up and in a hypnogogic muse say, No, Moonway, don't die, you can't die. He says, Yes, I am dying, Mom. You have to accept it.

By June of 1977, Moonway's court appointed lawyer had quit responding to my calls and letters, and I was getting so discouraged and impatient for some resolution to the legal charges against Moonway that I wrote to the Civil Liberties Union to ask for help.

> In April, Moonway was scheduled to go on trial. The Director of his ward at the hospital, advised him to plead guilty and take a jail sentence because if he is found not guilty by reason of mental defect or disease, he will get an indefinite commitment to SMHI. The courts tend to keep such patients hospitalized for longer than necessary. Moonway advised his court appointed lawyer from Northridge that he wanted to plead guilty. In court on the trial date, this lawyer requested to be released from the case since he could not go along with a guilty plea.

> The day Moonway was scheduled to go to trial, no one made arrangements for him to be transported from SMHI. It was done when court convened, so he did not arrive in court until 1:00 P. M. The rest of the day was taken up with releasing the lawyer and appointing a new one, Amos Myles, from Woodland, and listening to an East Northridge psychiatrist, state in Judge's chambers that Moonway was not mentally competent to stand trial.

> The result is that Moonway must now go through a competency hearing before he can go to trial. To complicate and delay matters still further, Mr.

Myles tells me there is no judge in the County Superior Court during July and August, and that October is probably the earliest date for the trial. That will be 10 months from the day of his arrest.

Bail was set at $10,000. We have not been able to meet that. Mr. Myles says he has been working on getting bail reduced and getting the competency hearing set without having Moonway spend any more time in jail. Presumably if he were found competent to stand trial, he would have to go to jail, or be released on bail, but could not go back to SMHI while awaiting trial. Mr. Myles has not accomplished any of that in the three months he has been handling the case. He tells me the case has become very complicated because he has to coordinate things with so many people.

Moonway is an intelligent, creative young man. He completed two years at ULN, majoring in art. He is continuing his art work in the hospital, but receives no encouragement from the staff to do that or anything else productive. He is restricted to the ward while awaiting trial except for occasional 15-minute, chaperoned walks which he gets to take if he cooperates. When I inquired about his therapy, I was told about these walks. From what I can see, he is not getting therapy.

I want him free to seek meaningful treatment if he can find it. I don't know if his civil liberties have been violated. I believe he has been treated very badly, both by the judicial system and by the mental health system. I don't have money to hire a lawyer or to pay for private hospitalization. I don't know where to look anymore for help.

Can you help? Please write or call.

I have no record or memory of anyone responding to this plea.

I have always had ambivalent feelings about Moonway's hospitalizations. Relief because I hope he is more protected there than out on his own. But then it happens, and it seems he is not safer there, but maybe in greater danger. He fears sexual predators and the temptations of illegal drugs there, and I have the nagging sense that much of professional care in the institutes—over-prescribed medical drugs and poor attitudes of incompetent staff—actually prevent recovery. Repeated hospitalizations make it hard to keep hoping for recovery; at the same time, I can't give up hope.

One day during that summer when I visited him at SMHI, he gave me some more of his drawings done there; they were more images of madness and torment. A few days later, I got out some of his more cheerful drawings and paintings done in college and put them up in my little house in Greenville. They were mostly landscapes, still lifes, and household objects in bright colors. I tried to talk to Shirley about the possibility of Moonway coming to live with us after discharge. Remembering his bullying during his troubled early teen years, she was afraid and upset at this prospect.

In early August, Moonway was discharged. Someone arranged for him to live with an artist in a town about twenty miles west of Northridge. He didn't stay at the artist's, kept returning to Northridge. He came to stay with me for a while in Greenville while Shirley visited with her dad. He said he was looking for a job, but he was smoking pot and acting crazy much of the time.

One day during a raging thunder storm, he dug out a folded rubber raft from the big back pack he carried with him everywhere. On the front porch of the house, he blew it up. Small as the raft was, it took up almost more space than was available with all his belongings scattered around on that tiny porch that doubled as his bedroom. He muttered all through his preparations about the limitations of space for his things and his need to get out on the lake in a hurry before the storm died down.

He wanted me to drive him down to the lake. Instead, I stood in his way in front of the door and pleaded with him not to go. "It's dangerous out there. You could drown." He pushed me aside and went off running toward the lake, struggling all the way to keep the raft from blowing away in the wind.

I called the police to come rescue him. I asked them to

please take him in for an evaluation. Very quickly, with the storm still raging, they had retrieved him from the middle of the lake and had him back at the house to pick up all his things before they drove him to Northridge for evaluation. As he often could be, he was fine at the evaluation, and they released him after an hour. He did not return to Greenville. No money and no place to live, he wandered back home to Richard's, and by Labor Day, I was back in Middletown for the new teaching year.

September 22
Dear Moonway,

Shirley said you called and want me to get some grease pencils. You can get them at Whitman Supplies. I have no place here in Middletown to get them, also have no money. I'm starting out the work year about $800 in the hole. That doesn't include the mortgage payment that is overdue. Even if I had the money I think I ought not to be buying those things for you. We agreed that it is time for me to treat you like an adult. I do have good intentions to do that.

Since the day I called the Police to pick you up on the lake, I have been pretty well convinced that you are in control of your behavior, are making your own decisions, are ready to take over the responsibility of taking care of yourself. I don't approve of you living with your father; I don't approve of your current lifestyle. But I have no control over it, not even any influence. You take the responsibility for it. I don't want it.

I'm coming to Greenville the weekend of October 7. I hope I see you then. I would like you to come visit me. I wish we could talk to each other.

On November 18, 1977, I went to Woodland to be at Moonway's sentencing at 11:00 AM. It was postponed again. Someone forgot to tell the Judge about the hearing, and he left before 11:00. Reluctantly, I gave Moonway $3.00 when he asked for money. When I got home, I wrote him a letter I didn't mail.

> Dear Moonway,
>
> Today you asked me for money and I gave you three dollars, last money I had until payday. I traveled 20 miles on empty coming home because I didn't have any money for gas, and now I worry that you will spend it for your "stimulant" and do something I will be sorry for. Whether I give you money or not, I feel guilty as hell. I am so tired of this. I guess if I wanted to enough I could walk out on it all.
>
> Instead, I sit here and mope. We are all crazy. Can't help ourselves, can't help anyone else. I'm sorry I'm not what I need to be, sorry I'm not what you need, sorry I have been dishonest to you about it. If I have. I'm not sure of anything.
>
> The phone interrupted this bout of self pity. I just talked to your dad. So, you took my 3 bucks and bought yourself enough drug-induced courage to throw rocks through the window. What now?

Neighbors called the police about the rock throwing; Moonway was arrested for disorderly conduct and incarcerated in Woodland County Jail again. I did nothing to help. In the many intervening years since this incident, I have learned that parents of children diagnosed with serious and chronic schizophrenia last about 5 years before they give up on them. At this point I was less than two years from his first diagnosis.

By January 12, 1978, he was out of jail, and he phoned me, Can I come down and visit you for a few weeks?

We would have to agree on house rules.

Only rule I need is, I got to have the place locked up at all times to protect my stuff.

Shirley and I go in and out all day. I can't agree to keep the doors locked all the time.

Well, if you can't even keep your doors locked, I don't want to come. I got stuff that has to be protected.

What stuff? I said, but he had already hung up.

On January 13, I was dreaming of him again. I am living with Richard, the kids are young—Marty and Moonway about 8 and 10. Although it is evening—dark at least—I am outside hanging clothes. Marty yells at me from the house to come help him with something. I think it must be homework, and I yell back that I will be there in a minute. I finish and go into the house. It is dark, no lights on but enough light to see Marty go running by me crying. Moonway is after him. They run into the bedroom where Richard is sleeping. I search frantically for the light switch. I must have light to deal with the situation. I can't find it. Marty's cries stop. Silence. I rush to the bedroom without light, but again I can see what is happening. Marty is cowering on one side of the bed, one side of his head bloody, hands over his face peering through partially opened fingers. On the other side of the bed, Moonway has a small bloody rock in his upraised hand. Richard is groggy and mumbling. I grab Moonway's hands, holding them firmly and tell Richard to call the police, we must send Moonway away. Richard mutters, Oh, that is not necessary. Moonway is writhing and crying, Oh, don't. I won't do it again. I'm through with it.

I hold his hands firmly and tell Richard, again, to call the police.

I tried all the next day to avoid that dream, puttering, skiing, finishing a book I had been reading. But it insisted. I was alone; there was no light.

Moonway, let's talk about your memories of the early years of your schizophrenia. You had a girl friend at the time you were first hospitalized?

Yeah. I didn't take it too seriously. I was too high on pot. Too gone. Colombian Gold, Mom, bought from Blip Blip.

A dealer whose name you don't want mentioned?

Yeah. I was doing pot, THC, Black Beauties. LSD. And Mescaline. I did enough LSD to singe my brain. That stuff's acid, more a Satanist drug, I think, from the Devil. It was a rush of chemical acid through me. Hallucinations.

Feeling good. I never did mushrooms. I smoked in my life a good two or three pounds of pot all together. By the ounce. Until I quit in '80 thanks to SMHI. I was doing Manson theater in the balcony of the town library when they locked me up the first time in the loony bin. I was suicidal then, awful depressed about the church. Their whole rip off. Money. AA is doing the same thing. They owed me theater money I was bringing them. Standing by the street, getting them business.

Ward C3 SMHI was interesting. Smoked a lot of pot there out in the woods, tripped once on the ward on LSD. Drank wine, too. Bought big jugs of it; we stashed it down near the old fire place. Me and Chris Brice, the dude that murdered his grandfather. He was my first godfather. Every punk needs a godfather when you've been locked up. Mahmud from MCFP is one. Manson's another. Both the godfather and I have repented. A nation that doesn't repent of its murders dies.

I was hospitalized twice that summer of '76. You got me out both times, didn't you? You raised your voice at the dungeon mast, didn't you?

I think you credit me with more power than I have. I picked you up when you were discharged. And I tried to speed up the legal process at some point, wrote some letters. But I didn't have any power to get you released.

Remember when I pounded on the table and started screaming, "Future shock. Future shock?" Those weren't pleasant experiences, Mom, none of them. I've had sane, insane, drug, and abstinent strategies and theories behind everything in my behavior all through my life. Once I was near a wall down here in Northridge, and I put burdocks all through my hair and beard. I did a leprechaun dance along Main Street. Hopped up on a car roof. It's not against the law, either, to hop up on a car roof. But I did some weeks in SMHI over it. I shouldn't have done that. That was itchy and awful. I shaved my beard off. Dad had me do it. Greased my hair down, too.

You know what else I did up at Sanders St. in '76. Dad wouldn't take me over to the Lumber Yard to get some wood for picture-frames, so I dragged that thing, and it weighed about a ton, all the way from the Lumber Yard up to 51 Sanders Street. Had a shepherd's crook. Had a sign that said "Woe to evil leaders who mock the temple of democracy and you churches, who remain silent." Publicly, I'm a doom prophet. Privately, I'm a major religion. Like Blake.

I sold that copy of Blake's art work you gave me. For dope, Mama. That's how much of a drug slave I was. I got $15 for all the books you gave me, and I'd like that Blake collection back. Joe, was it? The veteran up here at ULN. A student. Sold those in '76. You got use out of those art and literature books, then gave them to me. I don't know what I used the money for, probably tried to buy from him.

I ODed on Black Beauties once, too. Bought in a movie theater. Puked blood on that speed. I barfed blood all over the theater lobby. I bought them and gulped them down and went up in the grandstand at the fair grounds and just lay there and blitzed out. And the next day I puked blood in the movie theater. I wonder what movie was on. Ha, ha, ha, ha, ha. I'd like to find that out, Dude Brain. Bet it sold the movies. I wouldn't do it again Mama. AA jokes around a lot, and a lot of times they shouldn't. They joke around too much, in this area anyway. I need a lot of help with my addictions.

Moonway, is Dude Brain one of your voices that you're hearing now?

I dunno. I hitchhiked to D. C. to see Myra that fall, or early winter, '76. Smoked a joint with a trucker who gave me a ride from here in Northridge, great big bomb joint. Big black dude. He said I rolled the joint too big. He got stopped by the police too. I was lucky to get out of that one. I carried a hollow hand grenade on that trip. For protection. There were no explosives. I got stopped by the police for hitch-hiking, and they found a small flake of pot and the grenade. They let me go with the grenade where it was hollow.

It must have been soon after you came back from that trip that you stabbed your dad? Did you intend to kill him?

If there had been a sharp knife there, I would have done it, or he would've killed me, or we'd have killed each other. I was pissed off at him because he kept blocking my connections and prostitutes. That was all. It wasn't him. I'd go to dealer sometimes and try to get an ounce, and he wouldn't have any pot.

But that wasn't why I stabbed him or tried to kill him. I blamed him for my problems with women. I'm glad now he prevented me from going to prostitutes. I'm glad I never caught any form of STD. I was certain at the time he was interfering. I don't know if it was my insane certainty or it actually happened. I tried to make it up to you people. Everything I ever did. And I did six months in Woodland County Jail, WCJ, for that. And then SMHI. It wasn't crime, Mom. It was all just that damn dope habit of mine.

Assaulting your father was criminal? Illegal drugs were criminal?

Well, that was against the law but not criminal. The criminal stuff was stealing cans and bottles off trucks. Stealing gloves. I didn't do much criminal stuff actually. Other than dope. The thing with Dad was a big domestic dispute. It was. It wasn't financial or done for criminal reasons. I just couldn't take living in that hell. To tell the truth, I love the guy now, and I try to look out for him, but I couldn't take that, Mom. Just like you. You had to get out. It wasn't him really. Just no privacy. Not being on my own. But if I'd been on my own, I'd be dead as a junkie now, or all reformed and doing good art. But I'd a never got these animation techniques, or art techniques I thought up or got through the media, or having my cohorts spy on graphic art rooms through the media that I weaved all together, right up there.

I ODed on THC once during that time, too. I was 21 or 22, dropped out of college. Everything turned into blobs of color. Mauve. Dad came up to my room when I was ODing on that stuff. He had shaving cream and blood all over his face. I don't know what he wanted. I pulled out a knife I had strapped to my pocket with a rubber band. I didn't dare to hurt the dude though, glad I didn't. I don't know if that was fake blood or real blood. I didn't do it. It was all over his face, everywhere. I don't know if he was suicidal, the poor guy, or what.

Was it a dream? or hallucination?

No, that was happening. I just sat there and pissed and moaned and grunted and howled and screeched and hauled that knife out. I didn't use it though. I'm certain of that. I don't know if he was trying to tell me something or what. I don't know if he was on THC just to relate to me. And the music I was playing was making him do that. That's about the worst I've ever been concerning my sanity. Some of those experiences were pretty warped and bizarre. My own crazy insane drug mind. And I didn't know what to do. You got out. But I had nowhere to go. You probably didn't want me.

At the time of the divorce, you wouldn't talk to the judge and make a decision about where you wanted to live. And I think I understand why you would refuse. It must have been terrible to be put in that position. But the judge made his decision that your dad would have custody of you and Martin without knowing your wishes. Then later after you were diagnosed with schizophrenia, every time we talked about you coming to live with me, our talks broke down over household rules. And there was Shirley and my duty to her. I'm very sorry we could never come to any agreement about that.

Yeah. I'd a never got all these ideas I got if I hadn't gone through what I went through. I hope it's over, though. I hope they don't physically put me back into my childhood again, and all of us, like they're planning too.

I didn't hit bottom then though. You know what I used to do, Mom, early 80s pre or mid 80s. I'd eat a whole bunch of ice cream or popcorn, and then I'd puke it up so I wouldn't get fat.

My god! Bulimia?

Did you ever do that?

I have feasted on food until I was uncomfortable on holidays, but not like that. I hate vomiting, and have only ever made myself vomit when I was so nauseous from being sick with the flu or something, I couldn't stand the feeling. No, I've never been bulimic. I hope you don't still do that.

No. And I eat right lately, real good, make sure I get a balanced diet. Didn't get my fruit juice today though.

You still have time.

8. "How Terribly Doing Goes along the Earth" (William Faulkner)

In mid-February 1978, Moonway called my mother to see if he could stay at the family farmhouse in Greenville. He wanted room, he said, to spread out his paintings. It is a big old house, with only wood stoves for heat and no plumbing in the winter. Unoccupied except occasionally by family on vacation in the summer time, it is not a good place in January in Northern Lincoln for someone having trouble taking care of himself. Moonway did not stay long. Shortly after arriving there, he found a small stash of Mama's money and stole $100. As soon as the money was spent, he confessed to her and to me and apologized. He took his things and himself to my house in Greenville where heat at least was a bit easier to manage, though the plumbing was also turned off there in the winter. He had to carry water from a public artesian well and flush the toilet with a pail.

Later in February, after I spent my February break in Greenville, Moonway called me in Middletown at 3:00 A. M. to ask if I or one of his cousins on the Michael side were getting into his notebook that was among some things he had stored in a closet of my Greenville house. This cousin had never been in the house. I wrote to him, about as angry as I have ever been with him.

February 27

For Christ's sakes, Moonway, if you're going to continue to worry about your damn writings, would you get a box with a lock and lock them up. Your fears about me pawing through your things are completely unreasonable. As long as you have things at my house, I will probably make some effort to keep them tidy. That is the extent of my interest in your things unless you want me to see them.

Since you called at such a late hour I assume you were drunk or otherwise drugged which means that all of your good intentions lasted just about long enough for someone to bail you out of one more mess that you got yourself into. I very nearly didn't try to bail you out of this one. One of these times I won't. I hope before that time comes you will decide to control your own behavior.

I am very angry. I wish I weren't writing this in a letter, but I can't afford to run up there every time I get a crazy phone call from you, so this will have to do. I am angry because of the worry, the inconvenience, the time, and the expense that I go through in the hope that I can help. And that hope continues to be frustrated. I'm angry that you are wasting so badly your talents, your intelligence, and your energies. Your life is yours to do with as you will, of course. I don't even want to interfere. I don't want to support it either.

I will be coming home in April. Please scrounge around and find some way to lock up the things at my house in Greenville that you don't want me to see. Your mistrust of me about that is completely without justification. I feel very hurt as well as angry.

I wish we could talk.

Love,

Mom.

P. S. I will be sending the money you stole from Mom's house to her Thursday. I hope you have written to her.

I got a very angry letter from Moonway in response. I asked him to communicate, and when he did I was frightened to see how crazy he was.

Mom,

Tell people to keep their noses out of that closet.

It'll have to be a short letter because I've got to work on a church mural. I want to apologize for the following facts: All the water in those containers at your house is frozen. The house is in a slight state of disorder. I used very little oil, however, and there is bread there. As to your last bitter letter. <u>Someone did get into my notebook.</u> It was absurd of you to assume that simply because I called to check it out that I was drugged or drunk. This assumption is as savage as my AA counselors frisking me the other night under the guise of a pat of reassurance. I have collected all my writings and brought them over to Northridge. I <u>would</u> lock them up if I had a proper lock and container. In fact, if I had the money I would acquire a vault and a dozen tanks to guard it. But I don't. And tell Shirley thanks for nothing for that ridiculous Father's Day card that she sent the dolt you married (And you are on equal terms with him if you married him). The card implied I was a potential mother killer.

Moonway

Dear Moonway,

Better than apologies I would like you to clean up the house and take care of the frozen water before it bursts its containers and leaks all over the house. I hope you put anti freeze in the drains so they didn't freeze up.

Your interpretations of Shirley's card to her father are far-fetched.

Touch from your counselor is far more likely a gesture of affection than a frisking. Many of us like you and have faith in you, in spite of all. I would assume your counselor has no reason to frisk you and that he would want to reassure you.

When I get a few extra bucks, I'll buy you a container and a lock. It won't be for a while.

One of Faulkner's characters says, "I would think how words go straight up in a thin line, quick and harmless, and how terribly doing goes along the earth, clinging to it, so that after a while the two lines are too far apart for the sane person to straddle from one to the other." I was acting as though if I could just <u>say</u> the right things at the right time, the universe would fall into place, be rescued from chaos, be redeemed. Every time, Moonway's doings defied my logic. I moaned and shook my fist at the universe, which didn't give a damn; worse yet, I heard it laughing back at me in my own voice.

After that, I didn't hear much from Moonway directly for a while. Richard wrote to Shirley that he was better than he had been in a long time—really trying. I asked myself, Was it wrong or right to indulge my burst of rage, the worst that I remember with him? Or was it totally irrelevant?

In June, back in Greenville for the summer from Middletown, I heard that Moonway was down on the Lincoln coast somewhere washing dishes. Sometime during this period of relative silence between us, I wondered if I was finally severing the umbilical cord of my over concern, but I was only sure there was a change in feeling and that the new feelings were not less painful than the old. I sighed a lot.

In August, Moonway flipped out again and was hospitalized at SMHI on the criminal ward.

> Mom,
>
> I'm in the nuthouse again. Got drunk and threatened someone. Lost my head over a woman. Sorry I haven't written sooner. I guess I just need distance from the whole family right now that no one but myself can understand. I feel sick about myself. By severing communication I feel that I've somehow thwarted your lifetime infantilization of me. I will not feel good about living until I can pay Gram back and Dad for the windows and get on my own feet.
>
> I was doing good at holding down a dishwashing job in Southeast Harbor. The guy was actually trying to get me to be a cook. I still have a check for $10 or so there. I also have all my notebooks and art supplies down there. The woman I was seeing is supposed to be looking after them but she's planning on going to Philadelphia soon. I was planning on going there to live with her but I don't know what will happen now. Ward director Will St. Lorraine says it

looks good for my getting something worked out. If they give me jail time I might end up making some very loud statements like sliced wrists.

My main concerns right now are my notebooks and art supplies. If I can get back into college somewhere I could have a book off the ground within a year or less that should sell well. But I still haven't heard from Lori about whether she rescued my notebooks from the irate owner of the house she is renting a room in. I was staying there in an attic without paying rent. The owner told me to vacate several times and once threatened to throw my stuff out. Lori hasn't called. I don't know how she feels anymore. She doesn't like my drinking and I don't blame her. So what I'm wondering is if worse comes to worse, as is usually the case with me, could someone pick up my stuff for me and stash it somewhere? And if you see Lori please don't come on like "So this is the woman stealing my son from my bed." Schizophrenia has often reduced me to childhood in front of you and I'm sick enough of this whole Oedipus Rex crap that stems from Nephritis anyway.

Maybe Lori will come through, but I must plan ahead. I have $60 here and that check in Southeast Harbor. I'd like to get a typewriter. I'll call as soon as I hear from Lori.

I picked up his money, TV and radio, and other things in Southeast Harbor, and I took him the things he wanted in the hospital. He came down to the car, got them and started to walk away from the hospital grounds. He wouldn't talk to me. I went in and told the hospital officials that he might be trying to escape. Then I left.

Mom,

Just a note of apology for the other day. I lost my passes for two or three days for that stupid incident. I was just in a hurry to hide my pipe and seeds because I was afraid some idiot shrink or aide

would search me. I should have just put the
contraband in my pocket and returned to the ward and
talked with you. Someone saw me heading for the
woods and thought I was trying to escape. Which is a
ludicrous assumption. I would only escape if I was
confined here indefinitely. I was also irritated at the
outcome of my hearing. But all that aside, it looks like
I'll be going to a religious school in New Jersey
sometime. I'm more in control now and some of the
staff say I'm ready to leave. But it's all in the court's
hands now.

Whether I reported him or not, both felt like betrayal.
When I drove away, I was thinking I ought to get out of his
life completely. For me, or him, or both? I only told him
much later that I was the one who snitched on him.
   During this hospitalization, Moonway took classes in
art, woodshop, creative writing, and leather work. I was glad
of that, thinking it was likely the most therapeutic treatment
he could get there. He gave me a watercolor when I visited
him at SMHI in September and later sent me a sketch with a
note: "Sorry for the trouble I've caused you."

My Son, the Artist
         (continued)

In 1979, Moonway neither talked nor listened
to me. Recovering again, his painted
faces split, crumbled, fell and scattered
in pieces on bright tile. Blood streamed
from Christ's heart.

Moonway was discharged December 6 from SMHI,
just about 5 months after being admitted. One more time I
tried to find out what help he could get. One more time I was
told nothing could be done; he had been judged a sane adult. I
called Will St. Lorraine. He was out; I left word for him to
call back. He never did. I called the probation officer. He
could offer nothing. I spent a frantic weekend getting

Moonway established again at my house in Greenville with fuel and groceries to keep him going until Christmas. I also changed my plans for his Christmas gift. Instead of getting him a locked case for his writings, I decided it was impossible to get anything secure enough to make him feel safe; to try would encourage his fears. I got him typing paper instead and oil to heat the Greenville house, and I had the fuse box fixed. It was nearly one year after the dream of 1-13-78. Whatever crises came up with Moonway during the year, none ripped me apart like that dream and that time.

In late January, Moonway took an aborted trip to Boston. I talked to him briefly by phone to tell him not to go when he did unless he could get a place to stay. He did not call back before he left. When he returned, there was some sort of show down with Richard who told him he would have to leave by April 1st. He left that night to go to my house in Greenville. In early March, I heard from others that Moonway spent 7 days in jail for disturbing the peace. When he got out, he went back to Northridge for a few days and then on to my house in Greenville. I heard nothing at all from him. Richard wrote.

> Not much change in Moonway. He was home Thursday when I got home. I had a little talk with him Saturday morning when I gave him money for a pencil. Seems the only time he will talk is when he wants something. I didn't get any satisfaction out of him though. He said he knew what he was doing, didn't need any advice from me or anybody else. I saw him hiking for Greenville when I got out of work last night, walking in the rain, reading a book with his thumb sticking out. I still think he's hurting way down deep. He left a note saying he would clean his rooms this next weekend.

Easter Sunday in April, 1979, I hosted a family dinner in Greenville: two of my brothers with their families, Marty with his girlfriend Nancy, and Moonway. It was the first time in several years Moonway spent a holiday dinner with us, and it was nice. He was pleasant, rather withdrawn, and still fearful. But that Sunday, at least, the passion seemed to be absent from his fears.

Only in retrospect do I realize that during this time I began to take some concrete actions of letting go, to focus more of my time, energy, and money on developing my own mind and character. Before that, it seems, my detachment was mere sound and fury. Following graduation, Shirley went to Texas with my brother Keith and started her first job there, and I enrolled in two intensive three-week summer courses at ULK. I rented my Greenville house for the summer to help with my college expenses, and Moonway took all of his things back to Northridge. While in Kingston, I wrote to tell him to stop charging long distance calls on my phone in Greenville. He sent some money to help with the phone bill and a note.

> I did make some long distance calls on your phone. This was three or four months ago. I was trying to get into a drug rehabilitation center. They refused to admit me because I am still on tranquilizers. Then they had the nerve to send me a letter requesting me to help buy land for their new drug rehab center. I would like to apologize. It won't happen again.
>
> August

Mom,

> I was down to visit you about a month or so ago. I couldn't find where you were staying. I went all over the campus. I searched well into the night. Someone helped me look. We called some people on campus but nothing turned up. I went to Southeast Harbor and goofed around for a day.
>
> Fall is coming. The trees should be turning color soon. I hope to get around to doing some sketches and painting this year of the foliage. I am registered for a ceramics course. I should have access to the school darkroom, too, which will be great.
>
> I'm seeing a shrink. Probably will get into some group therapy sometime which should be interesting and possibly revealing. Looking forward to

seeing you.

Labor Day weekend, Moonway came to Middletown to help me load the truck to move to a smaller apartment so I could save money for graduate school. He was more communicative than I had seen him in a long time. It was a good time between us, and he loaned me his copy of Kenneth Donaldson's *Insanity Inside Out*. I wrote him later, "I have finished reading *Insanity Inside Out*, a very provocative book. What a lot of spunk Donaldson has."

My summer renters had moved out by mid September, and I went up to Greenville with a birthday present for Moonway. He was giggly and giddy, but Richard insisted he was doing better. When I was home again in Greenville in mid October, I tried to call him but got no answer. I stayed active through that fall, teaching full time, social activities, traveling to the University of Lincoln at Kingston, ULK, one evening a week and studying for my Modern Poetry course: Yeats, Eliot, Pound, and Frost. Although I missed Shirley terribly that first year she was gone, and I worried some about Martin in Florida, I was feeling happy about the interesting things in my life.

> November 14
> Mom,
>   I'm doing OK. It's snowing for the first time this year. I've been organizing my files and generally cleaning up the clutter of my room in anticipation of the end of my probation. I still don't know what I want to do. Maybe a little traveling. I'm still reading and doing my art work.
>   I was at UL, Northridge last night chanting stuff about Iran and anti Ku Klux Klan slogans. I ran into my probation officer. I thought I was going to be busted for disturbing the peace. He didn't bust me though. He was really nice about it.
>   I heard on the news that Jerry Rubin was on the Kingston campus giving one of his infamous lectures. He wrote some books about the 60's student

unrest. He's really a first class agitator. Could you do me a favor and see if you can find out how the Kingston people contacted him. I would really like to contact him and (or) his people. I thought that some of your student friends might know his address or someone at Kingston who might know how I could reach him with phone or letter. Don't go to a lot of trouble though.

I've been in contact with Eldridge Cleaver who was another radical, *Soul on Fire*. He did some time in prison. He is free now which is great. I'm really glad that he is willing to accept charges for my phone calls and talk to me.

I am going to write a letter to Shirley now. I haven't written her since she moved to Texas.

Moonway came to visit me for a few days in Middletown during my Christmas break. We had a good visit and closed 1979 looking to the future with optimism. By that time I had rented my house indefinitely which meant I would be spending less time in Greenville in the following years, at least through graduate school.

9. Diet of Worms

As Moonway and I advance and retreat in this dance of detachment and enmeshment between us, I wonder who or what is choreographing. Do I detach because he is less needy? Or does he become less needy because I have made other decisions about my time? Or do we simply advance and retreat in response to rhythms of personal stresses, each searching for a comfort zone and signaling to each other, unconscious as wild bees dancing a map to a food source?

In early 1980, Moonway told me that his "journey through insanity" was almost over. By May, he felt too far away, and my detachment no longer felt comfortable. I wasn't seeing much of him, and when I did, he was often stoned, his verbal communications mere grunts and nods, yes and no responses to questions interspersed with vacant grins. He

81

seemed burned out, and my whole life felt sad, painful, and unproductive. Still, I wrote in my journal: "I know these fallow times can be useful in the overall rhythm of life." At the end of that school year, I moved to a small efficiency apartment in Kingston, eager to begin a vastly expanded cultural life: art exhibitions, concerts of classical and folk music, a dynamic literary life.

I wrote to Moonway telling him I was looking forward to talking with him about his often expressed interest in Saint Augustine. And I asked if he would like to come help me paint my little house in Greenville during the weekend of July 4th when I would be home.

> Dear Mom,
>   We had a big thunderstorm up here. It stopped raining and the air smells fantastic. I probably won't be down to visit unless it's later on in the summer. I would be glad to help you paint your house. See you the 4th."

But we didn't connect much while I was home, and I didn't paint my house. I finished my Medieval Philosophy class and wrote to him, "Sometimes called 'The Father of Western Mysticism,' Meister Eckhart turned out to be my favorite." Like Moonway, I have always been, and still am, attracted to the visionary sensibility. I also yearn to know the divine in the thingness of our earthly life. I pursue the experience in meditation, inspirational reading, art, and music. Although these times have their own delights and are likely good training in being receptive, the divine presence mostly eludes me there, catches me up when and where I least expect it: one of Moonway's sudden insights in the midst of a flight of fancy so far out of my sense of reality, I have nearly stopped listening; the sudden appearance of a bear up the path of my daily walk; trudging up the hill toward home with my 5-year-old grandson, both of us carrying armfuls of heavy rail spikes he has been collecting in the railroad bed, him so tired from his exertions his face is red, but he will not let go of even one of them.

In early fall, I visited with Moonway and found him well, not taking any medication, very responsive and easy to talk with. In October, he came down to my apartment for a week to visit; it was another of the great times with him that keep me hopeful often when things seem utterly hopeless. We made plans for him to apply for admission to ULK. When he went back home, I wrote to him.

> The leaves are mostly gone. From my window, I have a view of the river now. Through bare tree branches last couple of nights I watched the full moon rise over the water. That's my psychedelic experience, my consciousness expansion. And Faulkner's *The Sound and The Fury* from my course last fall. Caddy Compson is my current favorite literary character. For part of the novel, she is a little girl who plays in the mud and gets dirty and climbs trees.

Mom,
> I mailed your books back. It will probably be two or three weeks before I know if I can get into school in Kingston. I hope I do. The snow is starting to build up which I don't like. I have always hated winter. I am enclosing five dollars for a Christmas present. Please don't give me anything for Christmas. Your Emily Dickinson paper is with the books.

Moonway was accepted at ULK and moved to Kingston in January 1981, but he only lasted a short time in the classes he began. By February, he was living in a small apartment a few blocks from mine, walking the streets with a painted face, and panhandling for spending money. He told me, Mom, I'm starting my own cult.

Well Moonway, that's interesting, but you should think about the price you might be paying in social alienation with your idiosyncratic behavior.

And you should stop feeling guilty about me.

We preached at each other, not quite willing, again, to let the other be.

In March we had a lovely snowstorm. I got excited about it and planned to do some cross country skiing with friends, but Moonway checked himself into the Alcohol and Drug Rehabilitation at Central Lincoln Medical Center. He had been talking to people at AA, got himself a sponsor and made the decision all within a few days. Without any valium, he was feeling so anxious about it that I decided to stick around. I didn't expect I could compete with valium for his anxiety, but his sponsor asked me to take Moonway to the hospital and be involved, and I was glad about that. People in the mental health system had rarely invited my involvement in Moonway's care; they frequently discouraged it. I felt hopeful, again, that Moonway had taken this step, a big initiative to help himself recover. I invited Shirley and Martin to come. They declined, but respectfully and with encouragement to me.

Moonway, before we begin talking about memories of the late '70s and early '80s, we need to talk about the team meeting Eleanor scheduled for next week. She and Dr. Long think problems with housekeeping, hygiene, and keeping treatment appointments indicate you are decompensating and maybe need some time in the hospital.

No! I'm OK, Mom—if the housekeeper would come when she's supposed to.

She says you are not answering the door when she comes.

Well, she needs to knock louder. These pills knock me out.

If you were taking them regularly as prescribed and only with your supper, you likely would be more awake during the day.

I do take them every day, every damn one.

When I was cleaning yesterday in the bathroom, I found a stash behind the curtain.

I need to save up some extra so I won't go into withdrawals if I run out. Mom, let's pick apart my time in Kingston like we planned.

OK. We'll talk about the team meeting some more

this weekend. I think we need to be prepared for what might happen.

Now, Kingston. When you said, "You got out, but I had nowhere to go. You probably didn't want me," were you thinking about that time in Kingston?

Yeah. We didn't have much of a time there in Kingston, did we, Mom? That was all my fault. I went down to go to college at ULK. And I wanted to see you. I thought you could make all things better for me with my drug problem, but that took a lot of work.

I couldn't do a thing for you with it, could I? You had to go to the treatment program for that? And you're right. I didn't want you to live with me the way things were. I couldn't tolerate living without rules and limits about house care and about your art and writing you had in my closet.

I thought you were getting into it and everything. I kept coming to check on it and wanting to sleep there.

And my agreement with the land lady was that I wasn't supposed to have any ongoing guests in my apartment.

That's what psyche and corrections does with the people they can't do nothing with. They live homeless. The homeless are probably some of the most incorrigible of society's people.

You weren't homeless there; you had your little apartment just down the street from me. But you would come in to my place at all hours of the night. I finally told you that you couldn't come any more, that I would come down to your apartment for us to visit. And I said if you were going to be paranoid about your art and writing, then you'd have to take it with you. I also told you if you were going to be so scared about it all the time, you should think about getting rid of it so it wouldn't haunt you.

I burned all those, you know?

Yes, you got rid of it, and it still haunts you. Did what I said have anything to do with you burning it?

I don't know. I understand it now. I didn't then. Now, I don't blame you. There are some things I won't tolerate. I'm not going to let gangs off the street in here, any more. I just refuse to.

Have you, before, let gangs off the street into your apartment?

We better blip here, Mom. Big, big old blip. Giant blip. I don't want to get anyone in trouble.

OK. You decide what you want to keep private. I was unhappy that I wasn't able to help you then.

This was before all the cities went rural in their thinking, or mellowed out anyway because of acculturation. It was hard times then.

You used to sit sometimes in my apartment and talk to the walls, things like that. I said to you, "If you are going to hallucinate, either you or I will have to leave. I can't be around it. It's too upsetting and scary." As a result of going through the treatment program with you and getting a sponsor in AlAnon, I was getting more assertive and direct about my feelings, needs, and limits, and without much anger that I remember. After I said that, you stopped hallucinating around me, or you didn't let me know. Which were you doing? Do you remember that?

I don't remember. It might have been related to pot. It probably was. And agitation. And culture shock. I've never killed anyone. Honest. Mom, I want you to have full, unconditional access to my psyche charts. Well kiss this jug: Poisonous cyanide for poisoning and drugging us.

I was growing dope in that little apartment and at Holman Cabins on Kingston campus, too. I don't regret the dope, Mom, just burning those notes. And I keep trying to force people to bring them back from the ashes, the fire. It's not impossible. Just might take time. A long time. And I don't want to force it on people, but I wish they'd work on it. That's my main grudge. The one grudge that nags at me. I've tried everything. I got even though, with the FBI for getting in there and toying with my radio and stuff. You know what I did? Down here at a beach in Maine, I burned a small flag that I stole from a grave yard. Right on the beach. I think I was trying to be a Mansonite yippie then. I'm more a guerrilla than a terrorist, Mom. Terrorists are slicker, more sophisticated. Guerrillas are involved in theater and everything going, every form of violence and masochism.

Pushed into it. I'm retired in guerrilla ways, though, other than propaganda, what you see here and there.

I'd like to get all my art and writing back. I burned some in Kingston, and some were raided and confiscated on K2 on SMHI. I stashed them in a closet in a pillow case, and they were gone when I went to get them, '80, '81 or '82. 3 main gripes in my life: the fractured arm, notes and artwork I burned under that bridge in Kingston, and the notes and artwork stolen, confiscated, burned, torched, or sent somewhere. I burned them because I thought I was becoming Adolf Hitler. I liked them, but they scared me down in that city.

Moonway, somewhere, in the transcripts of our conversations, you wrote in the margin that you wanted to kill me in Kingston. We ought to talk about that.

That was the FBI getting into my apartment, Mom.

I guess this is a hot issue, hunh? What were you mad about?

Oh. The FBI investigation is what forced it on us. You and me. They're quiet about it. It sure sucked, though.

Were you mad at me because . . . ?

You wouldn't let me in for shelter and food sometimes is why I was mad.

I kicked you out, didn't I?

Yeah.

And I was often afraid, too. I'm sorry . . . .

I'll live, Mom. Don't worry.

I'm sorry that hurt you.

I'll live. I made it through. I survived her. Thanks to Will St. Lorraine. And my attorneys. They been through this. There's got to be a better way than muscle from psyche and corrections. There are guns.

What do you think is a better way? How would you like to be treated?

Like a human being created in the image of God. They really put me through a Leningrad there on K2 and they did it deliberately. The charts, I think, and the medication. That's not a derogatory statement against Leningrad, either, considering the condition of these places, Leningrad would be

87

a palace. They made sly remarks, laughed at me, restricted me. I got something in my notes called Lowrey's Alternative Treatment Proposal as offered by Governor Lowrey. I designed the Alternative Treatment Proposal in this state. It was on the bulletin board there on Ward K2, SMHI. Lowrey's Alternative Treatment Proposal. They told me there was no alternative treatment though when I asked to be put on it. All the most negative stuff happened on K2. Mom, I'm curious: Do K1 & K2 stand for Klan 1 and Klan 2? KKK. Well, that's my opinion. I was probably resisting treatment, so it might have been my fault. They would gladly have given me drugs and weaned me off them. But I just Jonesed from all that pot and drugs all at once, and booze. My own stupid fault according to AA. I don't think it is though. I think it's the environment's fault.

That wasn't a very pleasant time in Kingston for either of us, was it, Mom? I hope these are better times for you.

And then the Drug Rehab, three months as an outpatient at the Central Lincoln Medical Center. I hated it, worse than SMHI. There was a counselor, black hair in a pony tail, I liked her then but not now. I remember the nigger that ran the program. I liked him then, too. But I hate his guts now. Being in all those places is no fun.

You and Dad had to go through that family meeting. My emotions there were all fake and tortured into me by that program.

It was difficult for me, too, Moonway. I went through the whole family program including weekly meetings with my counselor. I heard a lot there about tough love, and I still believe in it. Love has to be tough to endure. But it also needs to be soft and gentle a lot. Too many people, including some in that program, learn the tough a lot better than the love. Tough without love is punishment, just cruel. And it is really hard to fake love.

Initially, it looked like Drug Rehab was a failure for Moonway. He spent a couple of weeks at the inpatient unit and then was transferred to outpatient status because he wasn't practicing the program. He spent three to four months as an out-patient and remained withdrawn throughout; at best, he participated only in a perfunctory way. In hindsight, I see he was profoundly depressed, and I am impressed that he showed up every day and remained sober and drug free during that time, including free of psychiatric drugs. Knowing what I know now about the effects of withdrawal from that medication, it seems a heroic effort. In the weeks preceding Drug Rehab, he was often high on street drugs, extremely fearful of being wire tapped or robbed of his art and writing, and bizarre in behavior and appearance with strange hair and beard cuts, made-up face, and painted nails. Most of that behavior was absent during Drug Rehab. In the years since, I have often felt impressed at how much of the teaching from that program he remembers and often practices, and I believe he began there his long recovery from addiction to street drugs, often stumbling and slipping.

My own counseling in that rehab program was also rocky. My counselor was a big, burly recovering alcoholic always on the lookout for things to fix in me: my enabling, my life style he called too liberal, my emotions he called fake. I made an extra appointment to see him about that, told him not to judge my feelings until he'd walked a mile in my shoes. That confrontation may be the greatest benefit I got from him. But I did and do think the overall experience was a great benefit to me in helping me to live and enjoy my life in spite of difficulties and distractions, in spite of my imperfect practice, still, of detachment and tough love. It was a great relief to talk, like that program encouraged talk, with others who were going through similar experiences. And it got me started on a long and disciplined practice of the twelve steps that is still a central guide in my life. Even though the program was difficult and it didn't fix everything, I'm very glad I did it.

10. It's Hard to Find my Own Mind

Moonway left Kingston after drug rehab. He spent the summer wandering around the state with his only home the pack on his back and a 2-man, bright orange nylon tent tied to the pack with clothes-line rope. July 24, 1981, he wrote to me, "I have been living in a loner space here. The medications that I am taking make me throw up each morning, but I am still following my schedule. Marty and Shirl were up from Colorado, and we visited the woods with Dad."

In mid September, Moonway turned 25 years old and was, again, a patient at SMHI.

Mom, I been through the diet of worms in Kingston, you know? 1981. It was in the sandwich. I was so hungry and puking and barfing from bulimia that I ate a sandwich I saw with all kinds of aphids and maggots in it.

Oh h h. Who did it? What do you mean? Worms collect on the food after it's trashed. Did you pick it out of their garbage?

I didn't pick their garbage. I bought it at their store, that store down just the other side of Alfredo's Pizza there in Kingston.

Who would feed you worms?

On truce terms globally, all areas, including with the courts and judges.

Who fed you worms?

Some guy in Kingston. Some Italian, Mafia type. He didn't do it deliberately. He wanted to get out of the Mafia, so he fed me worms because I represent the Mafia. He did it deliberately, Mom.

I was hearing so many voices. I followed the voices a lot, right into the woods, out into the street. I slugged a dentist. He put morphine in the Novocain and was drilling my teeth too much. I know he was. They put me on Ward E3, the forensic ward, for slugging that dentist. I told Will St. Lorraine about the worms, and they de-wormed me there.

Long be the man of Will St. Lorraine.
Young be the man of Will St. Lorraine.
Protected be the family and man
of Will St. Lorraine of E3, SMHI.

Moonway wrote from SMHI, "I'm writing again to let

you know <u>I love you</u> and do still need your special guidance helping me make some right decisions, especially in things like finding a job." The University at Kingston is only ten miles from SMHI, so I continued to see him often, but my studies helped to alleviate preoccupation with his illness.

By December, he was discharged from SMHI, in Florida again, and he wrote from there.

> I called Gram Adams in Zephyr Hills, and we talked some. I must have sounded confused. It's hard for me to find my own mind through this microwave nightmare, but I'm struggling to do so. I think I've finally found the right type of medication to stabilize me and help me make some decisions about what I want to do. I should have been on medication some time ago anyway. I keep hurting people but unintentionally. I make choices I shouldn't. I've been praying more since I stopped wandering.
>
> Please pray for me in whatever manner you pray. I know it's hard putting up with me. Please send my bank money in traveler's checks to John's.
>
> A great big triple love to you, Mom. Please take out a double heap of money from my account for all the phone calls and for all you've put me through in trying to make me grow up and face the old big world like an old big man. I hope you keep glowing on with life. For the love of it all, I love you down deep inside of it all. I'm happy, hurt, lonely, and sorry. What I did to you was evil and somehow totally wrong.
>
> Double special love,
> Moonway

In mid-January, he wrote again.

> I'm leaving this Crisis Center next Thursday. I hope to get into a home for ex-mental patients. I guess Dad doesn't want me back and I'm rather glad because I'm 25 and need some independence. My theory is that somehow the family has been possessive

of me because of my illness, which may be a way of shifting the blame on my part. Anyway, I think a lot of what you said in the last letter about accepting responsibility for one's own actions. It makes sense. You are very smart. <u>I have never accepted this responsibility the way I should.</u>

Letters like these break my heart with sorrow, regret, and love. But sometimes it takes a long time for these complex feelings to become conscious.

Moonway roamed around again during that time, repeating again his journey from Florida to Denver and then back home, homeless much of the time.

Mom, on my way to Florida, I stopped in Greenwich Village for a while. Stayed there about a week. I remember watching a tribe do a dance, going to a Neo-Nazi shop, going to a place with all kinds of sado-masochistic books.

Last night I dreamed about David Berkowitz, Son of Sam. Ha, ha. He was in a mental joint in New York City right close to Greenwich Village. He told me not to talk. But we can keep doing it, Mom. Never mind the dream. He understands. I'm working on his release, too. I asked him if he'd ever been to Greenwich Village. He said, "It's there." I miss Greenwich Village sometimes. I didn't want to leave, but I was living in the streets, and I wanted a place to stay.

I went to Florida and lived at Johnny's and Grammy Adams' for a while. Then I was at the Crisis Center and Psyche Center at a University there for 3 months all together. Most of these joints I've been in Mom, there are positive and negative aspects to them. I'd have mass murdered, assassinated, or killed myself by now if I hadn't been in them. I know I would have.

Moonway, let me see if I understand your travel itinerary right. After Florida, you went to Denver where Marty was then? You were homeless there, too? And then you came home and went to SMHI for slugging the dentist? And then the next year, you were wandering around the country, getting more and more homeless? By the time I left

The University at Lincoln after I finished my Master's Degree, you were living on the streets of Denver again?

I lived homeless in the streets of Denver, Colorado for six months that time. That was hell on earth after a while. I think they did it deliberately just to get Denver some business, the cars and stuff.

Who did what?

Not the underworld, but business men there. Kept me there a slave in the streets. Faggots, Mom. I didn't do no sexual favors that I'm aware of. But they just do things with your mind. I can't describe it. I don't know how to put it in words. Horrible. I picked up a prostitute and got robbed by her pimp.

My checks came in a little bit, to Marty's place. I'd walk up there to get them. I walked all over Denver. Stalked the whole town, tried to. In building entrances, in the alleys, in the streets. I don't want to concede too much, here, but it's a good thing that mental institution, that mental box, took me in. A psychiatric place there. What happened, I was on my way to California to join the Mansons with a 6-pack of beer under my arm, and a policeman stopped me, and I was thrown in a mental joint. I came home after that. Did you get any phone calls from me?

I got a few, but not many during that time that you were gone. Those times are the longest periods of time when we have been out of touch. You lost my phone number?

In Denver, yeah. I think you were in Cincinnati.

Not then. I was in Kingston part of the time finishing my Master's degree. And in Greenville for the summer selling my house to Myra. Then I was on the road through the fall of '82 traveling around the country for adventure and to search out a place to study for a Ph. D. You were in Denver when I left. And I wanted to visit you and Marty there, but by the time I got there, you had gone back to Maine.

Mom, you don't recall any calls from me from Denver, Colorado?

You called once or twice while I was still in Greenville that summer. But I heard more from Martin about you than I heard from you. What do you remember?

I recall talking to you from a telephone, unless the FBI or CIA was running old tapes or something. You were gone on your cross country trip when I came back. Boy, didn't I turn my family into a nightmare bunch of tramps, hunh? I didn't mean to.

You didn't do it. I might not have left if you had been still in the state. But it turned out to be good for me. I loved the adventure of that travel, the landscapes, the space of the prairies, the Rockies, the Pacific Coast, the deserts. It's still a beautiful country even with all the environmental abuse. And I enjoyed it in spite of worries. That's the way detachment works for me. Much as I would like to, I haven't been able to stop anxious feelings. But they don't spoil good times. That's life, the yin and the yang.

Well, we're well traveled now. We can say that. I don't regret moving and traveling all over the place. But it wasn't much fun that 3rd time, after Kingston. And that time I thumbed down there to Massachusetts to be a mass murderer. Ha, ha. After I got pissed off in Newburgh—SMHI. I went down to join . . . Was his name Williams that killed all them niggers down there?

I wish you wouldn't call them niggers.

I didn't <u>do</u> any violence though. Too much training at E 3. Too much academics. I went to four other colleges after Kingston, in Florida and Colorado. I didn't take courses, but I hung around. And Mennonite in Harrisonburg, Virginia.

Moonway, this is the last chance we have to talk about the Team Meeting tomorrow. Eleanor, Dr. Long, and Victor Robbins might recommend that you be hospitalized.

No, Mom.

Well, maybe if it comes up and you would agree to spending a week or so at the County Psychiatric Hospital, you wouldn't have to go to SMHI.

No, Mom. I'm OK.

Well I hope you will be able to convince your team that you are.

I need matches for my smokes. Can you take me to the store?

I called Moonway to remind him of the team meeting an hour before the scheduled time of 3:00 PM. He didn't answer, and I left a message. I waited 15 minutes and called again. Still no answer. I called again in 10 minutes. No answer, so I drove over. When he hadn't answered by the third knock, I went around the side of his apartment, knocked on his bedroom window, and called to him. He mumbled, What?

Time for your team meeting.

I could hear him stirring, so I went back around to his door and knocked twice more before he opened the door in the same clothes he wore the day before—dirty chinos and once-white T-shirt covered all over in the cryptic messages and symbols he marks up all his shirts with using a black permanent marker. I said, You need to hurry, or we'll be late. Wash your face and hands and change your clothes.

I don't want to go, Mom. I'm too tired. It's all this medicine.

You better go. You said you don't want to go to the hospital, so you better meet with them and let them know what you are willing to do to avoid that.

He yawned. I'll get my coat, but I'll need some coffee.

He came back out of his bedroom wearing the same clothes, pulling on a dirty coat that was once bright yellow. He took a home-made hat off the TV and put it on. Both the coat and the hat were emblazoned with the same kind of graffiti, his art work, that adorned his shirts.

On the way to the meeting, I went through the Dunkin Donuts drive-through and bought a large coffee for Moonway and a small one for me, so we were late. All the other team members were already seated in the conference room of CMHC. We sat across the table from patient-advocate Cliff Worth wearing a frayed gray sweatshirt and Eleanor, the tallest person in the room. I always thought of Nurse Ratchett in *One Flew Over the Coucoo's Nest* when I saw her, which is unfair, I know. Psychiatrist Dr. Long was at the end of table on our right. Moonway's financial conservator (money manager) Victor Robbins was at the end of the table on our left. Sorry we're late, I said.

95

Eleanor: It's alright. I'll review with you what we talked about. Moonway, you haven't been letting your housekeeper in, and . . .

I let her in every time I hear her knocking.

When was the last time?

Week or so. I don't know.

Well, I called her, and she told me you haven't answered her knock in over a month. She says she hears music playing really loud. Other tenants are complaining about the noise. There hasn't been any cleaning for a long time. But just let me read down the list of other things we need to discuss at this meeting. OK? Then we will talk about them one at a time. You know I check your pill box every week, and according to my notes, you are not taking your meds, on average 2 or 3 times a week.

I forget sometimes.

Victor, eyes reflecting the bright blue of his dress shirt: And I found out today you sold the new computer you and Cliff talked me into buying for you. I knew it was a mistake. For $25 bucks! And you didn't even ask me.

Well it was my computer, wasn't it?

But it's just a waste. If you had asked me, I could have gotten a lot more money for it. What did you spend the money on?

Well, here's something. I want my money, mail and phone calls dating back to birth. I keep telling you guys I ain't getting them. When are you going to help me with that?

Cliff: That computer is water under the bridge. Can we focus on the issues that need to be resolved?

Victor: How he spends his money is my issue, and also an issue of compliance if he is out of money for food by the end of the month.

Eleanor: Your social-group facilitator says you are not going to social group.

I said, I worry too, Moonway, about you isolating, especially now that it is winter.

Eleanor: It's part of your treatment plan that you agreed to.

I got a right to refuse treatment, don't I Cliff? They

can't force socializing on me, can they?

Well, you know what the court order says. If you refuse the prescribed treatment they can send you back to the Missouri Correction Facility for Federal Prisoners. I know you don't want that.

Can I go smoke?

Eleanor: I think we have at least got through the list the things we are mainly concerned about, so you can go, but don't be gone long, and we will go on talking about these things while you are gone. Is that OK?

You let Cliff talk for me. Can I borrow some matches?

Victor dug out a book of matches and passed them to him: You better put your coat on. It's cold out there.

But Moonway rushed out the door without bothering with his coat.

I said, Could we talk about the med situation first. He doesn't like the way the pills make him feel. I believe that is why he doesn't take them regularly. The Haldol injections that he has every 3 weeks don't seem to do him any good, and I worry about the threat of Tardive Dyskinesia. Are there alternatives we could try?

Dr. Long: Risperdal might be available soon in long-term injectable form, but for now, Haldol is the only long-term treatment we have for schizophrenia. He is doing better with the shots than he would without them, because he is at least getting some regular medication. I check every month for tardive dyskinesia, and so far I don't see any signs.

Cliff got up and started pacing, one hand in his naturally-faded jeans, the other stroking his greying beard: If he is doing better with Haldol, why are we having this meeting about all this supposed non-compliance. And isn't Tardive Diskinesia only a matter of time?

Dr. Long: Probably, but I have some patients that have been on Haldol for years and so far no signs. And they like it. They choose it.

And when you do see the signs, it's irreversible?

Yes, but since he won't take pills regularly...

Well, is there some alternative to the pills that he

could try, something that doesn't make him feel like shit.

Any change in medication is risky. I won't make a serious change like that unless he is hospitalized.

Cliff stopped pacing: Why this chicken-shit attitude about risk? No change is risky, too.

Dr. Long rose, a small woman in a dark blue business suit, she glared at him: I will not tolerate being sworn at. She gathered her file folder, and turned to go, brushing against Moonway on her way out. She mumbled, Sorry, Moonway. I have another appointment.

I said, Moonway, how come you are not shivering? It's hovering around zero out there, and the wind blowing.

Cliff and Moonway sat down facing each other. Moonway said, I'm all out of smokes. Are we done? Can we go?

Cliff: Moonway, let's talk about what you can do to comply with your treatment plan. Instead of having to go twice a week to social club, could you go at least once? Would that work, Eleanor?

Eleanor shrugged her shoulders covered in a large shawl, a paisley print of olive green and red: We could give it a try, better than not going at all.

How will I get there? I don't always have a ride.

Eleanor: I told you, I will take you.

Cliff: Agreed, Moonway?

If I have to.

No, you don't have to. You can risk going back to Missouri instead.

No!

OK, now about the pills.

I don't remember. I would take them if I could remember.

How would it be if someone reminds you?

Who?

Eleanor: I could call you every week day before I go home for the day.

I said, I will call you on weekends.

Cliff: Agreed? Now about the housekeeping.

I don't hear her knock, honest.

Can you turn your music down a few decibels? That would help with 2 problems—your housekeeper and your neighbors. You don't want to get evicted, do you?

No.

And how would it be if your housekeeper calls you before she comes? Do you hear the phone over your music?

Usually.

Well, you usually answer when I call, and turning down the volume will help. So, have we got agreements on these issues?

If I have to. But will you guys get me some help with getting my money, mail, and phone calls? Dating back to birth? How come I got to do everything?

Eleanor, can you give Moonway a copy of these agreements and have him sign one for you and one for him to help him remember? And will you contact the housekeeper about calling?

I sure can.

Moonway: Victor, have I got money in my account for some tobacco?

You will have to call the office for that.

Outside by the car, Moonway said, Mom, Can you lend me some money until I get my check.

No, Moonway, I don't lend you money for tobacco products.

Well, take me up to Dad's then. He'll lend me money.

Cliff Worth was appointed Moonway's advocate by the court way back in the early '90s when he got into trouble for mailing threatening letters to public officials. Since he retired from his job with the Department of Health and Human Services, he not only helps out with the legal issues, but he is the one that usually comes up with the plan to solve problems with care providers. Dr. Long has been his psychiatrist for longer than that. One time when I was complaining to the state director of NAMI that Moonway only got to see his psychiatrist for a half hour a month, she said, You are lucky, most patients only see their psychiatrist every three months at best.   Moonway and I need both Cliff and Dr. Long.

11. Growing Mind Deaf in Here

Mom, I spent two whole years at SMHI right after Denver. After that incident with Dad.

What incident?

I'm not at liberty to say, not going to incriminate myself. One time on E3. I was sitting there drawing, and an intern came up and sprayed hair spray into my ear. Another intern took some of my art, put it in the trash. I wanted to hit her. Should have. I would never have been through this. I'd be out and free. But probably it's what she wanted, hunh? Some patriot wanting to be hit so she could stop my radical influence. And some guys were picking on me, so I hit one of them. Him and two of his buddies jumped me. They twisted my arm behind my back, broke it, fractured it. It won't bend. They had me down on the floor. I hollered for help. Some people separated us. They had me lift weights, Mom, they wouldn't take me to a hospital. I don't want an operation, though. I know that. And I'll never force medical stuff on you guys.

Who told you it was broken?

I know it is. It won't bend down beyond that point there. It kinked right up.

I think if you took physical therapy, exercised it regularly, it could get better.

It won't, Mom. It's broken.

I remember meeting Lee from the forensic ward when I visited you during that time. He said, "How come you are back in Moonway's life? You have been out of it for a long while."

I said, "I have never been out of it. When we are away from each other, we talk on the phone once or twice a week, and write regularly." I didn't offer any more information such as being out of touch with you for long periods of time during that year you, and then I, were wandering around the country.

Lee Green. Big fat guy with the beard. Looked like a

hick motorcycle gang member. Van Gordon, too. I hate their guts still for what they did, raping me like that.

Literally raping you?

Sh. Yeah.

Did you tell anybody?

No.

Do you have a memory of it actually happening?

No, but I have a feeling, a suspicion. Mom, what were you doing during your cross-country trip

I zig-zagged my way west, prospecting universities all the way for Ph. D study. Down south from Lincoln to North Carolina, across to Tennessee, northwest to Indianpolis and to Iowa, southwest to Martin's in Denver. Northwest to Seattle, down the Pacific Coast to Los Angeles. I met Myra there, and we traveled down to San Diego, back east across the Southwest, and up to Denver again. Shirley had moved there by then. We visited them for a few days, and Myra flew out of Denver back to Washington. Then I went to Austin, Texas and stayed for four months, worked on a construction crew rebuilding decks on condominiums, and waited to hear about my applications to graduate school. In 1983, I went to Oklahoma to study for my Ph. D. By the summer of 1983, I was teaching Freshman English and before long writing my dissertation.

At this time in 1983, Moonway had been hospitalized at SMHI for several months, and I received a letter from Adult Protective Services about his long term care.

Dear Mrs. Adams

The Department of Human Services has been requested to become legal guardian for your son, Moonway Michael. During the case study phase, we are required to contact all interested family members to determine their ability and/or desire to be guardian themselves. It is preferable that you respond in writing regarding your involvement.

Thank you for your consideration in this matter.

Lincoln Department of Human Services

I replied.

> Re. your letter of March 22, I would like more information. Who requested that your Department become legal guardian? Why is this measure being considered? What would it mean in terms of Moonway's welfare and his rights about treatment or confinement? Have you talked with him about this, and what is his response?
>
> I have been away from Lincoln since last September and have written frequent letters to Moonway but have only recently heard from him. His communications are erratic and confused. I realize that he is very ill. I also know that I cannot assume any sort of guardianship over him. During the last several years, I have had trouble managing even short term visits with him. I am not able to supervise medication or to exert any sort of control over his behavior. He will not allow it, and I have neither the physical means to control him, nor the emotional or moral authority to make decisions for an adult even though he is my son and judged by professionals to be unable to make decisions for himself.
>
> I am very concerned about him. Your letter poses a dilemma. I recognize my helplessness in dealing with him, and I believe that his hospitalizations have intensified his psychosis. From what I have seen, they offer little in the way of real treatment. At its best, professional care might at least serve a humane care-taking function. It has seldom done even that for Moonway. I don't see any good alternatives for him.
>
> I am enrolled in a Doctoral program in Oklahoma, so I will be away from Lincoln for the next several years at least, but I expect to be home some time this summer, and I would like to talk with you then. In the meantime, could you answer the questions I posed earlier?

I heard no further word from Adult Protective

Services. Instead, I received the following from the Director of Social Services at SMHI dated April 7, 1983.

> Dear Mrs. Adams,
>
> Concerning your son, Moonway. I thought you would like to know that, even without medication, Moonway is slowly becoming a little more cooperative and less disruptive. He continues to experience periods of strong delusional thinking, related to Christ, the CIA or Nazis, but this is less frequent.
>
> I can understand and appreciate your concerns about forcing medication and our need to pay attention to his physical and emotional health. We have not been very effective in helping Moonway in the past nor can I guarantee that we will be effective this time as so much depends on Moonway and what he wants for himself.
>
> I will continue to review with Moonway's treating Physician the need for a Guardian. At this time, an application for Public Guardianship has been submitted to the Department of Human Services but is held up by a legal problem concerning release of records.
>
> It was I that encouraged the family to locate you as I had recalled your positive influence on Moonway during one of his first admissions. I have not given him your address; I felt that was up to you to do. I do know he has contacted his father and brother trying to find you.
>
> If you have any questions or have any suggestions about how we can help Moonway, please feel free to contact me.

I wrote back.

> I am grateful for your letter of April 7. I very much appreciate any communications from people who have to deal with Moonway on the institutional level. I have had so few, even when I have requested

them, that a letter showing concern such as yours does rather overwhelms me. I am torn between wanting to hope and wanting to protect myself from disappointment again. I understand that so much depends on what Moonway wants for himself. And I still would like to believe that, if he must be institutionalized, it can be done in a humane and caring way. I'm still not sure why Public Guardianship is being considered now when it has not been in the past. Is it because of his refusal to take medication? Or is he considered much more ill?

As for suggestions about how you can help Moonway, I suspect that AA is the most effective means for motivating him to make any effort toward recovery. Does he have access to AA?

I never did get any clear answers about why guardianship was being considered then. Maybe issues of confidentiality play a role, such as the incident with his dad that Moonway doesn't want to talk about. There may be a variety of issues and incidents concerning his mental illness that I will never know because of confidentiality issues. I am ambivalent about confidentiality and conflicted in my own values about it. On the one hand, I hate to have people I don't trust probing issues I want to be private, and I think it is important to safety and self esteem to be able to set clear limits with such people. On the other hand, living with and keeping secrets is crazy making. This is one of the many important moral questions I have never resolved. How to live with moral uncertainty is one of the great tasks of wisdom that I have not mastered.

After I moved to Oklahoma at the end of April, I had a good, sane conversation with Moonway on the phone. Shortly after, he wrote.

I don't like this place. I'm sure you don't like what it is doing to you. You are at a new university. Maintain contacts responsive to your needs. Don't worry about me. Get me back north. I'm in revolt now. I have white hair. Now I am confident. I have started a small newspaper that I sell for one dollar. Could you send me five dollars to fund the Xerox copies I make of it?

I drove home to Lincoln in August. During that visit, perhaps for the first time, I began to see, in spite of his illness, bits of evidence of emotional growth in Moonway, more consideration for others, more expression of affection and respect. I wrote in a letter to a friend, "Visits with Moonway were relaxed and affectionate. I appreciate that without expecting it to cure him of his fears, voices, and beliefs at odds with the world. I enjoyed my time with him more than I have in years." Moonway wrote regularly from SMHI during the two years he was hospitalized there. In these letters I continue to see evidence of that emotional growth even through continuing craziness.

October 8, 1983
 I am trying to restrain myself to writing letters for now to subdue the cost to you that occurs from phone calls. I will try to be brief. I'm not getting a fair deal from psychiatry. Don't worry about me though. Myra said you worry about me.
 I feel like I am growing mind deaf in here. In fact I am. Could I have a little money?
January, 1984
 I remember something you said which is that tears have a natural tranquilizer in them. I finally accepted the truth in that. I still can't understand how I could have ever arrived at this state of loving, but I have.
June
 I have had some trouble. I need some prophylactics (male contraceptives). No one is pregnant or anything because I have been unable to purchase them, but I could sure use some if you could send me some. It must be very difficult for a woman when a man refuses his responsibility in using a

contraceptive.

Fall 1984

I will do some thinking about your expression about simple amends through expression of gratitude and apologies. Inner life is heartbreaking very often. I don't really want to be on these drugs because I am of this nature; I am talking about uncontrollable outbursts, etc. It is just too noisy. The human body can only take so much.

Hello,

Certain personnel seem to be redetermining our reorganization as a family. I mean you and dad. I haven't been allowed to escape this determination. Please cooperate. I now have a fractured arm.

Moonway

Mom,

It is surprising to me to see how much of my memory is returning. I remember feeling lonely sometimes when I was young around springtime. Old grass around a rural house waiting to be burned or rot away in preparation for the new springtime grass—things like that still make me feel lonely.

I LOVE YA,
SON

October 10, 1984

My arm feels better. A woman is using physical therapy on it. It hurts, but it feels more natural to me to be healed this way. I suspect the fight was programmed like much that happens around here. Often we are all television addicts. It is slowly healing however.

Love,
Moonway.

Mom,

You went out of your way to assist me that frightening summer. With your help, I remained hopeful and often I was cool and level headed. This helped me out a lot. You are a very supportive woman.

Lots of love
Moonway

Mom,

Consider all the good points in my life and save my letters to you. I am not afraid of death because I am eternal. I am only afraid of pain, and you have often comforted me.

Today, the 16th of October, 1984, I have been eating a balanced diet. I coped with the hospital court day the best I could, I am showering as regularly as possible and doing a laundry on my appointed day. I am trying to handle all stressful situations with the help of the groups I have attended.

Love, Moonway

When Moonway was in SMHI for so long, I was almost relieved, hoping, again, that he at least had a safe place to live and regular meals.

12. Pummeling on to Destiny

My Son the Artist
(continued)

In 1984, sometimes

Moonway brings me up to date on the progress
of his journey. Twice, playing his flute,
he says he hears dolphins sing.
Then he seems close by. He gives me
a gold-plated needle—emblem of mending,
tribute to my love of needle work.

By November 1984, Moonway was discharged from
SMHI and living at Nightsun, a Group Home supervised by
County Mental Health Agency, and he wrote me, "I don't
anticipate any insurmountable problems. I have a
Community Support Worker here at County Mental Health,
and I am going to stay with it this time."

He struggled with his ambition, longing for success
with his learning, art, writing, spirituality and recovery in AA.
He was anxious about failure, and he was often filled with
regret and remorse, indicating an active conscience about past
behavior motivated by schizophrenia and drug use. In spite of
this, he often expressed happiness in letters from this period.

Nov 28 1984
When I was in Newburgh, I was going to
seven meetings a week of AA, and adjustments were
easier for me. But I am slowly learning to use my
spare time. I went to the ULN library and listened to
Shakespeare's Henry the IV and Emily Dickinson's
poetry. I also did some art work and wrote some
poetry there. I hope you derive some satisfaction that
I am doing many things on my own now. I haven't
forgotten your kindness, understanding, and
compassion.
12-17-84
I sit in unneeded jealousy of every artist and
writer still in possession of his notes and artwork. I
feel a glad certainty in the possible and probable return
of mine in some form, but I really wish I hadn't
burned them. I followed your example tonight and
took a walk. I am in the Media Center of the library at
ULN, and I will listen to poetry when I finish this

letter. I feel a lot of self esteem, self respect, and validation of my own ideas. Everything seems possible to me now that I am sober.

12-28-84

I should be doing more to make amends. To make financial amends I have been writing letters to the government in an attempt to interest them in financing my ideas of instant success. I want to make up to you what I have deprived you of when I was abusing substances. Since the government is not interested or very slow, I guess I had better repay you for now with love. Thank you very much. You have sent me three of my favorite foods.

Please don't lose touch with me. I forget sometimes in my schemes to make something of myself so I can do something nice for you.

1-5-85

What got me in trouble before was impatience. I am reading the Alcoholics Anonymous Big Book. I find it is fascinating. It gives me hope.

January 18 1985

I have been praying as a source of inner strength. I am taking two courses at Nightsun here in Northridge. The real qualities of God that matter the most to me right now are spiritual essences like love, peace, joy, and security.

Drugs and alcohol cut me off from God, and AA is restoring me to Him. I hope these prayer sessions do not cease.

2-7-85

I feel happier every day when I pray. I would like to find the central location of God, but that is a major undertaking, so for now I will pray to remain happy.

I feel guilty about not writing Marty and Shirley. We are terrible strangers to each other, and I worry about them living in a big city like Denver.

March 19, 1985

I just took a shower and I feel great. I haven't

had any trouble with the police or Mental Health people. I have gained this freedom through cooperation. I am still building up a powerful addiction to the psychiatric drugs . . . but I strongly believe that if I continue to go along with treatment they will allow me to stay off these drugs as well. But that is the future. For this twenty four hours I am happy.

I feel guilty sometimes about the problems I caused you in the past. I'm sorry and very glad that I didn't go further in creating problems for you.

April 4 1985

I bought myself a small refrigerator and an electric typewriter to type my notes which can be very pleasant. Did you hear that Marty and Shirley are coming back here to visit in June or July? It will be nice to see all of you although as I recall I have seen you all more than I previously remembered (my memory is returning).

I am thinking about taking a watercolor course in May. I went for a walk. I am making a few friends in AA. So things are getting better for me.

In retrospect, it seems that the long hospitalization was helpful. Although he moved several times, the years that followed proved to be a relatively tranquil and successful time for Moonway. He sent me a poem.

> It arrives, painfully clean like
> walking on the sea shore.
> I feel guilt like a tornado, torn,
> mad, and afraid, the three
> horrors of my life. I dream about
> gang fights. I dream about my
> right hand being cut open.
>
> I chase God with my
> diminishing life and I have found
> that I am pursuing a mad man.

111

I am awaking to a powerful absence.
I miss my mother.

In May he sent me a Mother's Day note.

Dear Mom,

Happy Birthday and Happy Mother's Day.
I'm glad you were born and I'm glad you are my
mother.   Summer is here and things should be
blooming in a couple weeks.   Wish I had a girlfriend
and maybe a family, but I have to take it one day at a
time.   Alcohol and drugs burned out a lot of my
bridges.

Moonway enrolled in two college classes the fall of
1986, and he had his first academic success in many years.
Around this time, he moved from Nightsun to a furnished
room, and his letters mention cooking for himself, his photo
and painting classes, and his therapy.   In December, he wrote
me a sympathy letter following my hysterectomy for fibroid
tumors.

12-86

I am pummeling on to my destiny having
made slim and few amends to you.   You are an
inspiration and a quiet steady calming influence on
me.

I heard from Myra about your operation and
believe it or not, I actually empathized which during
my drug addiction would probably not have bothered
me until I had no drugs and then I would have cried
over how life and family was going on without me.   I
hope that surgery does not interfere with your goals.   I
treasure your support and friendship.

I still wallow in self pity and remorse, but I
have it great actually: I have a stable disability
income, a color TV now.   I still have sort of inner
shackles, wanting to do more.

I am wrapped up in the religious thing a lot: Eternal life, being brought back to life in the event of death. I often hope that you can find the same thing. With this new lease on life I don't want to lose you.

I liked what you said about the Higher Power thing. God can take my anger I guess. One term in Catholic theology for God is Absolute Being which is a concept new to me that makes me feel eternally secure. But life as it is frightens me.

Special Love,
Son Moonway

P. S. God is rather a disappointing being usually. Perhaps if He knew more about how He is disappointing me then I would be happier.

Merry Christmas.

By February, 1987, Moonway was struggling with tensions and temptations which would prove to be a prelude for further trouble that would last for several years.

February 1987
Dear Mother,

I am angry and probably still psychotic at times. It feels better sometimes to explain my anger but thus far I have encountered only unbelief at the reasons for my anger no matter how much I explain.

My community support worker has told me that she has a lot invested in my success which really makes me happy and makes me more self confident. I am still following the advice you gave me once about "not doing anything radical until you are sober for awhile." I have not had total success at controlling my behavior, but I am doing much better.

Love,
Moonway

P. S. I am very sorry that Myra's husband died.

2/24/1987
Dear Mom,

About 3:00 AM Tuesday, I took a stroll to a

store to buy a couple beers, but it was closed and I am glad. I now have to admit that I cannot take the consequences out of drinking or drugs. My sponsor is out of town having surgery done on a couple of veins. I am being honest with you→ I still feel divided on whether or not to drink and use drugs, but I am reaffirming my decision to you to remain sober. My support worker says I have a problem with delayed gratification. Do you have any supportive advice?

April 18 1987

I wish things in life could stay the same. I have been typing for three days now. I listen to rock 'n roll, watch TV, listen to the radio and also do artwork. I called two girls from group therapy tonight, but they weren't home. I call CMHC Help Line, go to AA, drink a lot of coffee and smoke too many cigarettes.

Dear Mom,

I seem to be on a mad pursuit for women. Also, I am materially greedy.

I made it through the last fall semester of school but had to drop out the second semester during spring because I just had too many personal projects going.

I can do it Mom. I know I can: I can be famous and successful in my own small way but it surely is demanding.

Moonway was suffering relationship stresses. His feelings about women resulted in the need for more intensive treatment that summer. I finished my Ph. D. in the spring of 1987 and was traveling in Canada for two weeks when he was hospitalized in June at CMC for about a week. By the time I arrived in Greenville to stay for two months with Myra, he had been transferred to an alcohol treatment facility where he stayed for most of the summer.

Dear Mom and Myra,

I am in the Residential Treatment Facility

located near Forest Knolls Air Force Base with military planes flying overhead, feeling hurt and discouraged, almost believing that people do care about me (in fact I know they do).

This would be idyllic to me, being in here for treatment, but I also want to work on cementing my relationship with Laura Collins. I am thirty years old, and I have been a slave to the intellect. I need the balance and masculine confidence that a woman brings and I really am quite in love with Laura. I need your support in this. Could I humbly beg six or seven dollars from you in order to make a phone call to her and let her know where I am? <u>Mom, on second thought, never mind sending me the money. I just called Dad and he will send me some. I was going to repay you when I get my check in a week but I will repay him instead.</u>

There are other ways that you can assist me in my relationship with Laura, like lending me your encouragement in our relationship. She is shy and sensitive; frightened of getting hurt again so it is crucial for me to be as assertive as I can in making contact with her.

Perhaps you might show Myra this letter since she seems to enjoy playing the Auntie Mame role with me. <u>Please</u>, if possible can you two help me pull this off with Laura ?

Sincere Love,

Son and nephew
Moonway

In late July, I moved to Ohio to prepare for a new teaching job at the University of Cincinnati. Moonway wrote me as soon as I had a new address

August

Dear Mom,

I got out of RTF yesterday. Last night I had a fit of depression and frustration but it was over during my AA meeting and the visit with Marty and Shirl and Dad tonight. I seem to have the support of my immediate family in this sobriety thing.

I hate the sedatives because I am missing much of life while I sleep. I have some gray hairs in my beard. I cannot accept aging or death. I wish that I could make it through college or school. I admit it that the grant money is my sole incentive even though I enjoy replenishing my education. I crave drugs, sometimes immensely.

In spite of his problems and tensions, Moonway enrolled in two more classes in the fall. He wrote me about his difficulties with sobriety, medication side effects, and focusing on his courses in Sculpture and History of Motion Picture and Sound; about his desires to steal Laura from her new boyfriend, about his continuing friendship with his AA buddy, Carl. He thanked me for presents of art supplies and money and said he really missed my influence. And he told me about tensions with his Dad.

The problem is Dad (Want to hear it?). He still receives some of my mail. I suspect a link up to stubborn postmen and the judge but I could be wrong. I try working my moral inventory which now takes up to 20 pages or so but just can't find the courage to confront Dad in a humble way. He doesn't understand how anyone could be angry with him especially his own offspring so I sense his sensitivity and think, Well I don't want to push him . . . so I just let it ride.

In responding, I tried to reason him out of his suspicions. "Maybe your dad still receives some of your mail because some of it is still addressed to Sanders St. rather than Kings St? Maybe the PO doesn't forward all your mail?"

December

Mom, if you run across any Islamic, Buddhist, or Krishna tape cassettes in English at your library, could you borrow them for me? I am mainly interested in direct scripture of these religions in English. I already have borrowed a tape recording of the Bible from the town library. When I told Dr. Edwards that listening to them gave me an ego lift, he seemed to approve.

I am gripping my sobriety by the bare edges, sometimes, and I am angry at the State which I feel is lazy about assisting me considering the damned hard heroic effort I am making to remain sober and drug free.

My moral inventory is expanding and it is as abstract and unbelievable as God Himself sometimes.

Love you,
Son Moonway

By the end of 1987, Moonway had completed four college courses over two semesters. These three years proved to be the strongest period of sustained recovery Moonway had known since he first became ill. His success in college classes, his friendship with Carl, and his interest in women all indicate mentally healthy attributes. And his fear of death and desire for an all powerful and all loving God to help resolve these tensions are normal human feelings. Paradoxically, all of this "normal" stuff—ambition for success, recognition, and happy relationships—also produces tensions that would become very difficult for Moonway to cope with in the following years. Reality is often a hard row to hoe.

Was Moonway doing better through this period because of his compliance with psychiatric care and medication? At times I want very much to believe that is so. But there are other times, as many times, when he has not been well while he was complying. All his psychotic episodes, whether complying or not, are preceded or accompanied by situational stresses he can't handle. And, to my knowledge, he has never received any sustained therapeutic help in managing these tensions. Maybe during this time he was complying better because he was more "normal," handling stresses better for other reasons such as the self respect gains he was making through education and active practice of AA principles. It is a mantra of mental health people that noncompliance with treatment, especially with medications, causes relapses. This implies that compliance causes better mental health. But maybe the cause-effect relationship is that mental health causes compliance more than that noncompliance causes relapses?

13. All Squiggled Up Emotionally

Problems with women, Mom, in the late 80s. That corrections official I had the sexual crush on. She was younger than me. I didn't tell her, but I proposed to one of them. She turned the letter in to a doctor. She was a mental health worker. Well, they all are corrections officers.

Did you get in trouble about it?

Not that I know of. It's so easy to get in trouble with these people. Anything you do is insane or delusional once you're labeled as mentally ill. They take your whole fortune, but in a way, they're just as bad. Turn coats. That corrections official, I think she was making love with Carl. Her name was Eliza Church. I thought he screwed her, and I got so jealous about it. But it was all her fault. She didn't have to cooperate with him. Me and Carl, we made it up. Fifteen years my AA buddy.

I was in the Woodland County Jail, '89 or '90, for phoning in bomb threats to the super market because of that corrections official. I was hurting, just like Sirhan and Jack the Ripper all in one, Mom. And I couldn't prove anything about her and Carl.

But you were feeling paranoid about it? Do you mind if I use that word, paranoid?

Yes, I do. I was hurt and angry. All squiggled up emotionally.

That is surely a better description of your feelings than "paranoid" can suggest. Thanks for correcting me.

I never talked to Carl about it. We just let it go. I met him when he flagged me into his apartment when I was coming back from AA one time. He's a great friend of mine now, my only human friend. My animal friend is Scandal, my cat.

This is interesting, too, about that time. I thought of getting a great big jar of gasoline or can and filling it right full of black letters, putting a long fuse on it, going around the corner and lighting the fuse. I wasn't going to do it. I just wanted to propagate it so others wouldn't do it.

John Nash has said, "Insanity is an escape." Moonway's stresses that have always preceded the most serious psychotic episodes are the same sorts of tensions we all have difficulty with: success and failure; friendship and solitude; inner desires in conflict with outer realities; and especially love and hate. In my own craziness, I escape from irresolvable tensions in myself by retreating into daydreams, a world of my own imaginative making so profound it blocks out external reality. At times that world is blissful and addictive; but it is always accompanied, sooner or later, by a crash into the real. The struggle to make dreams of success and love real can be a crazy-making enterprise. For Moonway, the late eighties and early nineties would be fraught with these struggles, accompanied by temptations to retreat into mental and chemical intoxicants, and frequent moves and hospitalizations.

Early in 1988, Moonway called me and said he wanted to move to Cincinnati. Remembering our time together in Kingston, I said, "I don't think it's a good idea for you to move to Cincinnati or any place else until you can cope better with reality." I followed this up with a lengthy letter trying to explain myself further, and I asked him to come visit for a couple of weeks in mid-July after I would be done with summer teaching, and I would drive him back. Moonway graciously declined my invitation to visit.

You gave me good advice about not moving to Cincinnati because I have faced my problems head on. I really like expressing my appreciation and love to you for being so patient and understanding. I am beginning payment on the treatment farm bill and am paying other bills on time, so I am growing up. My AA buddy Carl and I share a lot of problems and help keep each other sober. My interest in girls comes and goes. I am back into my artwork.

However, not long after, he wrote to me, "I wish that Dad, Marty, Shirl, you, and me could have some group therapy together just to resolve some hidden issues." Over the following two years, he repeated this request several times in different ways. Each time, I responded with some variation of my first answer.

> I don't see how we could all get together for group therapy since we are so scattered. But I do believe that you can work on your issues with each of us in your own therapy and in 12-step work. I am willing to talk with you about any issues you have with me—either in letters, by phone, or with a therapist if you would like when I am in Lincoln. Have you talked with your therapist about your desire to resolve some hidden issues with your family? Would that be a good place to start?

He also frequently indicated in a very oblique way what some of the issues were.

> I spent the holidays with Dad, Marty, and Shirl which was fun, but I didn't really feel like I fit in because they were all drinking, and I wasn't. I really may pass up Christmas at Gram Michael's because I love Dad so much that I just want to sit down with him and guzzle beer and make inebriated restitution to him. I know what you were fleeing when you left Dad. A mild suggestion is to just try admitting that you too are an alcoholic. Mom, have you ever considered re-marrying Dad? There, I asked the forbidden question.

I wrote back, "Yes, I know I am at risk for alcoholism,

and that is why I am not drinking at all now. No, I have never considered remarrying your Dad and can't see any possibility of ever doing so. It is not a forbidden question, and I am happy to answer it."

Eventually Moonway wrote me, "Mom, I just had a good family conversation with God during med management class and got some nice things cleared up." After that, these family issues disappeared from his letters. Resolved? Or replaced by mounting psychosis?

January 14 1988: "School is really a terrific pressure, so I am dropping one course which requires a 10-15 page paper. I had a slip last week, drank a bottle of wine on two days, but I am still determined to stay sober and am still starting to see light at the end of the tunnel. I feel terrific tonight and almost wish that I were on some anti-depressants. February: "I need some of my money. I'm locked in the nuthouse on unnecessary charges. Non existent? Out?" March: "I got over confident and bought a six pack of Budweiser and drank it after I got out of the psyche clinic Monday. Yes, they say that we all must die, but I don't believe them." Summer: "Another disappointment in romance. I have been disappointed in every romance I have ever had, but I better get over this one fast. This creepy world really bothers me." Sept 7: "Am cutting down on meds with intent of quitting. Shuffling my politics like a deck of cards. I will deprogram you from my little art cult if you want→ video education involves a lot of involuntary mental and emotional manipulation and twisting where books, lectures, intake and studying involves more control, relaxation, and voluntary intake." December. "I am really getting things cleared up through theosophy."

But, never one for consistency or a straight path to psychosis, Moonway could also be quite rational as well as creative. In the same letter in which he told me he would deprogram me from his cult, he wrote:

> I was at an AA buddy's house yesterday and they got into a real screaming argument. This situation left me with real gratitude concerning my relationship with you. We no longer fight and argue but rather have mature conversations.
>
> Carl and I are talking about renting a house together.
>
> Concentrate on the best parents give you in support and love and leave the rest to the devil to carry away into hell or wherever the devil does the dirty work of God, who I often call the great flipped blip.

During this time, he moved into and out of an apartment, lived for a time in a residential training home, and grew more and more fearful and angry: "I hate inside life because it is like a jungle, but I guess that the outside world is just as cruel and dangerous."

> January 1989
> Dear Mother,
>
> I find the filthy black man and Hebrew to be a plague on my creative endeavors. I also find Christianity to be interfering with much of my healthier sexual instincts. I toyed with Christians the other night by purchasing some Salem cigarettes and flaunting them. Mom, I am both a witch and a Christ; also, I am both a junkie and a narcotics informant.
>
> The folkish sorts I rub shoulders with in AA I no longer wish to associate with. My sponsor would not enjoy intelligent discussions, having married early in life.
>
> I actually have to appeal to the Ku Klux Klan to clear my phone lines. God knows, it may actually take the burning of black babies on crosses to clear my mail.
>
> Mom, don't be alarmed, and above all don't go to psychiatry about my racism because they are all

integrated scum.

Mom, do you have or can you acquire any modern books by Sazz or Laing?

2/5/89

Dear Moonway,

"Winners lose more than losers," said a wise mother to her child when he came home crying that he was going to quit playing a new game he was learning because he was losing all the time. Did I tell you this story before? Some impulse is moving me to tell it again today.

I feel upset—frightened and sad and angry—in reading what you wrote about blacks and Hebrews in your last letter. You know how I feel about racist attitudes and behavior. If you want to talk to me about your anger, direct it where it belongs (not at Jews and blacks who have caused you no harm), and be willing to also talk about how you can deal with it in constructive and healthy ways. The Ku Klux Klan is not a healthy or constructive way. Don't talk to me about it if you don't want me to oppose you in it. I talked to Shirley last week, and she told me you had checked yourself into SMHI. My prayers go with you for you to make a healing experience there for yourself.

Sometime during this period, Moonway told his friends on the Help Line that he wanted to burn down a lodge in the area. He was hospitalized at SMHI again in February 1989 with visual and auditory hallucinations and substance abuse. Through all these years, Moonway respected my wish not to hear him talking to his voice hallucinations after I told him in Kingston in the early 80s that it distressed me to hear it. Even in letters that were often otherwise incoherent with his disturbed thinking, he never let me know about hallucinations until I asked him when we started taping conversations in 2001. And even then, he mostly denied that he had them though he often reported them to health care providers. I do not pretend to understand this, nor do I know whether my responses to his paranoia were damaging or constructive for him, or if it made no difference at all in the course of his schizophrenia.

In May of 1989, Moonway wrote, "I have been writing letters to the government about my various concerns, and that has the approval of Mental Health. I am involved in law suits up to the god damned hilt. I am suing for three religious properties here. Mom, I wish that you had more faith in my intelligence and the credibility in my claims about all of this exploitation." In August, he began sending me copies of his "letters" to the government, typified in tone and content by the following.

8/19/89

The White Rabbi
Original Z.I.N.
Z.I.N. means Zerox it Now.
    Famous great artists opened sexuality to the myth of wop power and death to the buffoon the witch and the hypocrite in all extensions. Beware the patent office on that. It pays to stay abstinent and study Jehovah's Witness theologies of death clinic strategies. I'm growing up. I really am and to the capitalist experiments who have survived=money and control of their sub bureaucracies and to the communist experiments who have survived, guns and revolution against them. Now, comrade radical Satanists and comrade radical saints what is to protect us from the sub bureau societies which will try to destroy us? The swastika is a holy symbol of the Hebrews meant to free the Christians. The witch mediates between God and Satan and education mediates between God freaks and Satanists.
    In the name of reason and the global straight ima,bray!

The White Rabbi
Original, ZIN, Xerox It Now

If I'm forced to sleeze through it again, would you kill for me? He who hangs the minister hangs the devil and he who kills the priest kills the Antichrist. Among the dead of war lie thine and there also could lie thee. The great philosophers who are white and male live among the saints, and both the saint and the philosopher are eternal! Is it my fault that I am born again and that others are not and that the global orthodoxy in all forms is prosecuting and persecuting me? Now, on to better things like uniting these for global peace. It is obvious through the process of being created from the dust of the earth that we have the form of men and the instincts of apes! Argue with reason but find out the truth the hard way. All that superstitious shit, right? Some non worker pansy has a fight with his commune and/or relatives and is treated like royalty, right? What the fuck is the world coming to anyway. Top the glue and did it work?

Beyond the glue; rather vulgar organisms! Hey Mick Jagger, Ozzy Osborn, Voltaire, Mozart, Beethoven? Times are changing but not for me. Mom, save these letters.
Cogluft Moonway.
I love you,
Signed
Son Moonway Michael.
Cogluft Moonway Adams Michael
Love From Above Ministries

Cogluft is one of a number of pseudonyms Moonway used in these letters. Ironically, "Love From Above Ministries" began to appear in the headings and signatures of his letters at the same time that he was venting rage against his "oppressors" and using socially hated cultural symbols of power such as Hitler. The contradictions inherent in Moonway's symbolic system eerily mirror the contradictions inherent in the history of Christian practice with, on the one hand, its images of an all-loving Christ who embraces even the most cruel sinners, and on the other hand the legacy of Christian persecution of Jews, witches, Muslims, and others that continues to this day.

At times I would put such letters away without reading them immediately, but go back to them later. Sometimes it would take me weeks, but eventually I read and saved them all simply because he asked me to. Although I had come to believe that saving letters could be important to me personally in remembering and understanding life, I had no conscious intention then of ever using Moonway's letters for the public purposes he wanted. Over the many years of his illness, I accumulated many files of such messages.

I found out later that Moonway was actually, not just delusionally, sending his letters to public officials, and that he didn't send me the most violent ones although he sent me many in the following years up to 1994 when I moved back to Lincoln, sometimes 2 or 3 in one day. Aside from these copies, his actual letters to me became less frequent, sometimes very short and often very cryptic and incoherent. He was hospitalized for three months during this time. When he was released, he moved from the rooming house to a small apartment on Pitt Street in Northridge, and he wrote from there, "Am doing much better." However, included with that letter was a three-page Xerox of another "letter" that indicated otherwise to me.

14. Inmate I: Satan's Place

In March, 1990, the State Department of Human Services filed another guardianship petition with a treatment plan.

> Bureau of Elder & Adult Services
> State of Lincoln Department of Human Services
> March 26, 1990
> Dear Ms Adams
> As you are aware, the Lincoln Department of Human Services has petitioned the County Probate Court for an Appointment of Guardianship for Moonway Michael. A copy of the Petition, supporting documents and a Notice of Hearing is enclosed.
> Also enclosed is a Waiver of Notice form that I would appreciate your signing. The Waiver simply allows for the Department to expedite the service process. By signing the Waiver, you <u>do not</u> give up your right to attend the hearing and take part in the proceedings. You simply acknowledge to the court that you received your copies of the legal documents regarding Moonway Michael's guardianship. Please return the signed Waiver as soon as possible. A self-

addressed, stamped envelope is enclosed for your convenience.

If you have any questions, please do not hesitate to contact me at the above address or call me.

Sincerely,
Andrea Winston, LSW
Court worker
Bureau of Elder & Adult Services

This notice is directed to Moonway Michael. . . . Petition for appointment of Guardian for Incapacitated Person. . . . Pursuant to Title 19-A, M. R. S. A., 5-601, the Lincoln Department of Human Services serves as the public guardian for incapacitated persons in need of protective services when no suitable private guardian is available and willing to assume responsibility for such services.Moonway Michael is impaired by reason of mental illness to the extent that he lacks sufficient understanding or capacity to make or communicate responsible decisions concerning his person.

He carries a diagnosis of chronic paranoid schizophrenia. He suffers from severe delusional states which render him incapable of properly administering his financial resources to provide for his basic needs. He is constantly malnourished and unkempt. His delusional system also prevents him from understanding his mental illness and the need for his psychotropic medications. Virtually all his psychiatric admissions have been a result of his non-compliance with his anti-psychotic medications.

The Department is seeking a limited guardianship in an attempt to allow Mr. Michael some independence and to see that the following needs are met: 1) management of his financial assets to insure that his shelter, nutritional and personal needs continue to be safeguarded. 2) power to authorize all medical and psychiatric care and treatment, including, but not limited to, the use of an intra-muscular psychotropic medication. 3) authorization to place Mr. Michael in a setting appropriate to his medical, psychiatric, and safety needs in accordance with his mental health counselor and psychiatrist's recommendations.

Our goal is to work with the mental health agencies to attempt to stabilize Mr. Michael in the community by proposing he receive long-acting intramuscular psychotropic medication when deemed appropriate. This will prove to be a more reliable way to ensure compliance with medication.

Included with this notice were a detailed treatment plan for care from County Mental Health Center and the psychiatrist's detailed description of Moonway's mental disabilities that justified guardianship, both are summarized above and neither offered any new information.

It is hard to overstate the ambivalence I feel about guardianship for Moonway. I very much want someone to take over and do something that will improve his life. I have always known the deadening side effects of Haldol and other neuroleptics that are always absent from the recommendations. In addition, it seems to me that all attempts to force compliance have deepened his paranoia about "psyche and corrections." Finally, the evaluations always and only cite Moonway's medical noncompliance and substance abuse as causes for his suffering. They always ignore the psychological distresses and traumas that precede and/or accompany all of his major psychotic episodes. I suspect they do not even know about them, and I do not trust the opinions of those who so willfully and consistently ignore the psychological factors of mental illness. Unable to make a decision, I neither opposed nor supported this guardianship effort. I merely asked questions and requested more information.

Before I went home that summer of 1990, Moonway called from Woodland County Jail where he was incarcerated for "waving a toy gun and knife around in front of Burger King." I followed up the phone call with a letter.

7/30/90
Dear Moonway,

You ask me if I know that even psychiatrists have delusions. Yes, I expect they do have some delusions sometimes. I expect most of us do at times. We are all human and subject to error in our thinking. What is your point with that?

I would rather you didn't put swastikas and red ink on envelopes you send to me. I cannot see it is doing you any good, and I know it is not doing me any good. I don't mind if you want to, and I don't mind if you tell me you want to, but I do mind if you do it.

I believe you that you hate it in jail, in the streets, in institutions. I hate for you to live that way, too. And I also hate that you made the threats and do the things you do that make you suffer. I suffer when you do, I long for you to become willing to take better care of yourself and stop blaming others for your misery. I believe that you can start doing it today, simply by deciding to become willing and praying every day for your Higher Power's will to work in your life. Faith as small as a grain of mustard seed and willingness can make you well and free and happy.

I'm going to be leaving here soon to go to Lincoln, so don't write to me here again until September. You can send letters to me in Greenville. And I will come see you when I can after the 11th.

I love you.
Mom

Visits with Moonway in Woodland County Jail have always been very unsatisfying—severe time limitations, no privacy, Moonway angry or depressed or dopey from drugs. When I returned, he continued to frequently send Xeroxes of his delusions. He was still in jail and still raging about it when he wrote the following which I never saw until I researched the Federal Archives in 2001.

Nov 9, 1990

To the Entire Female Staff of the Office of Senator Hoffman:

Madness Network News, can you get me out of this jail? I didn't know work was a crime. I prefer exposing white collar crimes.

More cigarettes, Mattell, MacDonald's, Gremlins, Fzzzzz Shampoo, Fatal Perfume, Master Blend Coffee, Soldiers of the Future, Toys, Tracer Cars, I am a capitalist Protestant white racist imperialist chauvinist male.

Don't Bomb, don't Assassinate, Don't Arson, Don't terrorize, Don't (3 trillion) skyjack, Don't rocketjack, Don't deal porno. God reigns supreme over all. Don't vandalize. Don't deal drugs.

I voted for Senator Page, Senator Hoffman, Jimmy Carter, Ronald Reagan, and George Bush. And they are the only ones I am representing or lobbying for.

I want that original deal national with Page. I don't care who it involves. Mick Jagger and Ozzy Ozborn are my favorite musicians. I need money.

Am I making new friends?

I despise and loathe communism and socialism and both are evil. Oz in Booze. I need money.

Why do these statements go unrewarded?

The Michaels and the Adams are great, etc.

I am being tortured by socialists and communists and have been for quite some time.

You can't charge me with anything I write or say under the first Amendment and you are all guilty of double jeopardy. The Northridge Help Line told me I could write anything I want to. Unless you guys get me out of here, I'm going to have you poisoned to death and I'm going to do it anyway and have your balls and cunts and cocks twisted off with pliers on top of that and I gamble and I'll take any bets going that I will go through with it sanctioned by the global military and all of the governments in the world. And

that includes all of the judges involved in my "case."
Heil Hitler.

And you can also keep the police thoroughly
away from me! Do it real, bitch Page, or I'll live up to
the name of my rock group! And be careful and I
quote you, "No one can say since your conversion to
capitalism that relatives won't have to be killed." And
leave my relatives out of it or I'll go international on
living up to the name of my rock group called
"Assassin." And I'm the solo member!

Do it real bitch=documents confiscated or that
starts happening.

Madness Network quote= "For an ounce of
protection you've bought a pound of cure."

Moonway Michael

This letter resulted eventually in Moonway becoming
permanently supervised by the Federal Court. Specifically
cited in the indictment of January, 1991 were his threats to
genitalia. Before he was indicted, he remained in Woodland
County Jail for his threatening gestures with a toy gun and
knife and for calling in bomb threats from jail. Letters to me
from there are filled with rage, despair, fear, and longing.

Nov 14 1990:
I'm not happy inside! I don't give a damn about the
welfare of criminals, boobies, or psychos and I don't
want to join their unions or their reunions. The black
rap music over the summer was nice but it got me in
trouble! <u>Why don't you and Dad sue for guardianship
and let sub bureaus handle the financing with strict
accountable monitoring or something!?</u> I wonder if
Jesus Christ just got mad at rip offs when he drove the
money changers from the temple!

In reply, I continued to try to teach Moonway by sharing my
own experience as the practice of the twelve steps teaches.

Before he was indicted, Moonway was bailed out of
Jail. At some point during this time, the guardianship petition

resulted in a financial conservatorship. He often complained about his conservator: "Mom, my conservator Victor Robins won't let me get Paragon Cable TV." But over the years after, he came to appreciate having money all month long.

After he got out of jail, Moonway stayed for a while in a homeless shelter, then moved to a boarding home for transients, euphemistically called "Tourist Home," a short distance from Northridge in Crown City. His letters continued to dismay and confuse me, full of photocopies of things he was sending to many of his correspondents. A photocopy of the cover of the novel, *Lisa, Bright and Dark: A Novel of a Young Girl's Journey toward the Strange Hypnotic World of Madness* by John Neufield was included with the following.

Love from Above Ministries
Temporary Shelter for the Homeless

Holy

Spirit

MADD

SADD

FADD

Cigarettes

Crystal Night 'darkest chapter'

BERLIN (AP)—City leaders on Wednesday declared the 1938 Crystal Night attacks on Jews by Nazi hooligans the "darkest chapter" in German history.

The events of Nov. 9, 1938, became known as the Crystal Night after the glass shattered when Adolph Hitler's Nazi bullies ransacked Jewish businesses and homes in Berlin and other cities.

Walter Momper, mayor of former West Berlin, and Tina Schwierzina, mayor of what was East Berlin, made their comments in a joint statement responding to charges by Jewish leaders that Germans have forgotten the Crystal Night.

Momper and Schwierzina said that Germans should learn from the events of 1938. Photocopy from an unknown newspaper or magazine
Cogluft Moonway, The Theocrat-The Dictator-The Judge-The Doctor-The International Client

Who am I to criticize Adolph Hitler as a bona fide member of the Nazi party, cosmic and on earth, in heaven and in hell, and in the imagination of the world, perhaps the most flamboyant dictator and maybe the man who perhaps was the real anti Christ and simply responding to the call of the dirty work of the Vatican and Protestants, when no one else would, in doing the work of mental health globally, including prison and jail in fulfilling the role of Satan, Lucifer, Beelzebub, the Beast ,the dragon, the false prophet, and the full role of "cult" extensions of Christianity in the east and west because <u>even Satan has a place in the divine order and scheme of God</u>, if God does indeed exist? And who started all of this talk about revolution if not the saint or sinner known as (aka) Mary. Nuclear bombs are bottled energies.

In early 1991, Moonway was still decorating his envelopes with swastikas, and I wrote to him, "Please do not put swastikas on mail you send me." At times, he has explained such emblems to me as artwork or propaganda. He also says that he has had serious motives behind everything he has done. Like us "normals," he wants the power to control his world. He uses his art and writing in the service of propaganda that he believes will help him achieve that power.

I would read through his letters trying to figure out what was motivating him, and what he needed. But after a while, I admitted to myself that I could not understand; then,

I would skim through them quickly and do my best to ignore the violence of the content. No one escaped his withering commentary.

> Gram Adams, Mom, and Myra: The lurid assholes! Mom, truly I can say that I love every member of the family and the commune with Protestant Capitalist love and I'm sure that Adolph Hitler can reciprocate with Catholic Communist love and we both despise evil colored people and all colored people are evil because the Christian religion according to Saint Paul is a gift to the white Anarchist gentiles and I am a capitalist racist white Anarchist and Hitler is a communist racist white Anarchist.

For a time, I tried to persuade myself that Moonway was more rational in his letters to me than in the Xeroxes he was sending around widely. I couldn't keep up that pretense, and I was again relieved when he was hospitalized at SMHI.

I went to Greenville in July 1991. Moonway received some time out of SMHI and we went camping. He was very unhappy the entire time. Still having to face his trial for threatening public officials, he was moody and irritable, looking for more excitement than swimming, hiking, and my company offered. Sometime after I got back to Cincinnati, he wrote.

> I guess that Bourne is going to give some information to the DA. Maybe I should take your route and migrate and leave the whole mess behind since they are still locking me up against my will even after sobering up. If indeed it is my defense. The insanity defense, and who is anyone to stop the insanity defense, who the hell is to stop me from having a jury trial? I disapprove of violence myself. I really do, but shockers sell.
>
> As it stands now I am up on writing threatening letters to the government and I am to appear before his Magistrate Astor. I, too, have the

courts, and police and psychiatric profession on the following charges=Double Jeopardy, violation of confidentiality, no attorney present during questions, no hearing before incarceration.

Moonway became increasingly irritable with me that I wasn't rescuing him: "I wish the Michaels and Adams would take more of an interest in my case and treatment. Boy, I sure let go against you guys on a letter from Aunt Myra which I sent to the ladies at CMC."

1991 ended with no resolution of the charge against Moonway. In March 1992, Shirley sent me the following clipping from *Newburg News.*

Man Charged with Threatening Hoffman Staff Wins Insanity Plea

A Northridge man charged with threatening U. S. Sen. Hoffman's "entire female staff" at his Northridge office was found innocent by reason of insanity on Tuesday in State's federal court.

Moonway Michael, 36, who said he was suffering from schizophrenia, was committed to a federal medical center for prisoners for an indefinite time until he can prove he no longer is a danger to other people or property.

Michael had been scheduled to appear for a jury trial Tuesday morning, but as the jury waited for the trial to begin, the defendant waived his jury-trial rights and appeared only before a federal judge.

Michael, who is involuntarily committed at State Mental Health Institute, had pleaded innocent after being indicted in January 1991 on a charge of sending a threatening letter to Hoffman's Northridge staff in November 1990

During a brief hearing at which no witnesses testified, several exhibits were presented by a federal prosecutor, including two medical reports that stated Michael didn't know that what he was doing was wrong. One report made by a State Forensic Service psychologist stated that the defendant was "delusional at the time of the offense," said Karen Finnegan, assistant U. S. attorney.

After reviewing the evidence, U. S. District Judge Kent Miller concluded that Michael "did, in fact commit the offenses charged in the indictment," but "at the time of the incident . . . he was indeed suffering from a serious mental illness or defect."

Saying it was "the only possible finding," Miller, quoting the federal statute on the insanity defense, found that Michael was "unable to appreciate the nature and quality or wrongfulness" of his acts, and therefore was not guilty.

Defense attorney Jake Hubert . . . said that he was "pleased with the outcome—it was appropriate, and Mr. Michael is pleased with the outcome" of the trial.

The defense attorney said that his client's agreement to have his trial heard by the judge was a decision "reflective of the reality of the jury system." Hubert said that only one-half of 1 percent of all insanity pleas result in the defendant being acquitted.

"The evidence was just clear he was not guilty by reason of insanity, but there still was a danger the jury would reject the defense," said the attorney.

Finnegan said after the trial that the medical reports, which have been sealed by the court, would have shown "there was no substantial disagreement between the government's and defense's experts. In that regard, this outcome is justice being done," said the federal prosecutor.

In retrospect, it seems ironically appropriate and fits with a pattern of our relationship that, while he was going through all this, I was applying for and being denied promotion to Assistant Professor. When he was first ill with nephritis, I was caring for 3-year old Marty and pregnant with Shirley. When he was going through his troubled early adolescence, I was preoccupied with the divorce, the trouble that led up to it, and the aftermath. In the aftermath of this promotion denial, I felt once again mentally unbalanced myself.

Still, I found time to drive to Missouri where Moonway was incarcerated in a mental hospital for federal prisoners in April, to visit him. During this visit, he was as angry as he was in his letters and preoccupied by the wish to get out of the visiting room to go smoke, and by the raging desire to get out of MCFP entirely. Our visit was not very satisfying for either of us.

He received a conditional release from MCFP in May 1992. In June I wrote to him with enthusiasm and optimism about his release from MCFP, his transfer to SMHI, about my planned visits with him there that summer, and about his newly appointed advocate, Cliff Worth.

> When I talked to your advocate, he paid you a compliment; he was impressed with how well you got help for yourself with the situation of being put back in jail by mistake when you returned to Lincoln. Bravo!

A great thing about that summer visit for me was playing with my new grandson, Marcus, and it gave me something pleasurable to talk to Moonway about.

After I returned, Moonway sent me many postcards, sometimes several a day.

SMHI C3
Late July 1992
Dearest Mother,
> Can you make my relatives stop harassing me? I don't want you guys knowing much about my business or art or writing.
> Mom, did you deliberately pick up Dad and marry him to get you through college?
> A worker, Mom, for Christ's sake. How cruel! I'm intense lately. I'm stirring up the shit and

enjoying it.

8-11-92

Dear Moonway,

I have been getting your postcards and try to read them carefully, but you are trying to get too much on them, and I can't always make out what you are saying.

I ought to try to answer your question: Did I deliberately pick up your dad and marry him to get me through college? No. At the time I married your Dad, I had no intention of going to college. It's hard for me to really know or remember all my motives in marrying him. I think some of them were not good— not knowing what else to do with my life for instance, and back then marrying was the expected goal for a woman. But some of my motives were good: I felt love for him even though it was a very immature love and certainly imperfect, and I wanted to have children and never regretted that. I was an imperfect wife and mother, but I never thought that your dad would put me through college, and he didn't. I paid my own way with scholarships and work during summers and school breaks, and I even helped some with household expenses. When I think of the hurt the divorce caused everybody I feel very sorry. I wish there were some way I could have prevented it. If there was, I don't know what it would have been. And I wish that there were some way I could help with resolving any conflicts you have about it. I am willing to listen to your feelings, or to try to answer any other questions you might have, though I don't have a lot of answers myself about all the unresolved feelings. We can talk some more about this on the phone, and the next time I am home we could talk with a counselor also if you would like.

I will send some stationary supplies from time to time. I don't know if I can keep up with all you want. But I will try to send something each time you ask.

Since moving back to Lincoln in 1994, I have attended many of Moonway's treatment team meetings, but Moonway and I have never met with a counselor specifically to resolve tensions between us. He has brought up the issue only in letters at times when there was no opportunity to see a counselor together.

15. Inmate II: The Straight Gate is a Hole in the Universe

The conditions of Moonway's release from MCFP stated that he must fully comply with psychiatric recommendations as well as refrain from drugs, alcohol, and threatening behavior. He went to live again at Nightsun Group Home where he remained as far as I know, compliant with medication and abstinent from street drugs. However, this did not relieve him of delusions, resentment, and rage at restrictions of group living.

Nightsun

Dear Mom,

Things seem too buried in paperwork for me. Like the state never committed this injustice against me. . . . . I am doing without drugs or alcohol and letting God do the rest as far as all of the euphoria which perhaps is a basic search among all of us. If I can keep from making the bomb threats, I should enjoy typing up my book and getting back into the enthusiasm of doing truly what I want to do. Have been working on a central subsystem for myself but it takes work and hard headedness to keep it going. Have been competing with Salvador Dahli in using technology to simplify my art work but have to innovate to simplify my writing.

In January, 1993, I went to see an exhibit of Rodin's sculpture at the Cincinnati Art Museum. I liked his sculptures of Balzac. The nude of him looked like a clown. But I liked best one of Camille Claudelle's busts of Rodin which was more interesting than his popular *Kiss* or *Thinker*. She was his mistress and apprentice who spent the last 30 + years of her life in an insane asylum. By then, I had watched the movie *Camille Claudelle* several times. So, at the exhibit, looking for the greatness of Rodin, I kept seeing that last scene in the movie of her looking back at Rodin as she is being driven away from her life with him to an insane asylum.

I hoped that Moonway's placement in a group home with supervision would keep him safer and healthier than life on his own, and it meant I would not have to travel so far out of my way to visit him. But for Moonway, compliance with house rules at Nightsun proved to be too difficult. As he has always had with institutional life or with any group living situation, including home, Moonway had great trouble with the restrictions of Nightsun. I was teaching an early summer term in June when I learned that he was being sent back to MCFP for failing to comply with treatment and rules of the home, and for failing to refrain from threatening behavior. This meant that I wouldn't be able to visit him while home in Lincoln after the summer teaching. I wrote Lincoln Department of Mental Health asking them to please reconsider this placement. They replied, denying my request.

After finishing the early summer term of teaching, I sold all my furniture in an apartment sale, packed up my Plymouth Voyager with all the stuff I wanted to keep, and moved it to Lincoln. I planned to move into a furnished one-room efficiency for my last year in Cincinnati. Before I got to Lincoln, Moonway's conditional release was revoked, and he was returned to MCFP July 23, 1993 where he remained until April 1994. Prior to discharge, staff at MCFP wrote a "Risk Assessment Review" which included an extensive case history. I found a copy in in the federal archives in Boston. It was revealing in a number of ways.

According to the review, between 1976 and 1993, Moonway received a variety of psychiatric diagnoses and prescriptions: 1976, acute Schizophrenic Episode, prescribed Prolixin; 1979, Psychotic Organic Brain Syndrome, Lithium Carbonate and Valium; 1985, Chronic undifferentiated

Schizophrenia with acute exacerbation and Substance Abuse, Melaril; 1987, Major Depression, probable Substance Abuse and Chronic Paranoid Schizophrenia, Prolixin; 1988, Inhalant Abuse, Alcohol Abuse, Cannabis Abuse and Chronic Paranoid Schizophrenia, Haldol; 1989, complaints of suicidal ideation, hallucinations and homicidal ideations about government officials, Moban; 1993, Haloperidol Decanoate Injection, Benadryl, Ativan. This list is only partial. I remember also early prescriptions of Thorazine and later diagnoses of Bipolar Disorder and Schizo-affective Disorder as well as prescriptions for, Risperdol, Zyprexa, Trazadone, and Depakote. My memory, also, is only partial.

This Risk Assessment Review indicated that Moonway gradually improved during his stay, but I couldn't tell that from what he wrote to me.

> Mom Adams,
> Marty Michael with the photocopier and wood burning set:
> As Is
> Moonway Hitler and Jack Kemp of the Angel
> Garry Trudeau and Donald Trump of Doonesbury
> Greenville Hotel   Walton Jim
> Greenville Store   Buzzy's
> **Get me out of here.**
> Cogluft Moonway
> Moonway's SS #
> Moonway Michael
> **Biblio the Royal**
> Zerox corporation
> KGB + CIA +KGB
> Kolor 10 and Star Spearhead tabloid take over of the grassroots media.
> 1-800-452-1948 M's and B's
> Media—A but, phone c.b. hookup into sports stadiums and rock halls to broadcast. The Storyteller in sequel with several returns of $ to thee.
>   I'm not selling out.
> Hello Ladies,

Liege Lords of animal-human sex and animal rights: Homosexual military, govt, and church agents are our slaves in Liberation theology!

I need eye care and dental care. I'll try to stay loyal and keep exonerating yas. Can't stand theology, business and politicians getting away with this. To hell with these veteran stories except us. Disease is rampant in these places.

Dad, How is the home movie box offices doing? How is the "racket," very legal, of hiring women whites to phone 800 and 0 numbers for human rights bureaus in these places from a MNNM, IRT, SAM, Act? Win perspective with this message: "I am not at war with Micky Cruze. This is Love from Above Ministries under Moonway Cogluft Michael."
Saturn Bubble Gum

Mama, they are drugging people because of their skin color and nationality. I'm German English and French. Melvin and Jim are alright.

Signed

Moonway Michael

Dearest Mother,

Stay in contact with the psyche unit ladies of County Psychiatric Hospital in East Northridge.

Mom and Dad, petition to be my guardians. I want to keep thumbs down, re. revolution is my job.
KGBB Karl Luger   CIA   Third   Reich
KKK# 1   KGB German Luther

Who is to say that there would be rampant looting in Anarchy with legal centers for free money and needle distribution? Some wetback female doctor over me?: KKK WASP America and Third Reich have more respect.

"Nixon coming! Does your conscience bother you?" VIVA Nixon and could the global right wing give us our human rights in return for restored power and continued votes for right wing whites? Die nigger pig and nigger dog now.

Black Lucifer.

Through confinement and harassment from mental health and corrections, I and both of my families have been turned literally into animals.

Mom, Dad doesn't think much of Madness Network News but it should be the only shrink paper allowed in and anti-pop shrink at that.

September 28, 1993, I wrote again to him about guardianship.

Dear Moonway,

Moonway, I can't be your guardian. I don't know how. I love you, but I don't know what you need. I think if you don't want the state or government to control you, you need to find a way to control yourself, be your own guardian, deal with your anger in a way that does not threaten anyone and get you in trouble. I will do all I can in terms of moral support and encouragement to help yourself, but that's all I know how to do. I believe in your ability to take loving care of yourself, and I pray that you find the willingness and whatever else you need to do it. Perhaps you ought to give Clozaril a try? Is it any more harmful than what you have been taking? I understand your reluctance, and I know I can't be the judge of these things for you.

I have been working everyday for an hour or two on my novel. It is about an old Lincoln lady who paints pictures of the landscape and people around her and takes care of her disabled youngest brother. I've been working over two years on it now, slow work.

Thanks for keeping the address clear on your letters so they get to me. I have a new home address now, please note.

Strangely, as Moonway can be when confronting real life trauma in the family, his correspondence from MCFP became much more sane around the time of my brother Russel's final illness. In February, 1993 Russell had been diagnosed with advanced cancer of the colon metastasized to

144

the liver. By fall when he was near death, Moonway wrote.

Dearest Mother,
You don't have to send me money: I have
about $1000 saved up. Wish Victor Robbins was more
prompt about sending me money.
Don't know what I'm supposed to be learning
from all of this other than what a fake sham mental
health and corrections is.
Want to go home to see little Marcus so bad.
Want to have kids myself. Wish Shirl would marry
and have children.
Rather than blame anyone I regard your's and
Dad's divorce as a tragedy. Sorry about Uncle
Russell's cancer.
Ya son
Moonway Michael

This letter was postmarked Oct. 25, the day after
Russell died. He was the first of my five siblings to die, and I
drove to Connecticut to spend the last 2 weeks of his life with
him and his family.

Dear Moonway
I think I can relate to how you don't know
what you are supposed to learn from what you are
going through right now "other than what a fake,
sham," etc.
I wish I could go home and spend more time
with Marcus too.
I have been thinking for years what the
Buddha must have meant in saying the end of desire is
the end of suffering. I don't think he could have
meant that we mustn't ever feel desire or reach to
satisfy it. The human race would die out. I think he
must have meant what I learn over and over again–to
hang on to unfulfilled desire causes suffering whereas
to let it go into the free flow of feeling is the end of
that suffering. I didn't and don't want to let go of

some of my most cherished desires.

Well, dear Moonway, I guess Russell's dying
has inspired a lot of meditation on what is important,
how to live the rest of my life. I don't want my time
and energy to be taken up in resenting or desiring what
is not available. I want to let go of my professional
ambition, too; it doesn't seem important at the
moment. What is important? The golden rule. To do
my best to practice love in all my action. I doubt there
is anything else that is truly important. And that is
not always easy for me so ought to give me enough to
do for all my life.

Love,
Mom

It is in dying that we are born
St. Francis of Assisi

How do you help your brother die? I asked
the hills along my drive to see him.
What do you say? What do you do?
Wind rattled the windows, shook the whole car;
dry leaves whirled up and up;
forest vistas flamed with the fall.
I counted deer kills and prayed,
Make me an instrument of your peace . . . .

When I arrived, he played his old records
of Johnny Horton singing history
and talked of roles he acted long ago,
Riders to the Sea, The Cremation of Sam McGee.
Then he stopped talking for the rest
of his dying. He moaned or cried with pain
seizures, and I stroked his brow and arm
while the morphine was adjusted. We looked
into each other's eyes like mothers
and babies look. Past blushing,
past remembering.

146

Listening to his death rattle, I smelled decay
on his breath, the odor we brush away
every day. I whispered forgiveness
into his ear, kissed him, counted second
by second the faltering rise and fall
of his chest. The terrible grace of it all
flares sharp and brilliant as autumn leaves.

November 26, 1993
Dearest Mother,

I've been going to AA meetings and my
advocate Cliff Worth told me that I might be shipped
out of MCFP to the psyche unit in East Northridge
and then after two weeks transition there that I would
be shipped to the Forest Knolls Boarding home. They
made me take off a paper headband which I was
wearing and had made myself. Wrote a letter to an
old probation officer. I have also been writing to
Northridge Legal Assistance, ULN, and the *Newburgh
Daily News*. My Literary Art headquarters is 3
Greenside St. East Northridge, Me., USA, County
Psychiatric Hospital, CGH., psyche unit ladies; c/o
Liz.

Victor Robins, my conservator, bungled; and I
didn't get any money last week and may not get any
money this week; bad for my nicotine and caffeine
habit.

Hate to think that my letter writing campaign
is all in vain including the letters I'm writing to my
relatives. I think that you and Dad would make
excellent co/guardians along with Victor Robins. I
keep telling you guys to investigate and look into
things concerning the summary of the letters I've been
writing and you might find that I've earned multi-
trillions of dollars concerning the printed media and
the audio/video media. Not to mention my
commercial advertising, vote getting, legislation,
revival, and psychiatric/justice monies. But it takes
organized pressure to force them to deliver. I'm also

suing a lot of corporations and the mental health and justice systems also.

I don't like it in these places at all and I've only been allowed one 3-day furlough from K-2 SMHI about 10 years ago. . . .

I'M NOT SELLING OUT TO ANYONE, HOWEVER, MOM.

Tip: Live TV and radio tops literature and computer in educationeeze. Well, maybe not, because one could save a lot of money through computers instead of hiring research employees. The computerization of the global multimedia is growing at an amazing rate. I'm into Apple Computers in my advertising campaign. I'm still campaigning for the presidency of America and I want to continue to do so.

I lived a very quiet life my last year in Cincinnati, and I read a lot.

December 13, 1993
The candles in churches are out,
The stars have gone out in the sky.
Blow on the coal of the heart
And we'll see by and by. . . .
      Archibald MacLeish
Dear Moonway,
      It was good to talk to you on the phone. Thanks for calling.
      Archibald MacLeish was quoted in a book which has a whole chapter on *The Book of Job*, a long time favorite of mine, enigmatic, but its significance gets more profound with each loss and sorrow. So I read MacLeish's verse drama based on Job, Sarah in that play says to Job, "You wanted justice, didn't you? There isn't any. There's the world . . . . You wanted justice and there was none—only love." Amen. The world ain't fair, but do I want to spend so much time railing against that?
      I am looking forward to visiting you in

Missouri at Christmas. I'm spending my Christmas money on it. I'm not buying much of anything else for anybody. Maybe I'll make copies of tapes I made of conversations with Russell while he was still able to talk and give those for Christmas gifts to the family.

Love,
Mom

I was not only letting go of the physical presence of Russell, but also letting go, again, of all the loss and disappointment in life, including the inevitability of my own death and the limitations of the possibilities in life. I never do let go fully; rather I live in the process.   Moonway's next letters show, once again, his retreat from reality.

KGB + CIA + KGB
Don't leak and I'm not selling out.
Hello ladies,

Could you help me become an avid supportive fan of Bill Clinton?

I was told that I would be railroaded back here if I extend myself the dignity of failing the conditional release plan, which I don't anticipate. . . .   The medication is leading to Tardive Dyskinesia
Medicine—

Just ate two cans of oysters and ate 8 vitamins. Animal brains and guts when eaten raise the instincts and vitamins raise the IQ. Red stuff like tomatoes for the blood and Christ said that "the life of the flesh is in the blood."

My visit to Moonway at MCFP during Christmas break was a repeat of the former visit and no more satisfying. But I guess I wasn't expecting much because my letter when I returned was cheerful. "It was a pretty day yesterday to be traveling. I put in a Harry Bellefonte tape and sang along with him.   I'm glad I went to see you. Please see about getting to the dentist. Here's $10.00 for phone credits, and I'll send a little more at the beginning of each month."

149

Moonway wrote one letter with a dialogue balloon as a header that points to a Xerox copy of Doonesbury addressing a booing audience.

Straight is the gate; I am the messiah and I can't stay sober for my sheep and goats unless I am allowed attendance at a lot of the anonymy meetings to write beer, dope, and porno commercials for a nude High Times. The straight gate is a hole in the universe which leads to heaven and this will be sealed after the last saint has passed through to the judgment throne for damnation. I've already attempted to rocketjack through posing as a robbed beaten sky marshal for transportation. After the bottomless pit is opened which is a hole through the universe to the ghettoes of heaven, the ghettoes of heaven will revolt and this will drain all of heaven's energies so that the heavens will pass away. The Old Testament mentions this passing away of the heavens.

The new heavens and the new earth will be constructed by the ghettoes of heaven if they act soon enough to prevent Right wing reactionaries from getting in on the action of reconstruction. I still haven't got a lead on the Sea of Blood but it will materialize as I meditate. The peace and rumble of heaven are the peace and rumble of earth so pray for and act for peace.

Get me out of here and home to Lincoln. Please don't burn me the way others have and I'm not selling out! Don't leak!

February 1, 1994
Dear Moonway,

I have been feeling good lately, seems to be animal energy, happy for simple things—sunshine, food, smiles. Astonishing how one can feel happiness in the midst of the shit that happens all around. Thank God for the spirit of hope, and for the power of imagination. Talking to Shirley Sunday, while she was telling me about family happenings, I could see Marcus visiting for overnight with Shirley and your dad, could see Martin shoveling off my roof, could see Marcus being a rascal with Martin and Carol.

Happy Valentines Day. Here's some telephone credit to help you enjoy it.

Was I really as detached and cheerful as I seemed then, in strong denial about his prognosis, or simply too involved in my life finishing up my time in Cincinnati and preparing to move back home?

Dearest Mother, these aren't directed at you and are photocopies.
Hello Ladies,

Got your calculators because you are being shoved into the background by macho man and with calculators you can keep a record of macho man's corruption. I am depressed a lot unless I have money to spend on the photocopiers of MCFP's law library for the fascinating adventure of making my defense known. I am a psychiatric matter alone so I don't know what the courts, the police, the prison board, the U. S. Marshals and the FBI are even involved in my case for.

I want to go home immediately. I need money.
March 1994
To the entire female staff of MCFP, IRT, MNN, ABC, NBC, CBS, PBN, BBN:

The wrath of God begins against the church.

In the midst of all this craziness that Moonway was writing to me, it was determined that he was not a threat to himself or others and could go home.

I met with my counselors on a Thursday and this pre-release hearing determined that I could go home to Hazleton, Lincoln to a foster home. They're

151

working on the pre-release report after collecting a sufficient amount of signatures. I strongly think and feel that I am no longer a danger to myself or others or the property of others.

Cliff Worth met with SMHI officials on a Wednesday and it was determined that I need not return to SMHI, that I would go to the psychiatric unit for two weeks and then on to Forest Knolls Boarding Home. I want to remain as a spiritual mental health consumer network, my rights protected by advocates and attorneys and I have Medicaid.

Moonway   Adams

Morris Michael
Literary Art Headquarters, White Psyche Unit
Ladies of CMC CGH,
Hello Ladies,

Prophecy—On the morbid fates of those who would rule with a rod of iron and who would pollute the insane environmental man who does the derelict of the relative universe are visible to the insane philosophical eyes only through the absolute throne room of an autonomous and retarded god who does His work and bestows His revelations through the relativity of the mad environmental woman and child who opposes the goodness of abortions.

They want to stick me in a foster home yet. And would one of yous faggots do something about getting me out of here?

They won't let me use the library. Send money!

His letters continued to reveal a chaotic mental life; I could discern no improvement as a result of medication compliance. Did his release, then, depend on improvement in observed behavior, or did it occur mostly or only because of the aggressive efforts of Cliff Worth?

Near the end of Moonway's stay when he began to feel some hope coincident with real progress toward release I did see brief bits of relief from the terrible hold of his delusions.

Despite these bits, the mental retreats from reality through the late 80s, 90s and early 2000s proved to be the rule rather than the exception, and his health steadily declined. These were also the years of the most medical compliance with long-lasting Haldol shots on a regular basis and the most sobriety with drugs and alcohol. But also during these years, he abstained from the most egregious anti-social behavior that got him into legal trouble earlier in his illness. Is the long- term use of psychotropic drugs effective then for controlling the behavior? And does it also simultaneously contribute to the chaos in thinking as Robert Whittaker, *Mad in America,* suggests? Does he retreat so much because his legal status— permanently supervised by the federal court—has robbed him of some of the hope he had earlier, hope that somehow contributed to more frequent episodes of clarity and more sustained rationality, at least in his letters to me? Always more questions than answers.

16. Chance and Choice

I moved back to Lincoln in the summer of 1994. In the busyness of grandmothering, trying to work full time for a year on my writing, and after that on my teaching, I mostly abandoned my journal writing. And I visit with Moonway and talk to him often on the phone, so we don't write letters any more. In the absence of writing, so many of the details of what happens get lost in imperfect memory. We wrote our last letters to each other during the three months I stayed in Newburgh with Shirley when Jeffrey was born in late November.

December 1994
Now, once again, it is that time
of year when the cold triumphs, the night rules.
Every day the sun rises farther away.
It is hard to imagine him halting his march to the
    South,
stopping a little, resting in the black whirlwind
Of space to take new form, to be born again in a

153

barn.
But the shadowy barn has seen it happen
    over and over.
            . . . .
    I feel the rightness of it,
    the calm of those generations of beasts, the power
        of other
Hands on the beams, the light of the magic child
shining once more from the gathered summer of
    hay.
                (from Kate Barnes, "The Barn in
                December")
Dear Moonway,
        Shirley delivered tiny Jeffrey Michael Sage,
November 21. They brought her by ambulance to
Newburgh where (many say) they have the best
neonatal intensive care unit in the country. Jeffrey
weighed 685 grams, about a pound and a half, at birth,
about 24 weeks gestation. He will be hospitalized at
least until the due date in March. Both mother and
baby are doing well even through scary times with
respiratory distress, steroid treatment to strengthen
lungs, a nursing mistake with the glucose solution.
Still, things are hopeful with delights and joys every
day. He is making excellent progress, weighs almost 2
1/2 pounds today, is being weaned from respirator and
IVs, takes Shirley's breast milk through a tube.
        Jeffrey's birth place is dominated by very
different sounds, smells, shades than the barn of
Barnes' poem or the stable of the Holy Child's birth,
and still he is a poignant reminder of our
creatureliness. Every birth is surely both holy and
earthy.

                Chance and Choice

I feared my fear of life and death would blind
me so I couldn't see my grandson's birth

16 weeks early. A fetus this fragile,
law and choice allows, is not enough alive
or human to bear the right of life.
But almost against my will, I glanced
and saw, squeezed into folds like a raw brain,
                    the glistening crown.

Then I couldn't look away.
The head emerged, it breathed, it cried,
a mewl softer than a new-born kitten's
He slid out. I reached to touch.

His hand, tiny as a baby eagle's claw,
curled 'round my finger, clutched.

                    ~

Within minutes of his birth, his mother
had to choose. Resuscitate or not?
Without it, he would die, *mercifully*
many said. With it, tubes would invade him again and
again—through nose, mouth, veins
and arteries. 50% chance he might die anyway;
more than 30% of those who live have some degree
of life-time handicap—blind, retarded, palsied.

90% have major complications.
The only certainties—quick death if *no*,
months-long suffering and disease if *yes*.
She didn't hesitate—*help him live.*

Amid high-tech glare and urgency,
a tracheal tube cut off his cry.

                    ~

Her first baby. She'd never seen one
so small, so fully formed a human he seemed
a freak at 1 ½ pounds, seemed too delicate

to bear the sound of his own heartbeat.
Knowing the chances, what compelled, at sight and
sound of him, her unthinking, *yes.*

Her hand covered his whole back, she stroked
and murmered. Not able to hold him for weeks,
she yearned to put his whole foot in her mouth,
the mammal's urge to lick, the human kiss.

What but desire too deep in our animal brain
to voice, unspeakable joy, skin to skin.

~

Nature documents animal drives.
Several mother elephants struggle
in concert to save an adopted baby mired
in mud; in drought, a whole herd
halts its way to water and waits
in dust swirls for one mother nuzzling
one new baby, urging its pained effort
to rise on defective legs; they caress
a dead companion's carcass while scavengers
eat and flesh turns to liquid, dissolves
into earth. They carry the bones like babies,
rocking foot to foot. Animals

all, hanging on the cross of life and death
together, we get to choose surrender,

~

A nurse explained it is used universally,
the sound the placenta makes working
at fetal feeding. It's also the sound
of breath, mother's milk gushing,
the dark behind her baby's fused eyes,
his gaze when he opens them.

156

It's the sound of breezes and mist, sunlight,
microbes and worms working compost
into soil, water in the deepest currents.
It's the sound of sorrow's ebb tide.

To our feet, our rage, and our suffering,
the earth, our placenta, sings *shhh*.

———

In a letter addressed to both Shirley and me, Moonway
wrote a sane and sympathetic letter: "How is little Jeffrey
doing anyway. I think of the poor little guy strapped down to
that hospital bed with tubes all through him, and it makes me
sad." Such reality events bring out his best.

17. Exmate

Mom, After MCFP the second time and then SMHI, I
lived up to Cyr's Boarding Home in Hazleton.

That was the first year I was back in Lincoln after
Cincinnati. I visited you there often, and you would come
down and spend weekends with me at my little house in East
Northridge sometimes. We went to the police station to
introduce ourselves and find out if it was OK for you to sit out
in front of the library like you liked to do.

I hated living at the Cyr's.

I know you did. You agitated all the time to get back
to Northridge. Finally, they increased their price so much you
couldn't afford to continue there. Then you lived in supported
housing in Woodland.

In Woodland, I ironed things out to brass tacks. I
broadcast my whole rap there. Everything I ever did that was
illegal: attempted homicide on Dad, wounding him with that
scalpel; Z.I.N. is a bad burn.

Why is it a bad burn?

Xerox it Now is a bad burn because I sent out notes
and letters and everything encouraging everyone to rip me off,
break in, photocopy, film me. Sent out to everyone on "The
Summary" I gave you a copy of. Names and phone numbers

Moore Bowen

of lawyers, advocates, my financial conservator, judges, people from psyche and corrections. That's crucial to this book. Photocopied them, sent them out to all those people. That thing's crucial, the Summary.

For a long time, Moonway has been preoccupied with getting his history catalogued. "Index It" appears frequently on signs he makes and displays in public, in correspondence, on audio tapes he makes in private, and in his conversations with me.

Summary
by Cogluft Moonway Michael

So far, I have been writing to both of my families, the Cogs, Teen Challenge, Charles Colson, State Religions, State Government, State Universities, Bush, Clinton, Lawanda, Carolyn Smith, Carl Daggett, Duncan McVay, Jane Copeland, Floyd Grisham, Madness Network News, Issues in Radical Therapy, State Mental Health Centers, State advocates and attorneys. I've been phoning to free numbers and collect numbers which I got off the TV in Northridge, Crown City, and Woodland, Vermont, USA. I—Cogluft Moonway Michael, alias P. T. Clyde ZIN— control NYSE through 800. I control CIA, White House, Pentagon, Hollywood, and media through letters, being illegally bugged, and a two way TV. I control lawyers and underground through 800 and letters. I want to continue this iron grip of terror.

I have lived at 91 Kings St., Northridge; 95 Gentry St., Northridge; 51 Sanders St., Northridge; State Mental Health Institute; Woodland County Jail; Florence County Jail; US Medical Center for Federal Prisoners (MCFP) in Missouri; the streets, jails, and mental institutions of Denver, Colorado; airports and bus terminals; Hillsboro Crisis Center; County Psychiatric Hospital; 33 River St., Northridge; 22 Parsons St., Northridge; Cyr's Boarding Home in

Hazleton, Lincoln; Forest Knolls Boarding Home, the old hospital in Northridge under Dr. Jones; Greenwich and/or East Villages in N. Y. C.; a mission and bus station in Boston, Mass.; my mother's in Northridge; my uncle's in Florida. I have also resided at 13 Riverview Drive, Nightsun Transitional Living Residence, Northridge.

I have served time to my country and the world under psychiatrists, Dr. Long, Dr. Rash, Dr. Shane, Dr. Wyatt, Dr. Summers, Dr. Walker, Dr. McNair; police— Sargent, Rawlings, Parker; Psyche Personnel—Church, Marks, Butters, Gibbs, Walsh, Linda, Robert, Esther, Elaine and Jean, Perry, Mathis, Green, Rachel, Gold, Donald, Marvin.

My kriminal psychotic God Father is Chris Brice who killed his grandfather. I've been phoning State radio and TV stations collect, and I've been phoning State advocates and attorneys collect. I've served under magistrates Miller, Sanders, Weber, MCain, Wright, Austin. My attorneys are Lynch, Stevens, Enslin, Brown, Rice and Mayo, Murphy. My advocates are Baker, Worth, and Roth.

I have done art and writing on walls and doors in Northridge and Woodland, Lincoln, USA. Here are some shirts and T-shirts which I have lettered and worn: <u>Pentecost</u>, <u>Rubin Inc.</u>, <u>Manson is a Star</u>, <u>K. G. B. AAA Hero</u>, <u>C. I. A.</u>, <u>Eldridge Help</u>, <u>Krishna</u>, <u>Index It</u>, <u>I Request R. O. I.</u> I have carried and still carry a sign which says <u>Media</u>. I made paper hats in Woodland and wore them. One hat had a picture of Charles Manson on front and a picture of Skinner on back. The other hat had a picture which I drew on both sides. I have worn them, and I have worn dresses, make up and jewelry of women to broadcast the sexual and feminist revolutions.

Reading through his Summary literally takes my breath away—the reality of his fragmented life under psychiatric "care," the sheer numbers of moves, of transitions in "psyche and corrections," etc. And this summary is only a segment of the whole. I should say here, Moonway is typical, not unique, in this fragmentation of care.

I thought Woodland was a good place for you, Moonway. I liked your CSC, Gary, the best of all your case managers that I've had much contact with. He would give you rides from Woodland when you came to visit me which was a big help. I'm glad he's consulting with your treatment team now. I think he has the right priorities. He always expressed interest in you as a person with talents, not just a patient. He arranged art classes for you. Remember. I like the watercolor landscapes you gave me. You enjoyed those classses?

Yeah. After I came back to Northridge to live, they kicked me out of the Art Department at ULN, five years ago or so. Well, they didn't kick me out, but they told me I couldn't go back there.

That must have been right after you moved back to Northridge. Who told you that you couldn't go back?

Janice Hutchins, ADA officer, American with Disabilities Act. Damn her. She told me I could go to the Student Union Lounge and the library. That's it. It was probably all the propaganda I was leaving on the bulletin boards. And I'm not going to stir things up by going back in there. I'd leave something occasionally up there and on the street. I don't do that much in the winter any more. But Janice Hutchins got me working for traffic and industrial safety which I did down near IGA one day waiting for Dad or a cab.

The thing on the document she gave me banning me from certain areas of ULN, it was signed "Traffic and Safety" for Christ's sakes! They probably thought I was a protester and was blocking entrances. But I wasn't. I had that document posted on my wall there for a while or made a hat out of it. I go up to campus as regular as I'm conditioned to, but I haven't been going to the places she told me not to. Things have cleared up since I haven't been going there. For me and my relatives.

I'm not stalking women, Mom, contrary to popular

opinion or my publicity stunts. That's all feminism, Mom. No hustle, no stalking intended. That's all consideration for the feminists, giving them breaks, getting them up in the media. Publicity. 'Course they consider it pimping, don't they?

I suspect they consider it harassment.

Yeah. They consider it harassment because I'm so ugly and deformed, hunh?

No. Because it is unwanted attention. Do you need to find a better, more acceptable way to express your respect?

I been writing the presidents' wives and the president now for years. Maybe I should have explained it was all feminism, hunh? They might have lightened up. I did explain quite a few times. Of course I was hustling too and stalking in my writing. I don't do that anymore. Feminism. Mostly, that's what it was. That's the honest truth, just respect for feminism. Boy did I give the coloreds and women media breaks at Woodland County jail. KKK probably hates me for that.

Just think, Moonway, you have been living now for about five years here in your home town, doing your art and writing, and no serious legal trouble for you in that time. I like that self portrait. Could I make a copy for the book?

No. I'm working with it.

You need to finish with your current inspiration from it, hunh?

I did it from a photo you gave me.

My Son, the Artist
(continued)

1988, Moonway writes me,
Concentrate on the best they give you
  in support and love and leave the rest
  to the devil to carry away into hell
  or wherever the devil does the dirty work
of God, who I often call the great flipped blip.

In 1999, back home now for five years,

he greets the millennium with loud laughs
at jokes he says God tells him. He no longer
talks of journeying. Again and again,
he says he is sorry for the costs of his disease.

And I can't forget before all the sickness,
four years old, a hot summer afternoon,
he told me he was inventing a giant bathtub
with a fountain at the faucet end,
always spraying cool water, always full,

always draining, always flowing clean water;
he drew pictures and explained how water
stayed clear by filtering through
a network of gold piping arching the tub.

III
Psyche and Corrections

I'm an official, bona-fide labor union. Call it
the Resistance-Against-Psychiatry-and-Corrections Union.

18. Decompensation

In coping with Moonway's illness, I have learned over the years that a crisis is in my own mind. While there are still plenty of vexing problems that do not yield to ready solutions, not much feels like a true crisis anymore. But some continuing problems do escalate and peak at times. One such problem is Moonway's feelings about "psyche and corrections." In spite of planning and agreements made at treatment team meetings, Moonway continued to decompensate during the time we were taping conversations for this book. From the beginning of his illness, legal problems have been the chief instruments of getting Moonway into psychiatric care, and so psychiatric service providers and justice officials have always been linked in his thinking. I never fully appreciated his feelings about this situation until I witnessed this decompensation. I saw first hand how powerful and real "psyche and corrections" are in affecting the well being of all the mentally ill involved in the justice system.

1-16-01.

I'm a labor Union now, Mom. Adult Protection. I'm an official, bona-fide labor union. Call it the Resistance-Against-Psychiatry-and-Corrections Union. Now you babble. Say anything. Questions. Fire at me. Interrogate me.

I am concerned about how you seem to be hyper, and .

. .

Caffeine, Mom. I'm supposed to drink it and smoke it. And it's required in AA by the courts, you know?

No, I don't know that. And I'm concerned that you're so loud on your CB and phone. I worry about the neighbors complaining

Well, I like talking loud so the audience picks me up.

And you're isolating. It's winter, the dark time, and people need to get out, take advantage of the little light we have.

Don't worry. I like isolation. I like doing my art and writing, watching TV.

Eleanor is worried that you are "decompensating." I had to ask her what that word meant. Why do they invent a new word like that instead of the more familiar and medical "relapsing." She is still concerned about your self-care and that you are not going to meetings, not seeing Carl or your dad. It's hard on your mental and emotional life without any social life, isn't it?

Well, maybe if I keep showering, changing my
clothes, keeping my place clean. Maybe I can get some social
life. My rite of passage is showering, changing my clothes and
cleaning my apartment. And I am 45. Ha, ha. I should have
been doing this all along.

You did do it regularly before you got sick with
schizophrenia. You used to keep clean. Except for cleaning
your room.

Because I was made to. I was made to this time, too,
wasn't I? Psyche and corrections making me. Ha, ha.

I didn't have to force you to keep clean when you were
a little guy.

I didn't shower, Mom. I grew up warped. Always a
loner.

Moonway, you are throwing lit matches at the ash
tray, again. You can set a fire. It's dusty back there.

I shouldn't do that.

It scares me. Sometimes I put on my anthropological
hat and try very hard not to be judgmental about what you say
for the book. I'm not always successful, I know. But when
you throw those lit matches, I don't even try. I'm judgmental.

No wonder. More questions, Mom. Let's get back to
work on the book. I'd be better, you know, if the law would
leave me alone. Ted McKean came in today and harassed me.
Asked me why I was hollering on the phone. I was just using
a loud voice, talking to the psyche unit, the help line, and the
ARTS bus. He heard me from outside, I guess. Said he's
going to meet with me and Eleanor today. Plus he raised his
damn voice. I was afraid he was going to hit me.

He raised his voice about you talking so loud on the
phone? That's funny. But he is your Probation Officer,
assigned to oversee the "Conditions of Release" from the
Federal Court, so it would be good to cooperate, wouldn't it?

Talking loud is not against the law is it? I'm doing
OK, Mom, if the law leaves me alone.

Talk to Ted; be nice, and ask him what his concerns
about your behavior are. You've gotten pretty good at talking
to me about things that trouble you about me, right? Telling
me when you are angry with me, telling me not to nag about

smoking. We negotiate through these differences, don't we?

1-19-01.

Mom, I'm bumping in on the beginning of this one with a message from my Resistance-Against-Psychiatry Union. Extravagant returns to the Mansons and Abus for the right to prey on the stereotype of them, not directed at that airliner, their rights, or Dad. Let's get something else on tape here, Mom. Ted McKean and Eleanor Lee were in Tuesday. Ted was in twice. Eleanor was in once. They are threatening me with MCFP again. I guess they been getting complaints about the noise. So I agreed to sleep at nights. And I been sleeping nights since then. I think I know what was bothering Ted. I think it was so-called bizarre entries on some of my recordings. I modified them, censored them, blipped them. He didn't say that, but you start learning what they expect of you sometimes without them being here. There's got to be a better way than muscle from psyche and corrections. There are gains though.

Eleanor told me there was a problem because you hadn't followed through on the agreements you made with her for the day-care program and the psycho-social group.

I don't want to go there. That's exploiting the mentally ill, Mom. It's not allowed by the psyche unit in East Northridge. And, Mom, there's something more urgent here. The summary of addresses and phone numbers, if my mail's getting through to them, you could compile quite a book off of that. That summary is my little Capitalist Manifest, you know? This thing with all addresses, what I did, where I went. Who I been funding. Theaters. They're probably guarding that little piece right up there.

Yes, Moonway, I have your summary. I know it is crucial to you. Could we get back to the problem with Eleanor? She says it is part of the conditions of your probation that you follow-through on all that your care providers recommend. Did you think it was your choice to go or not go to group.

Yeah.

Did they talk to you about that?

167

No. Mom, you're not involved in this, too, are you? You're on the CMHC Board of Directors for Christ's sake.

I'm trying to understand, Moonway. Did they present it that way to you, that you would have to go?

Yeah.

And you made the decision anyway not to?

I'll go.

You don't want to, but you'll go if it's required? And you know, now, that it's required?

Yeah.

So are they going to set up something else for you?

I don't know.

Since one of their problems is you talking so loud, disturbing the neighbors, please lower your voice on this tape. It would be good practice for other times when you're alone and talking on the phone or your CB. This tape picks up things really well. You don't have to shout. OK?

OK. I love you guys. You know that, don't you?

I do know it. I love you. Do you know that?

And I'm trying to look out for you. But you gotta go my way a lot. I'd like access to my money, mail, and phone calls for the letter bombs, bombs, guns, contraband. And I'd like the guardianship and conservator-ship lifted. They don't call it guardianship, don't come out publicly and say it.

You are supervised by the court, so essentially a ward of the court. Is that what you mean by guardianship?

That's what the court said. Publicly, I'm a ward of the court. Privately, I'm a Michael and Adams and Morris and Grace.

You prefer your ancestral identity to the legal one? Makes sense to me.

Mom, I want to hear more from you in this book. What's on your mind?

Are you going to a meeting tomorrow night?

I dunno.

It would be good for you in relation to Ted McKean especially. Because he's the person with power in your life, right?

Cliff Worth says I'm the person with the power. I

think we better start focusing on *Madness Network News* movement, and lobotomizing judges and psyche and corrections officials, shocking them, drugging them, incarcerating them in jails, prisons, nut houses, concentration camps, globally. USSR, Red China, and the Old World. There's something else, Mom: Environment Police, lobotomize capitalist presidents without it affecting me. Emphasize <u>without it affecting me</u>.

Can I finish telling you how I feel about the problems you are having with Ted McKean and Eleanor?

Yeah.

This week you've only seen Eleanor and Ted on Tuesday and me. Right?

Yeah.

Have you been seeing your Dad very much?

No.

No one else? That worries me.

It don't worry me, Mom. I'm OK as long as I take my meds, though I'm being blotted out by these drugs, Mom. You're not going to enforce sociability on me, are you?

How could I enforce it?

Like you're doing through the courts and psyche. I don't know, Mom. Something's going on I don't like, though, in the background.

I do talk to your care providers. And I talk to you about everything I talk to them about.

Mom, let's focus on the book, OK?

You told me you wanted to hear from me in the book. So I'm telling you what is on my mind right now about problems related to your schizophrenia.

Are you on my side, Mom, against these people? You should be.

I'm not against these people. I am on your side, though we might not agree on everything about your treatment or about your beliefs or values. I want to help you find the best quality of life possible. Getting along better with all your treatment team, keeping them off your back would be good, wouldn't it?

PERC, Psychiatry Enforcing Resistance Corp.

Moore Bowen

<u>Madness Network News</u>. Not against the family, friends, relatives, offspring. I want kids, too, Mom, and a wife. State's preventing that, trying to. These parts and wires all through me, installed by the Pentecostal Church here and the CIA, not being run right. I got a leak from Eleanor the other day. She told me she was getting my mail at UNL when I was away. I want my money, mail, and phone calls dating back to birth, bombs, letter bombs, contraband, guns. I want all the dope. She said she was getting my money up at UNL. She told me that. It's no lie. And she also tried to frame me by telling Ted McKean I ain't even taking my meds when I been taking them quite reliably now, since about 1976, every damn one of them. Once in a while I forget one in the box, or it won't rattle right when I shake it, but that's about it. Been taking them reliably since '76, and I need them for sleep, too. And depression.

Eleanor looks in the pill box to see if you are taking all your meds, and she doesn't come up with the right number. That's why she thinks you're missing two to four doses a week? I think I understand forgetting once in a while. But she thinks two to four missed doses a week is serious. Do you think so?

I've done a lot of legal work for the Michaels and Adams, too. Mom, talk into the tape. Interrogate mental health and corrections.

I am interrogating them, and you don't like it when I talk to them.

Yeah, that's fine, Mom. You're on the Board of Directors. Exploit that to the hilt.

I'm not there to exploit, Moonway. I hoped I might be able to do something there to improve the quality of life for all the mentally ill. But I doubt that I have much power to even affect what I would like to. I certainly do not have any power to exploit my position to personal advantage. On second thought, we all try to exploit situations to our own advantage, don't we?

I'm not taking evidence on you, Mom. I'm just illustrating my medical chart, here. As long as you're on my side, Mom. And that's fine if you keep interrogating them. I think it's better for all of us, Mom, family and friends, if we have a bunch of legal services going during the book, too. This copyright and patented book with my eternal copyright and patent on it. And I'm trying to look out for yous, doing the best I can. See my drawing here, my hippy, dippy.

Ha, ha, ha. You drew that mushroom real fast.

Want me to keep cutting you in financially, too, with my legal services? Although I'm tightening up lately. Would you guys cut me in financially? It's all legal. This book should sell, Mom, with that drawing over there of Jack Nicholson. I'm not guaranteeing anything. Just like you're not guaranteeing anything.

I'm glad we both understand there are no guarantees, certainly not about what is going on with Ted McKean and Eleanor Lee.

I've over-timed for everything, Mom, including volunteer time. I learned my lesson. I never wrote another letter to the government. I want all of this speeded up without the aversive stuff. I'd like to have the Harmony Family Christian Center out here which I generated. I'd like to get my notes and art work back from Kingston and SMHI. Mom, all these psyche and corrections places need to be eliminated. All of them. Psyche Unit in East Northridge. Woodland County Jail. Florence County Jail. Places I ain't been in, too. Mom, this is a point I do want to emphasize. Mental Health does use control drugs that manufacture voices to torture mental patients who have abused them in the past. A lot of this is spiritual, you know. People hate religion these days. Demons, angels, evil, good. AA says we are supernatural agents of God. Maybe it is political, these voices. Yeah, that clears up a lot. OK, I want to ban frame, I want to ban ban, I want to ban those control drugs forcing us to hallucinate. I want to ban psyche sluts. That corrections official back in the late '80s. They're like Sid Fisher sang: "I don't want a baby that looks like that, and she don't want a baby that looks like me.

Thursday we will be going to Woodland for your Neuro-psyche evaluation. What do you expect to come out of it?

Oh. Proof of my sanity. Proof of my insanity.

Hunh?

And sanity. Both. I recovered a lot of sanity, but I'm still mentally ill.

Hmm, that's insightful, Moonway. It's time to close this session. It was difficult in some places, hunh? My fears about how you handle feelings about Eleanor's and Ted's visit interfere with my ability to listen without judging. I lose my anthropological cool, stutter, get defensive, lecture. Oh well, it's all material for the book, hunh?

2-9-01

Well, Moonway, we are on our way to Woodland, and I have the tape going so we can work on the book while we are riding.

Careful, Mom. Be careful driving, look all ways.

We have to make sure we get to the neuro-psyche evaluation on time, hunh? You are excited about this, aren't you?

Yeah. I was up all night.

Oh dear. That might skew the results, but you said you wanted to interrogate me, and I promised you could. Fire away.

Have you faced your fears, Mom? It's good to, so you can conquer them, do something about what might happen.

Hmmm. Sometimes I think I have made a lot of progress in conquering my fears. Other times, I feel like I haven't made any. My fear of other people's rages used to be a major control in my life, like an 11th commandment: Don't make anyone mad. And if someone was mad around me, I either tried to fix it or ran away from it. I'm still afraid of making people mad, but now, sometimes, I consciously risk it when it is important to do so. I risk making you mad when I try to influence you to try to cooperate more with Eleanor and Ted McKean. And I risk making them mad when I criticize the way they treat you. How do you feel about your progress in confronting your traumas and fears?

Good. Careful, curve coming up.

How about your fear about riding with me? Much progress there?

No. Nor riding with anyone. Seems like we could get some service keeping us safe going down and back and at home when you go from my apartment to your house.

Speaking about fears, I felt afraid last night about you posting your signs in the window, "for protection." You asked me if I believed your signs would protect you. And I said no. And then you posted them.

I posted up that I was stickering my signs, "Adults Only." The pictures and the bomb and the Manson stuff, you mean? The sticker?

Yeah, do you think that would protect you?

I think it would make the FBI withdraw or something.

Are a lot of your signs for protection? Is that what they mean to you? Protection from flipping a lit match at the ashtray, for example?

Protecting me from the underworld and assassins and re-arrests.

Oh. But you don't believe you were protecting yourself from fire

No.

Well, that's a great relief. It scared me that you would go on flipping matches and not be careful because you believed you were protected. That's one of my big fears, that you will set yourself or your apartment on fire.

I bought a lighter that goes out after each light. That's safer. I have to be safe with my nicotine habit. I know that.

I'm glad of that. I'm also afraid about your freedom which I know is really important to you. I'm afraid it can get more and more limited if you rely on beliefs about such things protecting you from the consequences of your actions.

What actions specifically?

You think you are just practicing your freedom-of-speech rights at UNL when you post signs with swastikas or other symbols that people find offensive. But can you see how they could make people feel threatened?

Haven't been posting propaganda or nothing up there. Haven't even been up there lately. Mom, it's just writing and art work. I wouldn't do anything to anyone.

I'm glad of that. We're almost there. I hope we are

going to gain some insight with this evaluation. I sure would like to find a way to help you live a happier life, take better care of yourself, stay out of trouble.

I want to baffle doctors some more with the supernatural insight of the Holy Spirit within me. I'd like to get the originals of all these tests and my psyche charts. They could keep photocopies of them. I might go right into miserly, barren, retracted secrecy, too.

2-13-01

I hope you can stay awake today and finish the evaluation, Moonway. Did you sleep last night?

No. Oriented neuro-psychiatric, behavior modification, no tricks now, boys, or I'll poison the white race. And I can do it. I'm glad I was tested, but I hope they don't alter the test results. They might, you know. Or they're probably sending it to the FBI, U. S. Marshals, or CIA.

They don't do that.

Yes, they do. I'm angry.

Because I don't believe you? Well, Ted McKean will see a copy of the report, so I guess I can see where you are coming from.

I'm glad I didn't give that cheap shyster a copy of our book. He won't give us a copy of the test results.

He said we would get copies, and if we're not satisfied with the results we can talk about it with him.

2-19-01

It's good we got the neuropsyche evaluation done with, hunh? Everyone seems concerned about you missing the psycho-social group. What's going on in that group could be material for our book, if you can tell me without violating the privacy of people in the group.

God forbid that happen.

Ha, ha, you're being sarcastic?

We got the tape on?

Yeah. Why do you hate the group? What do you remember about the therapy from the two times you went?

It just feels like such a goddamned death clinic. Us

poor patients sit there. None of them want to be there. We would rather be right at home. I don't want to go, Mom. How am I getting home?

It's about a mile. You can walk from CMHC. It's good exercise.

No.

Well, Moonway, tell me what you remember Ted McKean saying to you?

I agreed to go.

What did he say about the conditions of release?

Obey psychiatry.

Yeah, not only medication, but the treatment plan.

Yeah.

You can get the transportation director to help you. Sometimes I see him hanging around up there, transporting people and such. Call him and make arrangements. Could you do that?

No. Maybe later.

Can you think of any ways to make this a plus for you? If you can arrange some extra money, would that be a plus?

Yeah.

And like I said, your presence there could provide good material for our book, too. Pay attention to what's going on so you can tell me next taping session. What is it doing for you? What would you like it to do for you? Make it all a contribution to our book.

Yeah. I'd rather just forget about these people, Mom. They fractured my arm. I know how to tap the phone, Mom. As long as there's a recording service on the other end I can tap the media. They're going to wire tap me, they better expect wire tapping in revenge. It's all hush, hush, this wire tapping. Probably why I'm safe though and not using drugs.

19. COUNTY MENTAL HEALTH CENTER NEUROPSYCHOLOGICAL EVALUATION

Name: **Moonway Michael**
DOB: 9/18/56

DOE: 2/8/01; 2/9/01, & 2/21/01
Evaluator: Dr. Andrew Wellstone
REFERRAL INFORMATION

Mr. Michael received an Occupational Therapy assessment in 1998 from Virginia Sayers, OTR/L. She found evidence of "severe sensory defensiveness" and hyper-reactivity to environmental stimuli (such as light touch or sudden noises). She felt that such reactions might be responsible for his aversion to grooming, preference for layers of heavily textured clothing, avoidance of crowds, the need to define his personal space with warning signs, and his disturbed sleep-wake cycle. It was noted that Mr. Michael had problems with "gravitational insecurity," which were present in his wide-based stance, side-to-side shuffled gait, high level of pressure in handling of objects, poor balance, and heavy pacing.

Although he displayed a good ability to focus his attention and discriminate visual stimuli he appeared to have difficulty with novel problem solving and visual-spatial relationships. He was able to follow sequences, but had difficulty with planning and organization. Recommendations included tactile, vestibular, and proprioceptive stimuli to reduce sensory defensiveness; increased structure (consistent, and predictable daily routine; better sequential organization of tasks); use of a memory book and visual cues to retrieve information; and clear guidelines and standards for conduct.

PRESENTING COMPLAINTS AND CURRENT FUNCTIONING

Eleanor Lee, MHRT-II: Mr. Michael's Community Support Counselor said that before his medications were changed, he was averaging one hospitalization every nine months or so. In the last seven months, he has been hospitalized or needed residential crisis or respite care on 14 or 15 occasions. She felt that his delusions were having a greater influence on his behavior and had caused him to isolate himself. He will agree to follow treatment recommendations and then insist that he has the right to do what he wants. Although his delusions fluctuate in intensity, they generally are quite prominent during counseling sessions and he often talks about the FBI and CIA and how they are intruding on his life. She also noted that he now attends only two AA meetings per week instead of five. He no longer goes to the soup kitchen (he used to eat three meals a week there), and a male friend he used to see regularly has stopped visiting him. He appears frightened of his probation officer and will stay awake for days prior to their meetings.

She indicated that he misses about two to four doses of his medications each week. While this report was being prepared, she sent an e-mail to the examiner which indicated that the sanitation of his apartment had greatly deteriorated. She questioned whether he required a supported, residential-type placement where he could be more closely supervised.

Ted McKean: During a phone interview on 2/28/01, Mr. Michael's probation officer, Mr. McKean noted that Mr. Michael did not appear to be adjusting well to independent living. Although he has been more alert since his medication was changed last year, his overall functioning appears to have declined and there has been a noticeable increase in rebelliousness and defiance. His refusal to attend recommended psychosocial group meetings clearly was a violation of his conditions of release. Mr. McKean indicated that he overheard Mr. Michael screaming and swearing during an unannounced home visit in January of this year. He expressed concern that Mr. Michael's psychiatric status was unstable and could decline suddenly.

Victor Robins: Mr. Michael's financial conservator, Mr. Robins, was interviewed by phone on 01/26/01 He noted that Dr. Christian's recommendation for medical and residential

Guardianship apparently was not addressed by the Probate Court the last time Mr. Michael's case was heard. His description of Mr. Michael's functioning and the condition of his apartment was consistent with observations made by other members of Mr. Michael's treatment team prior to Mrs. Lee's recent communication about his apartment

Moonway Michael: Mr. Michael indicated that he often stays up all night watching TV or listening to the radio. He said he was paid for keeping watch on a "2-way station" that he had "invented" and noted that he had proof for this in his files. He felt that his medications have kept him from becoming violent and suicidal." However, he said he would like to discontinue Haldol because it causes "horrid nightmares." He acknowledged that he had been attending AA less often this winter and said that he did not want to go out in the cold. He also had stopped going to the soup kitchen because he felt that others had stereotyped him as a "destitute criminal and prostitute" and wondered whether the soup kitchen was making money by "selling some goods to rich people." He indicated that he no longer has command or visual hallucinations but only has "inner" visions of himself as an "Artist." He noted that he still hears voices mumbling in the background. He said he wanted to have his financial guardianship terminated so that he could have "access to money, mail, and phone calls dating back to birth." When asked what types of mail had been withheld from him, he questioned whether "a rocket launcher made of silver that I want to put on my wall" was being held for him at the post office; however, he added that he was uncertain whether this idea was a product of "my suspicions or delusions." He noted that his Federal probation officer nags him to clean his room, shower several times a week, and do his laundry. He said he now showers "every two or three days" instead of once a month. He does his laundry once every two or three weeks" when he has the money and brushes his teeth "once in a while."

He indicated that he did not want to live in a supported housing program (e. g, CMHC's housing complex) or have more opportunities for socialization (He stated that he did not care for the 'Sociology Department"). Being around other people disturbs his concentration and negatively affects his ability to do his artwork. When he socializes, "every thing turns blurry and ignorant." He still has a friend and sees this person more often during the summer. He noted that he occasionally forgets to take his medications but estimated that he missed only "one or two pills" a month. He said he was glad he moved back to Northridge where he could see his family and friends more often. He occasionally has memory lapses, which he attributed to his medication. He also has to favor his right arm because of an old "fracture," although be refused to discuss how and when this injury occurred. He noted that his cleaning lady hasn't been in to clean his apartment for a month and that he was unable to wash his clothes because he was out of laundry detergent. He also acknowledged that he carelessly threw lighted matches at his ashtray and said they sometimes fell on the carpet. He was worried that his probation officer would "send me back to Missouri' but felt this would not happen as long as he kept taking his medication, attended AA, used CMHC's Helpline for crisis support, and maintained a minimum level of self-care. At first, he seemed to accept the examiner's recommendation to use the soup kitchen to extend his limited income and improve his nutrition; however, in an unguarded moment in the next session he admitted that he had no interest in using this resource.

His current routine involves getting up around noon time, listening to tapes of his mother's published writings, editing and annotating dictated transcripts for his own book and making quick trips to the store across the street. He receives $20 twice a week for tobacco and incidentals and buys his own groceries with food stamps. His Community Support Counselor noted that he generally has an adequate amount of food in his apartment, although the quality of his diet is somewhat questionable (V-8 Juice, fish sticks, hot dogs, Vienna sausage).

BEHAVIORAL OBSERVATIONS

Mr. Michael was dressed in multiple layers of warm clothing, most of which were filthy and stained. His nails also were painted (he indicated he did this "to irritate society a little bit and to keep them on their toes"). During the first session, he wore a cylindrical paper hat, on which he had written a number of slogans and phrases (e.g., "The Rights of Experiments"; "Look Out And After Each Other"; "NASA"; "The Right to Refuse Pro And Con Treatment"; "I was a Test Tube Baby"). He also wore a "Voodoo" (his words) necklace consisting of empty medication containers, a whistle in the shape of an eyeball, and a five-star pendant. He said the hat helped prevent people from putting things in his brain while he wore the necklace "in case people try to poison me or overdose me on psychiatric drugs." During the second evaluation, he wore a cap on which he had written "E-Man Artist" and other acronyms ("ULN"; "MPI"; "UMK"; "KGB"). Undecipherable writing in faded ink also was visible on the back of his hands. He walked with a heavy, bouncy, and somewhat wide-based gait that was consistent with the observations made during his 1998 Occupational Therapy evaluation. While walking, he tended to look at the floor just beyond his feet.

His speech was high-pitched and had a "gritty" quality. At times there was an odd tension in his voice, as if his mouth was somewhat constricted and the words were being produced in the back of his throat. His cadence tended to be measured and he often emphasized individual syllables. Some words were difficult to understand because he did not articulate them clearly. There were no apparent problems with word finding or paraphasic speech. During the interview, his responses were relevant but on many occasions contained bizarre or delusional content or references. When asked questions, he frequently cocked his head and there was a significant pause while he thought through his answer. He had little difficulty understanding instructions.

When the examiner refused to let him take a smoke break at the beginning of the evaluation, he put on his dark glasses and gave vague or stereotyped responses until he was allowed to smoke. He also insisted that the examiner return samples of artwork and dictation for his book, which his mother had brought. Once these matters had been taken care of to his satisfaction, his mood quickly changed and he was friendly and cooperative throughout the remainder of the evaluation. He took numerous smoke breaks, but kept them brief and rushed back to the examination room to complete as much of the testing as possible. Good rapport was established and he appeared interested in the evaluation results. He often was aware of his mistakes and coped relatively well when he ran into difficulty. For the most part, he appeared to be putting forth his best effort although his responses on some visual tasks seemed rather hasty and imprecise. The samples of his art work reviewed by the examiner at the beginning of the evaluation were quite good and were far superior to his performance on visual-constructional tasks. When using the computer keyboard, he appeared to have difficulty regulating his hand movements, tapping the keys so hard at times that it eventually slid away from him. During an oral reading task, he tended to read individual words so rapidly that they almost seemed to run together. He displayed good concentration on many visual tasks, but had increasing difficulty retaining information in short-term memory on an oral arithmetic task as items became more lengthy and complex.

He indicated that he had stayed up all night prior to both evaluation sessions. His concentration started to lag part way through the morning of the first session, and he complained that a Haldol injection he had received earlier that morning was making him feel drowsy. That session was terminated part-way through the afternoon after he indicated that he was too tired to continue. He made a valiant effort to complete the MMPI-2 during the afternoon of the second session, but repeatedly fell asleep and completed the final 156 items portion in the CMHC Northridge office, two days later.

RESULTS OF TESTING

Emotional Functioning: Mr. Michael's rating on the Beck Depression Inventory-II indicated moderate to severe levels of dysphoric or depressive symptoms. He indicated that he feels sad all the time and has strong, negative feelings about himself. He feels he has had many failures and sees his future as "hopeless." He seems to feel that his psychiatric medications are a form of punishment. He reports diminished enjoyment in everyday activities, as well as increased restlessness, agitation, irritability, and fatigue. He is having greater difficulty concentrating and his energy, libido, and appetite are reduced. He reports that he wakes up early and is unable to get back to sleep.

There were extreme elevations on the F (120I) and FB (120T) scales of the MMPI-2, suggesting that his clinical profile was invalid. These unusually high scores may have resulted from his accurate reporting of chronic psychotic symptoms as well as a tendency to exaggerate or over-report psychopathology. There was no indication that he was confused or cognitively disorganized when taking the test. Inspection of Supplementary and Content scales indicated that he was reporting especially significant problems with depression, concentration, self-motivation, and fatigue, as well as conflicts with family members, feelings of persecution, and psychotic thought processes (including hallucinations and paranoid ideation). He also appears to be concerned about his health and tends to be nervous and fearful.

SUMMARY AND CONCLUSIONS

The test findings indicate the presence of mild to moderate level of cerebral dysfunction that appears to be most prominent in frontal-subcortical and possibly right medial-temporal brain regions. It is quite likely that his lack of sleep prior to both sessions and administration of IM Haldol on the morning of the first session negatively affected his attention, visual-motor processing speed, and ability to inhibit impulsive behavior. As a result, the test results should be viewed as a minimum estimate of his processing capacity. Despite his fatigue, his performance on many tasks was within or above normal limits. Although it was not always possible to make comparisons between the current and 1995 evaluation results (because different or updated procedures were used in the present evaluation), Mr. Michael does not appear to have experienced a decline in his overall cognitive abilities since 1995. There was evidence of changes in specific neuropsychological domains. He appears better able to learn and retain verbal information but is having greater difficulty encoding visual material into longer-term memory. He also seems to be having increased difficulty with motor skills (bilateral fine motor speed and dexterity). Verbal fluency, reasoning skills, and comprehension of cause-effect relationships in social situations appeared to have improved significantly. As in 1995, his attention was erratic (Dr. Christian also noted that his attention was "variable") and there were indications that his overall intellectual abilities were significantly higher earlier on in his life. This latter finding is consistent with recent research, which has suggested that some individuals may experience a decline in IQ score after they develop a schizophrenic illness. The reasons for the above changes in cognitive functioning, especially the visual memory and motor skills findings, is not clear at this time. It is possible that the increase in activation has enhanced certain well-established cognitive abilities (e.g., language skills) while interfering with other skills that require sustained attention and self-regulation (e.g., drawing). Medication side effects may also be a factor (e.g., decreased motor regulation and speed).

Mr. Michael's psychiatric status appears to have been less stable since his medication was changed from Zyprexa to Risperdal in the spring of 2000. He has had repeated episodes in which he has been unable to cope with his depressive, homicidal, and psychotic symptoms and has needed hospitalization or residential crisis services.

On the positive side, Mr. Michael appears to have abstained from the use of substances or has had relatively minor relapses. He has not been violent and has voluntarily sought help during crises when his suicidal and homicidal thinking became overwhelming.

Over the years Mr. Michael's delusional thinking and beliefs have become a significant part of his identity. Although his world view often puts him at odds with society, in recent years, he has been able to refrain from the kinds of aggressive or threatening behavior that would result in the loss of his freedom. However, his marginal lifestyle has at times jeopardized his health and psychiatric stability.

Mr. Michael appears to have done some of the difficult work that is necessary to maintain his sobriety. He now needs to build on this foundation and broaden the scope of his recovery by developing better routines and self-regulatory skills. The mental health services provided to Mr. Michael in the last four or five years appear to have been appropriate to address many of the concerns noted above. Given his unwillingness or inability to accept or follow through with these services, it is likely that he will require a higher level of support than he currently is receiving. His treatment team needs to maintain a united front in insisting that he do whatever is deemed necessary to enhance the quality of his recovery and reduce the risk of relapse.

RECOMMENDATIONS

1. It is recommended that Mr. Michael's treatment team identify specific changes he needs to make to reduce the risk of a serious decompensation. For example, Mr. Michael might be expected to attend AA 4-5 times a week, go to the soup kitchen 2-3 times a week, shower at least 3 times a week, allow his housekeeper to clean his whole apartment, drastically reduce or eliminate his use of caffeine, accept preventative medical and dental services and attend weekly psychosocial rehabilitation groups. The team may have to meet apart from Mr. Michael to achieve a consensus. The team should not expect immediate changes in some areas and should not try to address all concerns at once but instead should set priorities and determine what Mr. Michael needs to do to demonstrate "improvement" or "cooperation" as he works towards these objectives. A contract between Mr. Michael and the team might be written to clarify their respective responsibilities and the steps that need to be taken to reach these goals. The team also needs to spell out the consequences if he is unwilling or unable to follow through with these recommendations.

2. Mr. Michael should be referred to CMHC's Dual Diagnosis Institute and follow-up dual diagnosis counseling for additional support as he works on the areas of recovery identified by his team.

3. In working with Mr. Michael it may be helpful to look at ways that he can use his creative and

artistic talents to help him make more healthy choices and decisions. For example, he might be encouraged to arrange an art exhibition at the soup kitchen or at the site where the psychosocial club meets. He might also help other people who are struggling with mental illness by including a chapter in his book that documents his attempts to make positive changes in his own life and provides helpful advice for his readers.

4. The marked increase in psychiatric crises and hospitalizations raises the possibility that Mr. Michael's medications need further adjustment. If it is not already being done his community support counselor should provide his psychiatrist with regular (e.g., biweekly) updates about his current functioning and mental status. His psychiatrist should attend quarterly meetings of his treatment team.

5. The findings suggest that Mr. Michael will function best when he has a high level of structure and routine. He should be helped to set priorities and set aside enough time to complete essential tasks. Visual and verbal cues can be used to help him maintain a basic routine. For example, small signs or pictures might be placed in strategic locations to remind him to accomplish specific tasks, such as cleaning off his living room table, emptying out his cat's litter box, or disposing of matches and cigarettes properly. His daily routine can be posted in a prominent location in his apartment. Tasks can be broken down into more easily manageable components or modules (cleaning or straightening up one room each day).

6. Instructional methods should incorporate multiple stimulus modalities (e. g, written and oral directions, demonstrations; simulations, "hands-on" practice). The emphasis should be on developing practical solutions and helping him deal with problems and obstacles (including his

own delusions and oppositional attitudes). Counseling sessions should have a consistent format and only a few topics should be discussed or addressed. Information should be presented in a logical and clearly-organized manner. Important concepts, tasks, and "homework" should be reviewed at the end of the session and written down in a simple, easy-to-follow format that can also be used as a behavioral cue. Plans and programs might also be kept in a three ring notebook which can be organized into sections for reference. He could learn to routinely consult this book at specific times during the day (and indicate that he had done so by . . . initialing after the date on a designated page). Care should be taken to draw his attention to key points or subtleties (e. g, by highlighting) and help him make distinctions between concepts. It may be helpful to discuss possible scenarios that help him anticipate consequences. Skills should be practiced until they become relatively automatic. Tasks which require a great deal of strength or rapid fine motor skills should be de-emphasized and compensatory supports provided if necessary (e. g., modify the task or equipment, have someone assist him). It may be helpful to have his mother assume a more formal role in his treatment plan to assist him with certain activities of daily living (e. g., laundry).

7. If Mr. Michael is unable to keep his apartment clean and regulate his sleep cycle, it is recommended that he move to a placement that provides a greater level of professional support and supervision (e.g., CMHC's assisted living housing).

8. His treatment team may wish to involve the State's Intensive Case Manager in Mr. Michael's care. The individual who recently was hired for this position, Gary Gold, worked with Mr. Michael for several years at CMHC and has

extensive knowledge of his issues and needs.

9. If Mr. Michael is unwilling or unable to follow through with recommended changes and behavioral guidelines over a trial period of two to three months, it is recommended that his guardianship be expanded to include medical and residential functions. The appointment of a full guardian can be viewed as an "intermediate-level intervention that hopefully will allow Mr. Michael to remain in the community and minimize the need to use the "last resort" solution of involving the Federal Court.

Andrew Wellstone
Ph.D. Licensed Psychologist

When I first read this evaluation, I was very disappointed with what I read as the hopeless tone of the whole report. From the beginning of Moonway's illness, it seemed we had all been struggling against the sense of his disease as inevitably leading to a lifetime of guardianship and/or institutionalization. I interpreted this report as suggesting that our struggle was futile. I knew "a trial period of two to three months" was ludicrous to successfully implement the radical recommendations he made, radical in the sense that they would require far more changes from all involved than could possibly happen in such a short time, and radical in the sense that his professional care has rarely been consistent or frequent enough to accomplish the recommendations. I have never know him to receive the kind and intensity of counseling recommended by Dr. Wellstone.

In hindsight, I think Dr. Wellstone must have been convinced from the beginning that the effort to keep Moonway's limited independence was hopeless, so why should a trial period longer than three months be necessary? He knew Moonway's history before he started the evaluation, and his review of it confirmed that no one had been able to successfully treat Moonway's illness on a sustained basis in the twenty five-year history of the disease he was reviewing. I can understand that perspective and respect the effort Dr.

Wellstone put into the thorough evaluation and his later efforts to attempt to get Moonway a full guardian. He was doing what he believed was the best thing for Moonway. But I still feel angry at that impatient tone, and I still believe the desire of many care providers for quick fixes and their hopeless attitudes with "failure" constitute a great barrier to patients' recovery.

During the months that followed, Moonway's conflict with Eleanor and Ted drew in Andrew Wellstone.

20. Is Psyche Sucking Dream Spirits Right Out of You?

Chapter 20 and the last pages of Chapter 21 contain excerpts from monologues Moonway recorded at times of extreme tension during his conflict with the treatment team. The tension is evident in his voice on the tape and affects the quality to such an extent that I had difficulty understanding. It was also emotionally difficult to hear because of the violence in the content. To maintain my resolve to focus on problem solving and avoid crisis thinking, I did not transcribe these tapes as I had the others, usually in one marathon session right after each hour or so of taping. Instead, I listened to them repeatedly until I felt I had a good understanding of the literal meaning and had diffused some of my own tensions about them. Then I transcribed them slowly, seldom working more than a half hour or so at a time. It is still difficult for me to read through this and to accept that these thoughts originate in the same mind as the affectionate, outgoing, and creative mind of the little boy I knew in the late 1950s; the same mind I can still see at work, at times, in present behavior and talk.

For conciseness, I cut much of the repetition and content that didn't seem relevant to Moonway's conflict with "psyche and corrections," and I mostly selected only content that I later talked to him about. I have tried very hard not to censor violent or offensive content because I think it too important to the whole picture of Moonway's "decompensating" mind.

Even with all of that, I include these monologues with

a great deal of trepidation. In a workshop conference, an editor told me once about the early chapters of this book, "Cut all those dialogues with Moonway and tell the story as a straightforward narrative. You can't expect anyone to read through all that craziness."

Those chapters were mild compared to what happens in these monologues. I have worked extensively with them, but I keep coming back to the conviction that the truth is more important than any reader's sensitivities. They were recorded when he was the most psychotic that I have ever seen him. It is likely that he has been more psychotic at times, but I did not witness it as it was happening.

If we are ever going to understand psychosis better than we do now, we must try to understand these kinds of expressions from those who experience them. At present, they are mostly discounted as symptoms in studies of the mentally ill. Never in the more than 30-year history of Moonway's illness has anyone that I know about ever paid any serious attention to them. I don't pretend to understand them. I include them in the hope that, if you have stayed with us up to now, you will be interested in the most extreme experiences of Moonway's mental life. And I hope someone out there might read them with the respect I believe they deserve as important in themselves in illuminating understanding of psychosis.

Late April, 2001

Did a truce in my own blood about disco drugging of Jack Nicholson and Sid Vicious and prostitutes they attacked, which disco doctors did just to turn them against whores. If I ever went on a legal speed prescription, I know I'd kill a junkie. Because of the strings from the doctors. She's in blood you two, and that's as far as I'm taking her. Or can I take her further? Got a nuclear bomb contract against Hollywood and D. C. in blood. Blood samples and needles left behind by a nurse. And the only way I can see out of this Haldol drugging is getting convictions against these doctors for drugging me and the people who lock me up in those horrible places.

Song:
Uncle Ernie, Uncle Ernie, Uncle Ernie.
Oh, Bernie. Bernie and Uncle Ernie.
Everyone's got an Uncle Ernie in a closet.
Ernie's story: Just to have a guinea pig
or someone to torture and extract and extort from.
I'm Belinda Adams' and Richard Michael's Uncle
Ernie,

My only alternative is alternative medicines.
Ginseng's party approved.
All the anonymi did was get me covering up. They
tortured me into covering up, in fact, the butchering of my
original notes, replacement of folks that cared. Horrible
military experiments that were conducted on us. The
lobotomies. The shock treatments. The drugging. The
experimentation on me and others in my family.

Song:
Roll in the isles, boys.
Swing from the rafters.
Play with them snakes.
Drink the poison.
The more you can get of that snake venom in you,
the better off you are.
The world's coming to an end,
so eat, drink, and be merry
because I ain't no fairy.

Song:
The covenant of the Lord would say unto thee.
The Eve of Pentecost is past.
The wrath of Yahweh cometh down now.
The wrath of the fist has begun.
Remember the battle of the Bull Run, dear ones.
Remember the battle of the Bull Run.
Long remember it.
Joanna don't want me. Joanna don't want me.
No one wants me.

ULN wants me, don't you?
Don't you want me ULN?   Hee, hee, hee.

Get your halos, your judge's gavels, and your voodoo
necklaces made out of strings of all the pills you're on, and
start burning summons, and sticking Porky right in the gut
and the throat with switch blades. Get them skulls raised high
on scepters.

A political poem by Moonway Michael.
Little Chinamen, how to create a Kent State.
Passivism, violence, anarchy,
drugging the whole college,
poisoning the whole college, my little ARTS,
Pentecostal, AA. Proposal to Joanna:
If she don't want me, I'm going under as a junkie.

Poem:
Get the guard towers built now, dear ones.
Get the guard towers built now up there
at ULN. And get her built
at Harmony Family Christian Center.
Get Channel 1 going.
Get them Pentecostal campgrounds
stomping, now, stomping right silly.
Stomp out the devil. I need a Black Day
to oppose Jimmy Jones' White Knight.
I need a black day, now, dear ones.
This is Ron Mainline, Chai Com, woman daughter.
I got the ghost. Halleluia.
I got the ghost with the roast toast
and the host and the most high.
I got the roast toast.
I got the roast toast.
Mom wouldn't give me my bread.
She can have it. She can have it.
Got the roast toast and the most ghost.
I believe I'll have me a slice
of roast ghost delivered, right now.

I believe I'll snuff the world.
I believe I'll snuff the world.
Through revolution and war.
Through revolution and war.
Bring me my family. Bring me my family.
What a legacy. What a legacy.
Drink the wine dear ones. Drink the wine.
It has healing medicine in it.

Song:
I want to slice AA, Joanna's ghost,
soul and spirit, to eat.
I want it affecting me funny.
Bring me my family. Bring me my family.
What a legacy. What a legacy.

Song:
Bum Chichy. Bum Chichy.
Urby, Chichy, bum. Bum Chichy.
Bum Chichy. Urby, Chichy, bum.
Aztec, Aztec. Inca, Inca. Aztec Inca.
Bum, Chichy. Bum, Chichy. Chichy, Bum.
Bum, Chichy. Chichy, Chichy, Bum.

I want you to get the drug team going.
Set it on obstacle course.
Old tires laid zigzag on the sidewalks
up and down.
I want you to start training them.
There's a war on.
I want you to get up on the eves and eat,
heave and shit from the eves.
Everyone carry candles.
The drills have begun. The drills have begun.

The toy knife I had in Caribou and toy gun were
forced on me by an undercover narc to protect the criminal
law. They forced me to do it.
Got myself all designed here, boys, clones, family,

friends, kin, offspring. Got myself all designed, here, and I'm
not going to impose any laws on you, clones of me and us, or
try to convert you or do nothing to you. Wishing you the
best. You want a couple of roles. The runaway and the
confidence man. Me, I'm a junkie. Let's design ourselves.
What we want to look like. Where we want to live.

Privately we're Moonway Michael. Publicly, I'm
Cogluft Moonway. Who are you?

Images. The agony of the underdog. The ecstasy of
the Wop. H. P. Clyde never fails, does he girls? Does he?
He's me.

And I don't care where my sperm goes, through
masturbation, or sex, or how many children internationally I
have, regardless of background. Or who they are, what color.
Just hetero, though. And I want them all raised in contact
with me. Adoring me. Worshipping me. And last name,
Michael. I don't care who my sperm goes into as long as
they're women.

I've survived the streets, you know. That's the hardest
part, trying to survive.

Song:
I'm a runaway hero.
A royal old Nero.
Fascination the same.
Extortion's my game.

You know what the media's doing? Or, Alyce Cooper,
is psyche sucking dream spirits right out of you? Creating
whole new races that way. Taking our songs and claiming
them as our own. The sons of bitches. Sucking creative
spirits right out of you. Psyche techs do that to Alyce Cooper.
Alyce Cooper did that to me. No chain of command for me. I
have no role model. I don't even obey God half the time.
Taking our names, aliases, and addresses, using them as their
own. They're not getting much out of it other than torture.
What next? Extracting the pleasure nerves out of us.

The goal of exmates and inmates should not be to
flood the prisons or the outside but leave it a choice. This is

the writ of the great schizophrenic Luther, here.

Art-psyche stream-of-dream consciousness is being blocked against my will by psyche drugs and parts and wires.

Friendship. Keep Carl Daggett and me off illegal dope and illegal deals and aversive therapies. Keep our benefits and checks coming in.

It was pure cruelty from society against an intellectual artist and alcoholic and drug addict that forced me into what happened under the bridge in Kingston, Lincoln.

The other night I dreamed that I was with a city gang in the urban woods. They said it would cost me 2 million for 2 ounces. They bladed me and tested me with a silver hand grenade. I thought of gold and silver hand grenades, military gold helmets. That's disco, ain't it? I'm a terrorist. Last night I dreamed that I was with some psyche tech women wearing my Hitler mustache. A German was there and he tapped me on the foot. I told him that the Nazis had competition with the mental patients on the scene. I said, "Another true set?" Then the German and I were with a giant he developed into other teams. The Germans said I shouldn't wear nail polish, but I'm gonna.

Visions of people on staff side who tortured me in SMHI.

Throughout my life, my relatives have abused me and had me experimented on by doctors and shrinks against my will. Psychotic cry. There is a problem with mainstreaming mentally ill alcoholics because they are subjected to all forms of cures and crucifixions by the churches and academics. But I'll take freedom, no matter what.

> Song:
> Needles and pills are disco.
> It's in the smoke which ain't disco.
> White supremacist rock is all too terrorist.
> Colored rock is outdated.

> Poem: Willie's Cape
> Oh, wretched, perverse,
> and wicked red youth,

how pleadest thou
in thine atheist dilemmas?
Anyon speaksia.
Singest thou the anarchist poetry of enigma.
Banish it from the face of time
and orbits of Kap destines
To come in the sons of heretica.
Only the economist deities
await those who stop the wrath
of the assassins and slayers,
spoke facts with all their mind's
heart to speed. Herald the plagiarism
of this dark day of profound ignorance.
Or the slayer woman will arise
from the shadow land of fraud
and assassinate the media eternal.
The Michaels, Adams, and Morrises
are my purloined and literate family, now.
So leave us wretched oppressors
lest we send thee to the lake of fire.

    Criminal psychosis. Most hits' sons, psychotic delinquents which come from psyche and corrections are ordered by celebrities as cover-ups because most runaways are cooperative rats.

    As a teen, I was separated from my real parents and brother and sister by opportunist shrinks who gave me a genetically engineered replacement family. I want the genes of the replacements which came from my original relatives stored in guarded PERC laboratories. I want my original family returned to me. Or do I? My real brother Martin tried to call Kap shrink and Dad tried to call Kap military. Real Mother tried to call the Reds. And real sis Shirley tried to call the school. But to no avail. This is the original family, and we're in the opposition's hands and shoot the dope, and drinking ill. My mother and I went through the same thing. My real mother anyway. Only it was environmental with me, and it was all internal with her. Boys, let's bottle both in wine and rum bottles and give it to shrinks without the other RXing them.

Uh, uh, uh. Uh, uh, uh.

Last night I dreamed that I was in Canada with Polly Marks. We went to nursing homes and found that our mail was going there. We had some trouble getting into Canada because I called the border guard a homo French: "You're a fucking fag, ain't you?" He said, "Who's a homo?" I said, "I apologize and meant homosexual." Before the nursing homes, we were in French Projects, and I put down the pollution and Kapitalist countries. Also, at the Project was a photo of Bush. I told Polly, "Ever think of shooting him? I have." Then the image of old Bush moved and Bush said, "46%, Moonway. What is this? You want to be a nukie? Just let me know any day. Revolution and nuclear war is what I represent, against all mankind."

I want my real and replacement families, nationally and internationally all young and safe and kept alive forever on their terms.

Poem-Song:
Don't laugh, church of the drug revolution
because you could be a junkie, too.
Don't laugh at Solzhenitzen titty thing, either
because look at the way the Kapitalist free world
is rapidly becoming a dictatorship.

That all happened in the past, real folks. Sanity and insanity by praying, preaching, and going to church. I did this, also, by going to college and using tranquilizers to become educated and sleep off 25 years of horribly hard times for the world.

Psycho autobiography. In total violation of the Nuremberg code, psyche and corrections is trading parts and body fluids from client and resistor both and implanting and injecting these into themselves. Both sexes and both races are involved.

Snakes and cut-open brains make the same sound which is s-s-s-s-s. Eat worms and maggots from the black panthers' music scene. My real family are all church, state, and media experiments. I've been butchered throughout my life and been brought back to life. I need a Miller Light so I can buy reality and real hate. Why are you killing me? I'm a doctor of death.

Yea, in the crypted book of blood called Enigma, ye should abandon blood and join all that is evil. I don't want the past because the future's a blast.

Last night I dreamed that I was on THC on a bus. The hippie next to me pulled a knife which I used against him to stab him in the heart and throat. Then he pulled a gun, and I pushed it away. The gun went off, and I took a bullet in the head. Lawyers become involved, and I became involved and I confessed.

Isn't Satanism part of Christianity, the evils defined by religion part of that religion? Or just something religion wants to avoid? They named them, though. Ain't that part of the religions?

Manson, LaBaron, Karesh, Jones, and I all need love. This is all art and poetry. All art-work documents.

All art and poetry? Yes, and covered by the first amendment, for most of us, but not for Moonway or thousands of others with paranoid schizophrenia who are criminalized. Should we judge them by different standards? Should I? I can read this sort of content written by strangers and advocate passionately for their first amendment rights, but I am still debating the wisdom of publishing this book out of concern for Moonway's freedoms.

May 22, 2001

Moonway, in your April monologue, who is Uncle Ernie?

Ernest Hemingway.

What does it mean that you are Uncle Ernie to me and your dad?

Well, I'm better off in your hands than in Mental Health's.

But you feel like you're tortured and extracted from and extorted from by us, too?

No. What I mean—I don't want to be a guinea pig any more. That's the next generation's job. Mom, I got a lot of health tips for you, like V 8 Juice, milk, meat. You probably eat OK though, don't you?

Yes. With "sticking Porky" and other comments, are you threatening?"

Another publicity stunt. Anger at psyche. I'm being blotted out by these drugs, Mom. I don't want to drink, though. If I stay on the road to recovery, things should clear up for me. Maybe I joke around too much, but I don't want to stop joking around.

Is there another real mother?

Mom, I don't know what's going on.

Do you believe there's another real mother?

Yeah. Is that psychiatric brain washing?

It's probably your schizophrenia? Maybe your whole monologue is your reaction to all that's been going on with you and Eleanor and Ted, and now Dr. Wellstone. It's very stressful, isn't it? I feel stressed by it, too. Tell me what you mean by blood samples left behind by your nurse.

Well, there was a red plastic box, and it was full of needles which had tubes to pull the blood. Not right full. Just plastic extensions on them which had some blood in them.

Did you call the nurse?

No. I just left it there, and she took it away when she came back 2 or three weeks later. The only problem I got with these doctors now are these Haldol injections, Mom.

I know they must be uncomfortable. Why would the nurse have the blood samples in here if she didn't take your blood?

I don't know. They didn't take it from me. I don't know, though. Maybe they did try it once.

This isn't just a story, hunh, just art and propaganda?

No, three times they left needles, Mom.

Could it be a delusion?

No.

That seems really strange. I'm alarmed about it.

Mom, listen a minute. This is kind of crucial, too. You know what I did with syringes they left behind? I put one on that voodoo necklace of mine with the pill bottles on it, went out to the winery, and faked shooting up. You don't have to worry about me really doing it as long as I keep going to AA. I just like having a say in my treatment coming first. If they're going to drug me with needles, I'm going to drug them right back.

I talked to the nurse about this, asked her if she ever left hypodermic paraphernalia behind. She said, no, she always puts the materials in a bag she carries for the purpose and takes them with her to dispose of elsewhere. If that is true, where did the syringes that Moonway wears around his neck come from? Where did the needles come from that I saw when I swept down his stairs? Though Moonway says they came from this current nurse, perhaps they all came from an earlier one, and he has gotten confused about how long he has had them. It might occur to any objective observer that they may have come from use of street drugs. I am his mother and likely have blind spots about Moonway, but I do believe and try to practice evidence-based judgments. This includes regular scrutiny of my own motives and of my ability to see clearly regardless of how unpleasant the sight is. It is clear to me that Moonway is delusional in many respects about shots. But it is also clear how aversive Moonway has always been to needles in his body, and I do not believe that he would use street drugs by injection. This is a nurse Moonway likes and trusts. I want to believe and trust her, too, but after I talked to her about this issue, I saw no more hypodermic paraphernalia.

21. Who's Forcing all this Treatment?

By June, the probation officer, Ted McKean, was in the process of petitioning the Federal Court to reconsider Moonway's release from MCFP for noncompliance with the conditions of release. The treatment team was still trying to get Moonway to comply with their recommendations. The more he was pressured, the more Moonway's anxiety mounted toward greater psychosis. The relationship between Moonway and Eleanor was deteriorating. His advocate, Cliff, was away for three months at the time; when he returned, he participated in a dialogue about treatment planning between Moonway and Eleanor which Moonway taped along with another monologue after they left.

July, 2001

Cliff: Moonway , we're going to work on a treatment plan for the time period from now to Thanksgiving. You're agreeing to the following personal/social activities: Shower twice a week. Take all meds as prescribed. Refrain from abuse of alcohol and drugs.

Do you guys refrain from alcohol?

No.

I do.

Good for you. Were we going to put something on the table about cleaning the apartment?

Today I swept the living room. The cleaning lady ain't been coming in, Cliff. I phoned today and they said the door was padlocked, but it wasn't.

OK. We need to work on that. Sweep the apartment how many times a week?

Twice.

How many AA meetings?

Many as I can get to in the summer.

Minimum.

Two.

How about going to the soup kitchen?

I been going, but it's closed this week.

You can't be responsible for that. How many times a week?

Three. No groups. No crossing out on these papers. No censoring the tapes.

What kind of medical services are you willing to get?

When I got a medical problem. NO, on the teeth—the right to refuse treatment, ACLU. I like keeping my teeth and gums. OK?

That's why they have to be attended to. When was the last time you went to any kind of a dental professional?

I went in Houlton. They cleaned my teeth there.
And how horrible was that?
Awful. They took a tooth.
While you weren't looking or what?
No.
Did they tell you they were going to pull it?
Yeah.
And what did you say?
I said NO.
Eleanor , could we get his dental records?
Eleanor: I don't even know who the dentist was.
Gary would know. Moonway, is Gary the one who
hooked you up?
Yeah.
Eleanor: I might have documentation in his charts.
If we can find out what the records say, Moonway,
let's leave it that we'll decide based on that. If the records
have recommendations . . .
No, Cliff. I don't want any teeth pulled.
No one's talking about getting them pulled. How
about getting them cleaned?
How come?
Because they need to be cleaned.
I'm angry.
Well, no one's going to make you do it, Moonway.
All I'm talking about at this point is let's see what the
recommendations were back when you went. You were
saying that you're going to get an EKG?
Yeah.
Eleanor: But he's refused to allow me to make an
appointment with the doctor.
Eleanor, I can't get there.
Moonway, I told you I will make an appointment. I
will arrange it. And I can take you, myself. So you could go
get a physical, and you could get your Previcid. And he could
give you an order to have the EKG.
They do it in the office. So, Moonway, are you
agreeing to that?
Cliff, how come all this is being forced on me again

against my will? ACLU.

Well, Moonway, you can say *no*.

I say *no* then.

There's a lot of things I want to say *no* to, like painting the house. I want to say *no* to that. But the consequences are what make me say *yes*. You understand?

Yeah.

Now some people might say this treatment plan is just an attempt to pull the wool over the judge's eyes about the upcoming court session, make a good impression on him. But I don't think of it that way. If we could walk in there on the 6th of August, and you could say you had a physical . . .

Cliff, who's forcing all this medical treatment and psychiatric treatment and corrections treatment on me, anyway?

Your government.

Which figures? Who?

When you were found NGRI, not guilty by reason of insanity, you were basically given to the Attorney General's office under the oversight of the judge.

I need names, Cliff. For my lady list and black list so I can wire tap back.

One of the names on your list is yourself because you are the one who chose real strongly to plead NGRI. Right?

Yeah. Glad I did.

The second name is the Attorney General's office. Now, it would be Ashcroft.

Yeah.

The third name would be the judge. Because what the judge could do is say, "Maybe you should stay in Springfield, MCFP." What the judge is saying instead is, "You don't have to be in Springfield if all these other things take place. It's not really forcing you, Moonway. It's a bargain. Just like we're bargaining back and forth, now. They bargain with you: We'll let you out, but you gotta do this stuff.

Yeah. It's a strike, isn't it? It's political, isn't it, Cliff?

Yeah.

I want to withdraw services from the political figures and educational media, and the religious figures doing this to me—metro, bourgeoisie. I do.

Luckily for us, Moonway, nowhere in your order does it say you have to . . .

And I like you two, to tell the truth, Eleanor. And the folks. Mostly I'm looking after Mom and Dad right now.

Eleanor: I can see that, Moonway .

Long as you don't force things on me, I'm OK. I realize this is all military and political. And they're forcing it on you. I'd like to put Bush behind bars.

Eleanor: I think you need to listen to Cliff right now.

Cliff: You understand the trade-off, Moonway ?

Yeah. OK, an EKG.

And a physical. Before August 6. Can Eleanor make the appointments, or do you want to make it yourself?

But she's gotta get me there.

Eleanor : I told you I would.

Cliff: I'm writing this down. We can put all this down about refraining from threatening behavior, but I don't think you've engaged in it. I'm not going to put that in.

I quit broadcasting, and I'm calling it on my swastikas, and I been sleeping at night, within reason like you said.

Eleanor :   Tell   me   what   <u>within reason</u>   means, Moonway .

About five hours a night.

What time do you go to bed at night, on average.

10:00 or 11:00

What time do you get up?

5:00 or 6:00. I'd like to start setting my alarm for 9:00 in the morning, too. That would do it. Except these dreams from these drugs are interrupting. And that's so unhealthy, Eleanor .

What kind of dreams?

Just nightmares. Light dreams, too.

Like what?

It all comes from these parts and wires in me not being run right.

You sure? How many nightmares do you have in a week?

Three or four.

That's quite a few.

Cliff: How long has this been going on?

Years now. Ever since John Toomer prescribed that Valium.

It's consistent, hunh? Moonway, as far as I know, there's not much that anyone can do about that because you've had about a million med changes. Well, Eleanor, if Moonway was able to do all this stuff between now and Thanksgiving, you think he'd be in pretty good shape?

I don't know, Cliff. Can't hurt.

We are going to have to make a plan for the winter. And you know that's coming, Moonway, right?

Yeah.

You're going to have to keep your activity level higher than last year.

I need money, Cliff. 250 grand was involved in putting me behind bars.

You might be right about that. But money was not getting you out last winter

Eleanor: Well, Moonway has a point, Cliff, because he was not receiving his checks on time. The steps weren't being shoveled, and the postman wouldn't deliver the mail.

I got a shovel, now.

Yes, and your Dad came and your Mom to shovel. But it took close to two months to start getting your checks regularly.

Was that deliberate, Eleanor? You got anything on that?

I know the checks were sent from DHS.

Cliff: But Moonway, after it got straightened out toward the end of the winter, you still weren't getting out. Even after the checks were coming. What do you attribute that to?

Eleanor: When he says no money, he's partly right. It takes money to use the ARTS bus. But County Ride doesn't charge.

I been using that.

Eleanor: I know. This past winter your mom and dad both offered to take you to AA. But you were refusing. Said you were on strike.

Cliff: So, Moonway, this fall, we're going to have to formulate a plan for the winter. But we need to be thinking about it now. The problem last winter was not just that you weren't going to meetings. The problem was that you were isolating from all social activity. So if you can think of something else you can do, it doesn't have to be group therapy.

Eleanor: Except I would like to see him go to psychosocial group. That isn't necessarily focused on mental illness. It's focusing on socializing with peers. That would be a good thing.

No. I have the right to refuse treatment.

Cliff: Moonway , you have a right to refuse treatment, and the Judge has the right to send you back to Springfield.

Is that a legal right of his? Is it on the books? Law? What about rights laws, Cliff?

Moonway , once you get into the Criminal Justice system, which even though you're not guilty, that's kind of what you are in, you lose some of your rights. Why can they lock you on the unit in Springfield? Because at your hearing, the judge found that was the place for you. The government passed laws that provide for that. Do I agree with all those laws? No. Laws say they can keep people locked up even after they have done their time, which, to me, is insane. But until they change the law, you're pretty much stuck with it. So you can be a martyr.

I'm not going to be.

In that case, psychosocial group might be the best of all possible worlds. Doing nothing and isolating is definitely the worst of all possible worlds. If we can find something in the middle that keeps you from getting too isolated. . .

Going to restaurants. And I do. But it takes money.

By yourself?

Yeah.

You socialize with people when you go there?

I sit there and write. I take in people.

Well, Moonway, I got to go now. See you at the team meeting.

Bye, Cliff. Thanks Dude.

Eleanor: I checked your meds and they look good, Moonway .

I been taking all my meds. And I need them regulated so I won't pop them all at once.

Good, good, good. That does make a big difference. Especially with Risperidol. If you get up at noon and pop all your meds at once, your Trazadone would put you to sleep. We'll get you back on Previcid. Hopefully, I can get you into Cliff's doctor. Is there any way you would see another doctor instead.

No. Just Cliff's doctor. Is he a Red?

I don't know. I don't think so.

I'm a Kapitalist, you know. But I support Reds. Eleanor, why can't we shift this shit against the government doing this to me, so we'll all be in agreement?

You brought this on yourself, Moonway. You were doing things that were very frightening to people. That's how you got into this pickle. That's why you have to go through what you are going through right now. Because of what happened then. This is going to go on forever, Moonway . A lifetime. No end date on it. We're going to be doing this over and over and over again. But like I told you, don't worry about it. It's like a formality we have to go through. And it's all for your own good. We're not trying to hurt you in any way. We're trying to make your standard of living the best we can. It's for your benefit. I'm heading out of here, now. I'll be back next Tuesday. I'm going to try to make appointments with the eye doctor, and a physical. OK.

Thank you, Eleanor .

You have a good weekend.

Right after they left or later that same day, Moonway taped another monologue.

Eleanor Lee and Cliff Worth were in today. They said they want a renegotiating of the court order. I'm withdrawing services to SMHI if I'm subjected to the indignity of having to go back to court. The McCarthys are involved. I think you'll find the trouble that got me into the Federal system was just me situated in Caribou, wanting to sit there, become stationary as a former runaway, thrash her out, just thrash her out there. And I tried to, but things got out of hand. The Eliza Church/Carl Daggett thing. And I want them both safe, warm, cozy and free as long as they're both not out to get me or squawk at me. Otherwise than that, everything is cool except for the lack of money. Getting along good with my folks. Love 'em to death.

So scared of new drugs, or being returned to my childhood and subjected to those drugs. So scared of drugs and alcohol, legal or illegal.

Listen, stem cell research, cloning: most people know in this country that we're researching the image of God.

I don't want women who are forming their own State Legal Associations, SLAs, against Civil SLAs to brainwash men. I don't want to be a victim of women and Fence anymore, no matter what color. Well, ain't the feds a bunch of frauds and con men?

I work for a living. Hard, too. Growing up, too. Manual and intellectual. Never did make a very good terrorist or radical, did I? Just an old fundamentalist criminal. Lord Christ, please keep taking me over on my terms. The Lord Hebrew Christ. The real one up in Heaven, or wherever you are. Concerning us Pentecostals, it could be said we're tempting the Lord where Satan said, "All first things." Also, the prophets' worlds—strange, bizarre, nuts.

Who the fuck is AA to preach to Pentecostals for handling snakes and poison. Lord has a purpose for us all. I'm up here drinking arsenic and cyanide. Ain't she good, though? Ain't she good—this arsenic and cyanide, hunh?

There's something here, something else, real slick, real slick. Listen, the key. I'm all prepared, ain't I? Snake bite on my left arm. Survived her, didn't I? Ha, ha. Didn't I? Survived her. I should carve a snake and raise it. Moses held up a snake in his staff, didn't he?

World, mah sikah reekee.
Mah ketee tah ah es, ma seetah reekee.

Mah keetah rahmah, mah koree aku.
Mah sheetah reetah. Mah suriah.
Mah shend ah reeah. Mah soto.

Moses' snake eating up the Egyptian snake.
Halleluiah! Glory! Are there any southern cousins to handle
snakes and poison yet? Just found Christ tonight, the real one.
Has a great influence on me. And when I do handle snakes
and poison, I want to give it to others instead of myself. Rak
ah sheeto. Translation: Christ said, "Let the dead bury the
dead." Yet, he raised the dead.

I warn you, I'm not the lunatic. I'm the drunkard.

While I was on C3, was my clone on K2? Have I got a
clone in Denver? Is there a clone of mine in Hillsboro Crisis
Center in Florida?

Ain't that awful, CIA and Carter, another bombing in
both New York and Oklahoma? That's tragic and awful, aint
it? That's just so atrocious.

At least we got a tour going, don't we, Michaels and
Adams? Although we're being tortured for it, we're evolving
down into Florida, up through the Rockies, and back East here.
Surrounding Washington, D. C. so we can shoot the
president. Blast his head off with a sawed off. Ha.

Voices heard: High vice, Lord. We're proving it.
High vice, Lord. What's this, Dad? What's that, Dad? What
did we do? What's stopping Al? What's that? What is this?
No, Christians. Although it's a strip.

Voices heard: See what they wanted to avoid. Why
do you think I'm a pacifist? I like freedom.

Voices heard: Are the voices traveling, Moonway?
Child abuse. What's that, Moonway?

Voices heard: What do you think we're doing?

22. Court

United States District Court for the District of
Lincoln
Petition for Warrant or Summons for Offender
Under Supervision

July 2, 2001
Name of Offender: Moonway Michael
Name of Sentencing Judicial Officer: Kent Miller,
L.S District Judge
Date of Original Sentence: 03/10/92 Committed to
Custody of Attorney General
Original   Offense: Mailing   Threatening
Communications (U.S. President and Other Elected
Officials)
Original Sentence: Not Guilty by Reason of Insanity;
Attorney General Commitment: Conditional Release
Type of Supervision: Conditional Release (Life)
FBI Arrest: 01/02/91
Date Conditional Release Commenced: 10/28/92
Revocation of Releaser: 06/16/93
Date Conditional Release Recommenced: 04/28/94
Asst. U.S. Attorney: Dennis Miller, Esq   Defense
Attorney: Jake Hubert, Esq.
==
PETITIONING THE COURT
To issue a summons
        The   probation   officer   believes   that   the
offender has violated the following condition(s) of
conditional Release:
Violation #   Nature of Noncompliance
    1. On June 14, 2001, the Supervision Team
        received reliable information suggesting that
        the defendant had been failing to take mental
        health medications as prescribed. Therefore,
        the defendant violated condition no. 3 which
        states in part; "Defendant shall continue to be
        medication compliant and take prescribed
        medications as ordered."
    2. Beginning in late 2000, the defendant showed
        signs of emotional/mental instability and was
        hospitalized on a number of occasions. Since
        that time, he has refused to participate in
        mental health and support programs and
        therapies as instructed by his Supervision

Team. Therefore, the defendant violated condition no. 4 which states in part, "Defendant shall participate in mental health and support programs and therapies."

3. The defendant has consistently refused to sign release of information forms to allow his County Mental Health Center (CMHC) counselor to schedule medical and dental appointments for the defendant and to allow the counselor to communicate directly with medical and dental practitioners. Further, the defendant has refused to sign such releases after his supervising Officer directed him to do so. Therefore, the defendant has violated condition no. 6 which states, "Defendant shall be supervised by the U. S. Probation Office who shall act as a liaison between the Court, treating mental health professionals and the Patient Advocate. Defendant shall consent to the release of information to the supervising officer by the mental health staff."

4. In January 1999; the defendant telephoned Congressman Kreiger's Office in Northridge, Lincoln, and alarmed that staff. In June1999, the FBI in California received information that the defendant had written a letter to the staff of a mental health institution in California which frightened that staff. In October1999, the Newburgh Police Department received information that the defendant had been repeatedly calling Renwick & Associates, Attorneys at Law, which resulted in the issuance of a Harassment Notice to the defendant. Therefore, the defendant "encroached upon" condition no.8 which states, "Defendant shall commit no local, state, or federal crimes, including, but not limited to, threatening calls, threatening letters, or otherwise threatening behavior.

U.S. Probation Officer Recommendation:

Suggested Action/Modification by the Court (To avoid recommitment):

1. A Person should be named as Legal Guardian of the defendant.
2. The Defendant should be reprimanded by the Court.
3. The Defendant should comply with all conditions of the Order, undergo medical and dental treatment, sign releases, attend all treatment sessions as directed, and take all prescribed medications.

FURTHER PETITIONING THE COURT TO ISSUE SUBPOENAS TO THE SUPERVISION TEAM: Mr. Cliff Worth, Patient Advocate; Ms Eleanor Lee, Counselor; Dr. Rachel Long, Psychiatrist; Mr. Victor Robins, Financial Guardian.

7-17-01

Mom, Cliff was over today. Ooh, I better open that window. Too hot and stuffy in here.

It's not too hot for me. But I like the fresh air because of the smoke.

I'll open it then. But I don't like the environment, the hecklers.

Do you want me to go to court with you?

If you won't offer aversive testimony. Jake and Cliff seem to think you would look good. Not against me, though, Mom.

I don't intend to be aversive, but I don't know what I might say that you might take as aversive. Here is a copy of the memo I have written for the court.

> From: Belinda Adams , Moonway Michael 's Mother
> To: The Federal District Court, Newburgh, Lincoln
> Subject: Moonway Michael's Treatment Issues
>
> I wish I knew what the right treatment is to help Moonway recover, but the more I see of his

illness the less I know with any certainty the right thing to do. In spite of that uncertainty, I do have a wish list.

I would like Moonway to have treatment changes implemented one step at a time, rather than all at once as the latest plan is structured. I would like him to be more involved in treatment decisions, or at least be given choices about treatment. For psychotherapy, instead of requiring him to go to both psychosocial group and Hope group, I would like him to begin by choosing one option from several: one-to-one therapy, or psychosocial group, or Hope group, or other therapeutic options.

I would like more focus on improving the quality of the relationship between Moonway and his care providers. I would like more respect from providers and less negativity about failures; continuous reminders about mistakes—forgetting, isolation, socially unacceptable behavior, and refusals—do not help him to recover; these frequent reminders reinforce low self esteem and fears that "psyche and corrections" are out to get him. I would like providers to give more hope and encouragement to do well.

I would like them to pay more respectful attention to Moonway's strengths and talents and to give ongoing help with channeling his artistic, political, and spiritual impulses into constructive work, help such as Gary Gold provided several years ago when he helped Moonway enroll in an art course. That course was a bright spot in Moonway's life, he attended every class, and he was doing productive work during that time.

Moonway's providers are insisting that he must take responsibility. In some way, I, too, believe he must. And yet, responsibility for the quality of the relationship between him and others belongs at least half to others. I'm asking here that we focus more attention on changes we, as the others in his life, can make that might improve the context and give the best opportunity to increase his ability to make healthy choices for himself.

These are changes I attempt to make myself using as a guide Xavier Amador's book *I'm Not Sick; I Don't Need Help*. This book thoroughly documents with research that the lack of insight of about half of people with schizophrenia is caused by an abnormality in the frontal lobe of the brain that affects perception. It is neither denial nor a moral flaw in character. Dr. Amador provides a common-sense guide to respectfully treating these patients in a way that gets their cooperation in treatment by focusing on what will give them more of what they want.

Moonway, is there anything in that memo that you think is aversive?

Oh, you know what C. S. Lewis said? He said Milton's graveyards are being destroyed because of folk art, people taking people out of themselves, getting them in touch with people. I don't want to socialize unless I select it, Mom.

I would like to see you have more choices, too. That fresh air sure feels good, Moonway.

It sure does, Mom. That's all I needed was a touch of fresh air, wasn't it?

It helps, doesn't it? We've been getting some weird storms, huge water drops fell on my windshield as I was driving over here, scattered, not raining hard. Then it would stop suddenly. Then it would rain hard for a few minutes. The Weather Man's trivia question today was "Which months do we get the most precipitation: July, August, November, or January? How would you answer that?

July.

Right on. August is second. I completely missed it, thought it would be either November or January. Moonway, I'm sorry I can't agree with you about social isolation. I can agree, though, that not all kinds of social life are equally beneficial. I don't know if what CMHC is offering for group therapy is good for you.

This court stuff is not narrowed down to just me. I'm not walking back into that electric factory. A lot of staff want out of that, you know? They shock each other. You know that? You know what mental health does. It puts us on each others' program. The clients and families, gets us all mixed up that way: incest, domestic abuse. Did you know that?

Help me understand. Can you give an example?

I can't explain so you would understand. I'm going to have a problem in that court room. I'm going to take coffee with me. That is legal, great big gallon of coffee. Drink her on the way down, drink her there, and drink her on the way back. Two pots right in that jug. That's what I'm going to do. Mom, why does this keep happening to me when I haven't been violent in twenty years?

State of Lincoln
Department of Mental Health and Mental Retardation
Office of Advocacy

To: Jake Hubert [Moonway's Attorney],
Date: July 26, 2001
Re: Moonway Michael
Dear Jake,

I am sending you a marked-up copy of the DSM IV (Diagnostic and Statistics Manual for diagnosing mental illnesses) because I think it's very important for the judge to understand that schizophrenia is an actual illness and what its symptoms are. Moonway is in fact simply exhibiting an exacerbation of his symptoms, and this simply raises the issue of what the treatment team is doing to assist him. The fact that Moonway is refraining from any behavior which poses an actual risk (and has done so for years) is to his credit.

I also think the judge needs to understand that stress (such as that created by the stress of this hearing) only increases the likelihood of the symptom exacerbation. Any hammering of Moonway at court (even if in his so called "best interests") will only serve to increase the likelihood of his symptoms worsening.

This is not to say that he can't be encouraged to work

harder—only that threats are likely to be counterproductive.

It is a hard thing to have schizophrenia, and his illness makes all the things we are asking Moonway to do inherently much more difficult than we might ordinarily expect. Things need to be done in small steps with awareness of the variability of Moonway's symptoms. Just living with (or through) schizophrenia is pretty heroic.

It is worth noting at the outset that there were some significant changes in services to Moonway—He was receiving supported housing services from CMHC, but this position became vacant and is still vacant. His visiting nurse changed (this was for the better.) His homemaker services were, I believe, disrupted. Through the winter he had problems with the checks sent by the Department of Human Services, and this caused a lot of stress (checks were not arriving, etc.).

The fact that I was absent a lot during March-June (due to my parents' illnesses and deaths) was also quite significant. At the time all hell broke loose (for me), Moonway and I were working on a response to Dr. Wellstone's neuropsych, and many of the issues could have been controlled short of the court's intervention. Since I have been back and working with Moonway we have made a lot of progress with structure and compliance—see attached plan of 7-17-01.

Simply put, because of my role and my longevity with Moonway, I am the one with the closest thing to a therapeutic alliance with him; and as such I am an essential part of the team. The others on the team don't always involve me enough in a preventive way, and my absence can be blamed for a lot.

I think it's interesting that Ted McKean refers to us as the supervision team when we are actually the **treatment** team. As the supervision team the burden would be on Moonway, but as the treatment team the burden is on us to work with Moonway at finding effective methods to manage his symptoms. Simply demanding compliance misreads our role completely, and Moonway shouldn't be receiving consequences for the team's frustration or temporary inability to develop or implement effective plans. (At the same time, at the most basic level the plan is effective.) Dr. Wellstone's report came out in March, and Ted decided to go to court in June. I was pretty much out for the intervening three months. That is pretty precipitous action.

As to the actual violations:

1. According to Moonway's mother, the med issue is a lot more complicated than stated here, and does not reflect major noncompliance. The psych record also reflects overall compliance, and so does Moonway.

2. As the psych notes, Moonway sought appropriate hospitalization on his own. I believe I have addressed the other "noncompliance with treatment" issues above.

3. Moonway signed these releases on July 12. I facilitated his agreement, and this underlines the importance of my involvement (or the involvement of the person in my role).

4. The Kreiger stuff doesn't state a real claim of violation, neither does the California stuff. I'm not saying that Moonway should be doing it, but how people react doesn't equal a threat. I've reviewed the paperwork from the Newburgh police about Renwick, and this is more like entrapment than anything else. They told Moonway it was OK to call, then appeared to get fed up with him, and, without asking him to modify his behavior, just called the cops, depriving him of the opportunity to do the right thing. Also, the fact that there has been none of this since 1999 is more of a recommendation of the effectiveness of what the team and Moonway have been doing than anything else.

So, Jake, all in all things look good. Moonway is already doing much of what Dr. Wellstone recommended, and we are even looking at some possible med changes, once some medical clearances are done. I am more worried about the tone of the court. I worked really hard to get Moonway to see that, in some sense, Judge Miller was on his side. If there is any way I can do the same for Judge Gunther, I will, but he will have to be respectful of and delicate with Moonway if I'm going to have a chance. It's in everybody's interest for this to happen. If we work together, including together with Moonway, I think we should be able to get everyone's needs met.

Sincerely,

Cliff Worth, Advocate

8-6-01

Moonway was very agitated, anxious, and angry for a couple of weeks before the hearing. Those feelings intensified the last few days. Shirley invited him to the Michael Family Reunion. He went, and I think he got some respite from the court tensions there. She went out of her way to arrange transportation and mediate between Moonway and their Dad.

The morning of the court hearing, we were up at 4:30 A. M. to drive the 150 miles to Newburgh for court day because we needed to be there by 8:30 to meet with Jake and discuss the concerns relevant to the hearing. Moonway rode with Cliff who was going to stay in Newburgh for a few days, and I followed in my car. We had to wait for nearly an hour at Jake's office, so there wasn't much time for talk before we had to be at Court at 10:00.

At the Federal Building, Cliff, Moonway, and I sat on a bench outside the court room and talked about the marble wainscoting and mahogany woodwork lining the halls. Moonway went to the rest room and was there when Jake came and sat down with us. Cliff and Jake reviewed the situation for a while, and then Jake said, Moonway has been in the restroom quite a while hasn't he?

He's probably smoking, I said.

Oh, he can't do that in the Federal building.

And he rushed off to get him.

When he came back, he and Cliff went down to the second floor to talk to Ted. Cliff said later that he jumped all over Ted about drawing up the petition while he was away and couldn't give any input. While this and the following discussion in judge's chambers was going on, Moonway and I waited on the bench. Dr. Wellstone came in, wearing a black suit, white shirt, and tie. He greeted us briefly and went down to find Ted. I heard from someone that he was calling around last week wanting to know why he wasn't subpoenaed. Maybe he got himself a subpoena or just came anyway to try to give his expert opinion. He seemed to want very much to control the outcome of this proceeding.

Victor Robins, came by in a dark green suit, and shook his head at Moonway: All you had to do was a few small things to prevent this all from happening.

Then he went to find Cliff, Jake, Ted, and Dr. Wellstone.

Eleanor came out of the courtroom, talked nicely to Moonway, most positive I have ever seen her with him. As soon as Moonway left to go to the restroom again, she said, I'm very worried about Moonway. His place was in very bad shape when I was there last. He didn't have any food and no food stamps—they don't come for a couple more weeks.

Then she went to get releases for Moonway to sign in case she and Dr. Wellstone need to testify. She never did come back with them.

Finally in the courtroom, Jake whispered to us that they had resolved most of the problems, at least for now, in Judge's Chambers. The district attorney spoke first, saying that, in view of Moonway's improvement since the petition had been filed, the petition was being withdrawn contingent upon Moonway's continued improvement. It could be reactivated at any time things get troublesome with Moonway again. Then the judge spoke directly to Moonway; the tone and content of his remarks were encouraging rather than reprimanding. He compared Moonway's current functioning to past problems and congratulated him. He appeared to know more about Moonway than many of the care providers who work with him.

Later, Cliff said, Judge Gunther has done his homework, read the whole file. He could see Moonway was not currently behaving in the threatening ways he had been ten years ago. He suggested in chambers that the petition be withdrawn.

8-11-01.

Thanks, Moonway for mowing my lawn. You want to snap these beans for supper?

Yeah. You still got your pet toad down cellar?

I haven't seen it much this summer, not since spring. Maybe it's because I am down there so much with all the extra gardening and watering I am doing in retirement. That court day turned out pretty good, hunh?

Yeah. When Cliff and I were going down, I did the most talking, sat there mumbling, yapping, and blabbing away. He said I gotta do better, comply with treatment, so I'm trying to. They're just laying way too much on me. I don't know what I'm going to be able to do in the winter without wheels, get to the soup kitchen and AA. It's cold out, Mom. I'd keep turning to AA for more services, but they would just lay shit on me. I remember in the court, they told me they almost sent me somewhere. Did you hear that? They put Cliff under prison sentence, too. I'd like to get some names of people doing this to me.

I didn't hear that.

And us. Doing to me and us.

I heard that if you don't continue to improve then they would consider guardianship before another time in Missouri at MCFP. I didn't hear they almost did send you to prison.

They better stay in contact with the ACLU. It might not have been just the railroading. But I hate this.

You hate doing the things you have to for treatment?

Not that so much. Just being railroaded from court to court and institution to institution. When is it over with, anyway? I'd like to dig up all the hate mail and hate calls I've received. Beat them at their own game. Put them in the pen for that. That'd be getting even. All they gotta do is mind their own damn business. Drop it. I'd like to get The Angel going. But it probably is going right, in God's hands. I don't know why it has to be God all the time, doing every thing for us, though. Why can't people pitch in and do for us, too. Boy that smells good. Pizza crust?

Yeah.

Smells good raw. I hope I'm forgiven by you folks for every thing I did, Mom. I know I still get hot-headed and pissed off at you. Still, I love you.

I know. I love you and forgive you. I hope you forgive me for things you have been mad at me about. I hope you forgive yourself.

Yeah.

Want some raw carrots while we're waiting to eat supper?

Mom. I been complying. All the meds I take now—Zoloft, Trazadone, Risperdone. The Haldol sludges me out. The other reason I take them is to stay in control and stay young. Seems to be working so far, plus nutrition.

Do you think that's enough beans for 2 servings? Split half and half?

Yeah. It's enough for me. Can I have another carrot?

Have all you want. Moonway, I don't believe Eleanor's judgment that this situation has to be forever. It's possible to keep on recovering, ask your higher power and the people you trust for the help you need, seek out the best that is within you. Another acronym from the 12-step program: Where Is The Help I Need? WITHIN. Whatever Gods may be must be found there. But that doesn't mean without reference to what is also without. It's another paradox to me. Job finds no help from his friends with his troubles and with his persistent "Why me?" He demands a face-to-face encounter with God; and, in contemplation of the power and mystery of Creation, he finds his place, his solace, and his happiness. What could you do to help improve your relationship with Eleanor?

Hit her in the face. That's what I should do, Mom. Chop her head off. Put her in the guillotine. I'm going out to smoke.

Pissed off, hunh? But you're joking, again, I hope? Seriously, what can you do?

Don't phone AMHC any more. Show up for appointments though.

Showing up would be good.

With Dr. Long, anyway. One thing I remember bringing up in Jake's office, since they're holding the letter I wrote to Senator Hoffman's office over me, is digging up the hate mail and hate calls I've received from the government. I think I'm getting them from both sexes and all colors and races. Three months in SMHI for swearing in a letter. That was highly illegal?! It's not illegal to swear.

No. But it is illegal to threaten, slander, or harass in a letter. And sometimes the legal line is a thin or fuzzy one. All freedoms have limits when they butt up against someone else's rights. You like mushrooms and olives on your pizza?

Yeah.

It's about ready to put in the oven. Thanks for your help.

IV
The Presence of the Past

Put pictures and pictures of me, a time line continuum.
The wall art I'm generating could be protective.

23. Pictures and Pictures of Me,
a Time Line Continuum

Mom, how're my nephews: Brett, Jeffrey, and Marcus? How're the rest of the family?

Marcus got a cold, a bad one, stayed out of school all week. Shirley had a test for Lupus.

Damn it. That's running in Dad's side of the family, ain't it? Grampie, Uncle Roland. I don't think a lot of these diseases are genetic unless images are transferred to children from images in the reproductive semen and ovum creating babies that are passed on to them.

From the DNA, Moonway. And that's passed on through the semen and ovum.

Well, I disagree. It's OK to disagree with people, ain't it, Mom?

Sure.

Let me do something for the family, Mom. Knowing CIA, now calling out WICCA. Melt them. Cover up. In treatment: Steven King. Fighting for APA, USSR, Kodak, Child Protection Rights.

Doing your own thing to take care of us, hunh, Moonway? The biological influences are surely important, also social and cultural influences.

You were important when you read me those fairy tales and fables in childhood. Got me educated. That's what spring-boarded me getting into ULN up here. Dad's important for disciplining me, slightly. Grammy Adams' religious training of me was important and all the religion that flourished in the Adams' family.

Religion flourished in Mama's family, the Morris side.

The Adams were never very religious. Daddy was an atheist all the way, died not believing. Another of those big differences between my parents that caused turbulence. Several of Mama's siblings were fanatically religious.

One aunt went to an Oral Roberts revival meeting on crutches from an automobile accident. At his healing touch, she threw the crutches in the air, sang out "Praise God!" and walked out without them. Uncle Dan later remarked on the strange coincidence of this miracle occurring so soon after she received an insurance check. Uncle Dan was the most stable-minded sibling of that family. One of my heroes. Kind, cheerful, helpful. Practiced the Christian virtues without ever preaching them. I doubt that he even believed in the literal "truth" of the Bible as history. He was a strong moral influence on me.

Aunt Annie, in her manic highs, proclaimed her faith publicly wherever she went. Aunt Margaret became a Jehovah's Witness. Following one of Annie's visits to Mama in Florida, Margaret performed exorcist rites to rid Mama's place of demonic influence brought there by Annie.

One time Uncle Calvin backed Darin and me up against the house and preached at us. I was four, Darin was three. Morning sun in our eyes, his tall gaunt frame in black silhouette looming over us, his arms waving in the air, Uncle Calvin preached the damnation wages of sin, the joy of salvation. His fervor scared me more than Daddy's rages; it was so much more incomprehensible. I went numb. The scene froze in my memory, and I never witness any strong expression of religious passion without flashing back to that scene. However, I came to know him later as a kind and gentle man, a thoughtful and caring husband and father, a help to our family in times of need. Thanksgiving, he would drive 52 miles to fetch all eight of us back to his house for the day including a big dinner and then drive us back, over 200 miles all together in his rattletrap old car. He, too, practiced the Christian virtue of being a good neighbor, and he didn't preach to call attention to his own goodness; he wasn't self righteous. He just loved to preach, got high on Jesus.

I think Calvin preaching at us like that must have

influenced me to declare myself an atheist at twelve. I asked Aunt Kit once how he managed to get money to buy property and build a house for the family after their mother died. She said, He was a boot legger.

We human beings are sure complicated creatures, hunh?

For a long time Mama resisted the appeals of her fanatic siblings. When I was little, I remember being with her at Congregational services at the Greenville Schoolhouse. She would debate with the minister, using Daddy's arguments about the evidence of evolution, all the counter evidence to such literal beliefs as divine creation, virgin births, bodily resurrection, miracle cures. But a couple of persistent questions seemed to trouble her most about the Christian belief she heard: "How could an all powerful and all merciful God create and allow suffering, sin, and death? Why does God give us such strong desires and then say 'Don't?'"

When I was thirteen, she started going to a fundamentalist church in Northridge with a neighbor. She soon converted, was baptized, and tried to preach the faith to Daddy. He scorned her attempts, her beliefs, and her passion: "Man evolved up from apes and God didn't have a damned thing to do with it." She soon quieted down a good deal with her passion, but she never gave up her faith. Although she turned all her doubts over to "the mysterious ways of God," she also never ceased wondering about the central questions of her doubting years. I'm glad she influenced you to find faith, Moonway. I doubt we can live without faith in something, no matter what we believe that something is.

Mom, this is a picture of Grammy I did, a photo with fashion on her. I put blonde hair on her. I hope you don't mind. Right here, that's a chair.

I wouldn't have recognized her, but now that you say that, I can see it. The blonde hair is deceiving.

Aunt Myra was important to me for putting up with me when I just showed up on her doorstep that time. She flew me back home. Was she reimbursed for that from Pepsi or Coca Cola? Or Budweiser or anything?

No.

From Jerry Falwell or anyone? Jimmy Swaggart? Pat Baker?

No.

$120 might do it. To my Auntie Mame Myra there in Greenville. All of yous in one. One and all. Jim Walker, Christian therapist, got me my check. He's probably insuring it. He did transactional analysis with me; going back to Dad's house after TA wasn't too good. Hard to believe all that stuff with him was OK. I'm beyond that now, Mom. I'm in behavior mod.

Would you like to find a behavior mod therapist?

No. Calvin Hogan, art teacher up here at ULN, got me doing concrete art instead of just that abstract shit. I would take more art courses at ULN, but I don't think they want me up there, Mom. I've been trying to have the place shelled by a rocket launcher.

Maybe you don't want to tell the wrong people that?

No. Don't tell anyone. Put it in the book though. It's covered by freedom of speech. I wouldn't actually do it. I'd have it done though. Not through paying people or giving orders. Just influence. I don't really want to do that, either.

You don't have control of rockets.

How do you know? You don't know the half of it, Mom. I don't do much propaganda at ULN in the winter any more. Probably will next summer, I'd take a course up there. But the only way I could do it is if someone helped me and it was in the afternoon. I know why I haven't been doing my art work and writing. I haven't been dropping in on ULN. No money to get there with all my laundry I'm doing, trying to catch up on laundry. Hickey Roo, common martyr, is also one that I chanted up there at ULN. I want a free education from ULN.

They won't let you have a free education?

No. No free lunch for them either. I'm withdrawing services, going to Northern Lincoln Technical Center, NLTC, and charging for this free education I been given except the red countries. I go there and hang out. I'd've been crucified if I'd've done that at NLTC, putting up propaganda and stuff. I'm not going to do it anymore at ULN, so no one knows what

227

I'm up to. I have permission to go to the campus center and library there. That's pretty good. Mom, see this picture. The caption says, "Here she comes." That's supposed to be a woman in childbirth. Here's the hands. This is the woman. It says, "This one released with Doonesburial's permission."

Doonesbury is a big influence, hunh? Oh, there's another self portrait, too. Gee, you have been doing a lot of art work, Moonway. Can I make a copy of that?

No, I'm going to leave that up there, Mom. I did it from a photo you gave me. Put pictures in the book of my bloody wrist at Bangor International Airport when I was shackled on my way to Missouri. Put pictures and pictures of me stabbing myself in the leg in Florida and pictures of me with safety pins all through my nipples, stomach, and chest in front of that 1226 store down the street from Martin, brother of mine there in Denver, Colorado. Moberg's E-man gave me $20.00 there. Mom Adams Myra Belinda, the wall art I'm generating could be protective if we keep becoming Native Indian inside us. I only relate to Vincent Van Gogh, but my real aspirations lie with Bosch and Blake. Listen, I could use all the pictures and frames from all those photos of me at all ages I been through. Mom, what I'd like to do is get photographs from you of me growing up all through my life, a time line continuum. And I'd like copies of pictures of all my ancestors dating as far back as they go.

I can make copies for you of what I have. Please be patient with me; I'll have to do a little at a time. Keep reminding me.

I know, Mom. It's taken me a life time to get where I am. You know what Alyce Cooper sang, "It took 18 years to get this far."

Yeah. It's taken me 63 years to get this far. You want to make a picture autobiography?

No, I just want to use them in my art work. I had a picture I did of you. Remember that picture I did of you when I was an adolescent? I got a photo of it in there somewhere and I did some art work on it that was a real tribute to John Lennon. But I filed it away.

Your art work is intimately tied up with your

propaganda, isn't it?

Got some on the wall there, with that picture of Jack Nicholson in it. That little portrait of Jack Nicholson with blonde hair. Take it with you, make a copy for the book. But get the original back to me. That's one of the best pieces I've ever done. That's modeled after Dunesbury's Duke. Looks like Jack Nicholson a little bit, don't it? I'm loyal to all these superstars that are haunting me, Mom. If they're loyal to me. Maybe they're behind a lot of this stuff, but a man's gotta forgive sometime and incorporate like Marilyn Monroe finally had to do. Elvis. Judy.

I don't want to travel anymore, I know that. Never yielded nothing, except culture. Well, that's something. I wish they'd get some philosophy and art and poetry on TV. They been important to me. I can't get much on ETV anymore. It's all gone kids and upbringing and raising, psychology or psychiatry. Mom, you don't have to go all out for me. I'm doing OK for myself actually, considering some things.

What do you want me to stop doing?

Nothing, if you want to do it, go ahead. There's no guarantee on this book thing though.

No.

I'll try to dig up some art work. Here's a sculpture, a jug here with words taped on it— Speed, LSD, Cat, Soma, Mescaline. It's just water, and a little fruit juice, but I don't want the public knowing that. Publicly, it's all dope. Privately it's just water and fruit juice—art work. I don't want to stop the spread of my art style, but I want a tax for everyone using it. Superman's using it.

Really!

Carl's important to me, a great friend of mine, my only human friend. My other animal friend is Scandal, my cat. Carl and I run the roads, summer time anyway. Go to AA, but he dropped out of AA. We went to the movies a couple of times. His girlfriend was there. I don't want any gay relationship, Mom. That wasn't directed at you. Just people thinking I'm queer.

I don't think that, and if you were, I don't have moral

scruples against it.

I'm not queer. Mom, I want to get copies of *Madness Network News*. That was real important to me.

It is defunct

Yeah. But I could be getting back issues of it. There's a book of it up here at ULN. *Madness Network News Reader*. I wonder why these little magazines go under. Suppose they get infiltrated with dope and plagues and disease and STDs and stuff? That's sad. There's something else I wanted to say. Just because these underground and underworld periodicals go under—that don't mean they can't go to # 1 slots and be propagated through interested well-wishers.

I wonder how addicted the world is lately. I don't know because I go to so many anonymous meetings. Maybe I do know because I go to so many of those meetings. I pity these poor underground people that die of drug addiction. Whole subcultures and sub-empires go down into nothing. They're so valuable. That *Madness Network News* was eliminating so many aversive conditions in asylums. Yeah, that was important to me, Mom.

24. Mind and Art

Mom, let's pick apart your academic experience. Want to? That was important to you, wasn't it?

Yes, it was, and is. A major influence in my life and important to whatever mental health I have. And maybe to whatever mental illness I have, too.

You started out here at ULN, University of Lincoln at Northridge.

If I go back further, I started out up in the little Greenville School, two-rooms with two three-holers attached, one for the boys and one for the girls.

We need more of those home-schooling and rural-schooling houses. Getting back to basics. Dress codes. That would be quite the tourist attraction for the city people coming up here to escape the violence in the city. Be good for them. How was ULN for you?

If I'm going to review my academic life, I want to go

back to the Greenville School first. Rural isn't necessarily good. There were many things not good in those rural schools, things that have important effects on psychological development.

Did the teacher hit you?

She didn't hit me, but she used to hit some of the kids with a ruler on the hand. That wasn't unusual back then; it's no excuse either. And she had certain kids she picked on. One whole family. She would use any little excuse to use that ruler on them. I don't remember that they ever did anything I would consider worthy of corporal punishment. I suspect they frustrated her efforts to teach them.

I've had that happen to me. And on the head. I used to get in fights all the time in early high school. Before I got reformed.

I had it happen once to me, too, in high school, I was being mouthy to a teacher, basketball coach about the relative importance of competitive sports, and he hit me on the head, shouted, "Sit down and listen."

Did it hurt?

I don't remember the physical hurt, but it shocked me.

That's where revolution against the education system begins, Mom.

I know.

Changes things. This calls for a J.

A J?

A joint. Ha, ha. Just kidding. This is just tobacco.

He was my geometry teacher. I was living with a family in South Greenville at the time, working for my board and room so that I could be near the high school and take part in extra curricular activities. They were outraged, wanted to get the teacher disciplined in some way. I asked them not to. I was embarrassed at the fuss and just wanted it to be over. I quit trying in Geometry. After that, I had to take Chemistry from this teacher. I was even lazier in this class than I was in others, felt like I was getting revenge on him by refusing to try. I should have failed both classes, but I got one of the highest scores on a standardized test in chemistry, and maybe he thought he couldn't fail me because of that. Or maybe it was his guilty conscience. I hope he felt guilty. I hope he didn't apologize just to save his own skin. That test suggested he was a really poor teacher because the highest scores were in the 60s. No one was learning much chemistry. The year after I graduated from that school, they made him the principal.

But I'm getting ahead of my story. The teacher at the Little Greenville School House had her pets and her victims. I was neither. I kept quiet and out of the way.

There were good things, too, that happened there. I was the only one in my grade most of the time I went there, and I didn't get much grade level attention. Mostly I did the work of the grade above me and helped kids in the lower grades. That's how I learned reading and writing and arithmetic. And it seemed to work for me. I liked going to school, maybe because it got me away from the tensions at home. Six grades in one room. We didn't use the other room for classes. It was a kitchen where we could heat up Campbell's Tomato Soup for lunch.

Did you learn fast?

I don't remember having trouble learning. I also don't remember being required to do much. My grades were not great, and I don't remember feeling smart nor stupid either. I really liked the plays. We started practicing as soon as school started for a Halloween play. After Halloween, we started practicing for a Thanksgiving show. After that, we practiced for the Christmas pageant. Then there was Valentine's Day and Easter. The teacher played the piano and she liked performance. The whole village would come. We would make costumes and scenery, bring props from home. Did you do any of that in school?

I remember one play I was in at the Greenville Grammar School. I lept off the stage and said, "His pajamas done fell down." That's all the drama I remember from my entire school life.

We did a lot of it in the Greenville School. At the end of the school year we had a picnic at Bear Mountain. The whole community would go, and I would stuff myself with red hot dogs and chocolate marshmallow cookies. In sixth grade, I was still the only one in my grade, and there were no older kids to pay attention to, so the teacher sent me down town to the Greenville Middle School. I went there in Sixth and Seventh Grades. What I remember most from there was something that I still feel ashamed of. One of the girls skipped a grade, and I was part of a group of jealous girls who followed her home one day and taunted her. We got in trouble at school because of that, and rightly so. It was a lesson I have never forgotten. In Eighth Grade I went to the High School in Northridge. I don't remember much about Eighth Grade except a boy I had a crush on, a friendly redhead; I thought he was the nicest boy I ever knew.

When I was a freshman, one of my teachers right away took an interest in my mind, thought I was too smart to be in the secretarial courses I signed up for. He said I should do College Preparatory classes. Six weeks into the school year, he had me switch to those classes. He was responsible for finding me the place with the family I stayed with last two years of high school. A huge influence. He was the one started me thinking maybe I was smart. A couple of other teachers paid attention to me, too, and encouraged me to develop my mind.

I never had one teacher take an interest in me. Until the art teacher in college. He was the only one. Everything I did was hard slave labor.

I didn't realize how lucky I was at the time. I liked the attention, but I didn't do much work, really lazy. However, they planted a seed that never died.

ULN's the only education I ever enjoyed, except that I didn't have much of a social life. I studied hard and made up for past poor education.

Yeah, I studied hard, too, in college. Years after High School, after I got my MA in English, I visited that English teacher who first encouraged me. I thanked him, told him how much I appreciated his help. He said, "At the time, I felt like I was harassing you. The Latin teacher told me you would not be ready to hear what I was saying for another ten years at least." I think maybe at the time I felt harassed. He must have been very frustrated with me. But as I got older, I appreciated it more and more. And ten years later I was in

233

college. By that time when we moved to Northridge, I was really motivated to do well, and I worked very hard and loved it.

Me too.

I have many fond memories of my experience at ULN. I fell in love with poetry. I got fascinated by literary theory there, tried to figure out the answers to the many questions I had, didn't, of course find solutions I was seeking, but . . .

One final solution. Heil Hitler. Ha, ha, ha. He sure got to the bottom of things, didn't he? He never achieved his goal, though of getting restituted until he killed everyone off. I better not do that, then.

No. He died in disgrace.

Horror. Horror and disgrace. Did you ever have an affair with a teacher? Don't tell me. That's your private thing. I didn't.

No. I had a crush or two, but no affairs.

It's illegal, isn't it? Or shunned.

Shunned at least. Not so much when I was in college, but it certainly is now.

The only affairs I ever had were with prostitutes. They sure will learn you the facts of life quick. Good thing I stayed clean, never caught anything. I lived an immaculate, fundamentalist life up there at ULN and at Dad's those four years from '72 to '76. Absolutely virginal perfect. I hated it, but I didn't want to go to hell. Another reason, I didn't want to become 666, or The Beast, or the Anti Christ. The fear of God was in me. God is Love, right? Mine was Hellfire and Brimstone. Now, God is a dictator to me sometimes. Tells me what to do and I jump and snap my fingers and get going.

Hmm. Sometimes I hear an imperative voice, too, urging caution and patience, sounds curiously like my voice, sort of an alter ego during times when I want to rush in where angels fear to tread.

Well, He's different to every person. He's got a different plan for everyone. I liked the studying and learning up at ULN though. What about your academic life in Kingston?

Did I finish with ULN?   One of my most memorable experiences there was a fight I had with my British Survey professor. Near the end of the second semester of that year-long class, I went to pass in a paper early because I was going to miss the class when it was due. She chastised me, treating me like I was chronically absent. I said, "Don't bully me. This is the only class I have missed all year," and I walked away.   The next day, I went back to her office. She must have thought I was there to apologize, and she turned on a broad smile. Instead I said, You have not passed back my last four papers. I want them returned.

You can't talk to me like that. I could take you to the Dean for this and for the way you talked to me yesterday.

That sounds like a good idea. I would like to talk to the Dean about this course. As a matter of fact, if I don't get my papers back or if I am not satisfied with the grade, I will go to the Dean with all my complaints about this class.

I walked away again. A few days later, she returned all my papers with the predictable B she had been giving me all year. It's a shame that is an experience I remember in such detail when there was so much that I liked about my years there, my Shakespeare teacher, a course in American Literature, an advisor of independent studies in poetry theory who wasn't a very good teacher but a great human being, an advisor of independent studies in literary theory.

Same thing in Kingston where I went for a Master's Degree in English after Shirley graduated from high school. One of my most vivid memories of being there is reading a critique of some of my poems that I showed to a poet on the faculty. He wrote a full page torn from a yellow lined legal pad. He told me to "get rid of the dead hand of the iamb" and to focus my efforts on academic writing.   Fellow graduate students, too, were mostly discouraging of my creative attempts when I tried to share with them. One said, Oh, I see you're into consonance. I can't identify. I'm into assonance.

And yet there was so much that I appreciate about that time at ULK, courses in John Donne, Modern Poetry, Philosophy of Art, my thesis on Reader Response Theory, my thesis advisor I have kept in touch with occasionally ever since. William Faulkner is a course I will never forget as much because of the teacher as because of Faulkner.

Light in August, Mom, that book you gave me, I read part of it. I don't recall if I ever finished it. The world is so anti-intellectual these days, just like C. S. Lewis said. And Tolkein and Williams. Anti-intellectual. All the intellectuals are turning Nazi and Red. And bitter capitalists. No anarchy. My poetry career has been butchered by politics. Little snotty, bratty pukes in town want me to run for office. Leslie Gardner. A twirp I went to high school with. Nothing overt.

Oh. This is what you are imagining? Sometimes I have wondered if I imagined the disrespect I felt in Kingston. But Oklahoma State University for my doctorate was very different, and I'm sure I wasn't imagining the respect I felt there from the beginning. When I got there, I was told I had won a tuition scholarship without even applying. In Oklahoma, I had courses in Literature of the Bible, American Literature, Literary Theory, Poetry Writing, Fiction Writing, Screen Play Writing, Linguistics, and much more. I won money awards for my creative writing. The fiction writing teacher there still writes to me, still encourages my work, complimented me on this project I'm doing with you. Most enduring and valuable literary friend I could ever hope to have.

Mom, is this exhausting you? It's not meant to be an interrogation.

No, I'm enjoying it. People like to talk about themselves you know? And Oklahoma was a creative blossoming for me.

I took a film class at ULN. I got a B in it. I liked that. After I was converted at 16, I used to preach up here at Dudley. We went on three or four rallies on backs of trucks. We'd stop in a town, preach, go on to the next town. It was so embarrassing, going up to Greenville and doing that in front of my old friends. I wasn't embarrassed then, but I am now. I thought every one in the world was going to hell but me.

People who talked to me about it were impressed with you, Moonway. I was proud of your style and passion. And I was relieved that you found something that seemed to be helping you to recover from your troubled adolescence.

What else about your academic life?

Those are the highlights my academic life in college. My teaching experience is another story, other rewards and frustrations, encouragements and discouragements. Now that I'm retired, I'm thinking about taking courses again, maybe studio art, painting or sculpting. More philosophy or some science. And I will teach again, too, part time, because I like so much the regular discussion of literature.

But learning takes place everywhere, Moonway, not just in schools. My whole life is a learning experience. Education and writing helps to show me how to create meaning, or at least significance, or at least value, out of everything, even the shitty stuff, especially that. And I, too, have a dark insane side I need to own. It's why I need art and poetry.

And it's good to butt up against intellectual limits regularly. I need to push knowledge to the place where I no longer know or understand anything. Only then can all the most important stuff— love, faith, beauty—penetrate to every cell nucleus.

25. Belief and Power

"Came to believe that a power greater than ourselves could restore us to sanity" (Step 3, from the 12 steps of Alcoholics Anonymous)

Moonway, I know you don't like me to talk about your delusions. Can we talk about your beliefs?

Yeah. Yeah. That's fine. That's what delusions are. Beliefs. I want mine to be central notions. Of my reaction to culture. My work with poor people, the mentally ill— so-called, the workers, the rich, liaisons, arbitrators, diplomats. Mom, I don't think the Adams or Morrises have got to cover up—or do we?—for anything in this book, with my power. Ha, ha.

We don't have to cover up anything, but I want to respect privacy. As for power, I know you are doing what you believe will influence the situations that concern you.

Well, I do believe in my power. I am powerful, Mom. I'm not in prison, am I? It's been the law right down the line. It's been the law and rights I been researching and reading and quoting, and jitting and jotting about. That's been it, honest. That's why I'm not in prison. I want control over my own business. Psyche and corrections are not minding their business, and I'm just minding my own as a former incorrigible run-away.

What you call your propaganda, what you display, the things you do in public, is it mostly designed to get what you think is some control over your situation?

That and to clear up a lot of social problems. You'll find all the rockers concerned with social problems. All of them right down the line, punk rockers, all of them, addressing major social problems in the world. But Jack Nicholson never should have hit that whore. Shouldn't have been taking it out on her. It should have been Janet Reno dangling by a rope or wire. You learn loyalty in these death clinics, Mom. In these Ghettos. These jails, prisons, mental health institutions. You don't cross each other very much. You shouldn't either. When you do, you protect each other. You look out for each other. You help each other financially, legally. And when you don't, you blame the right people, the staff and the landlords.

What do you have against Janet Reno?

Reno put me under guardianship. I think it's the Salvador Dahli thing. He was put under guardianship. I'm neither a revolutionary, terrorist, square, nor oppressor, Mom. I'm beyond all that. I was a right wing Republican all the way there for a while, a real war monger, and they stopped that, so now they gotta deal with this. Now, they gotta deal with stuff beyond terrorism. It's their fault. I've seen to the presidents and assassins, seen to their protection and welfare, all of them. Seen to violence and pacifism both. Seen to Horticultures and trees as filters for biological animal and human life.

That's a pretty big job.

It is, but I'm doing it. Honest, if you want to look into it, get it all on tape and listen to it. I don't know if I want you having everything. Some things I want left private. A lot of things I want private—my finances, a lot of things. Special.

Moonway, can I change the subject here? I'm curious about hallucinations. Are the ones you got from drug use the same kind as from schizophrenia?

I don't have hallucinations from schizophrenia, Mom. That comes from my art work. I don't have any more from drugs. That's all worn out of me. You don't hallucinate from verbatim schizophrenia. That's a myth. I never did from so-called mental illness. The only reason I go to Mental Health is for protection and for treatment of my drug addiction and alcoholism.

When we were making out that survey for the Schizophrenia Project, I asked you if you have been hallucinating, and you said yes.

Well, sometimes when I do a lot of art work, I'll see things. I hear voices sometimes that could be from the burn-out in my brain from the drugs and alcohol. Not from the schizophrenia. Or it could be from being warped into being a mental patient. It's not genetic. It's other things. I like seeing things for my art work. I think the voices are CIA manufactured, Mom. To torture mental patients. I think the CIA is trying to twist me into something. You don't believe me do you, Mom?

I believe that you believe what you are telling me.

Or maybe the voices are from the Nazis that don't know what Hitler represents. Mom, where I call my rock group Assassin I get the real scoop, the real truth. Assassin's a rock group I'm trying to form. Not as a booth or to hurt anyone.

I got a closet right full of broadcasting and media books in three locations: names, phone numbers. But someone censors me every time I try to phone them. I was thinking what if my CB broadcast went into theatrical and film production? I'd like to collect off it. Money. I sure would like to get copies of Steal this Book, Abby Hoffman; Do It, Jerry Rubin, and Revolution for the Hell of It, Abby Hoffman. Maybe I should stick with the underground. Mom, let's blip the over-ground, play up the underground. Underground to me is the streets. Over-ground is Ron Reagan. Authority, rules, regulations.

Things that are hard to control?
Yeah. Hassles. Harassment. Maybe I should stick with the underground. Should I, Mom? I got over-ground and underground things going. State pays my check. Keeps that money coming in. I think they're stipulating I retire, though. As long as I keep the check. But I'm retired in guerrilla ways, other than propaganda, what you see here and there. Making deals with the government, the CIA, Hollywood. I think, anyway. Don't quote me. It would bear investigation. And sometimes KKK so they'll talk. I'm sure disappointed in coloreds and women for lack of support, where I upped them in the media there at Woodland County Jail the last time I was there. They're not getting me my money, mail and phone calls. I know that. Maybe that's 'cause Gorillas are a little ahead in the game. Or are they? More advanced than women or coloreds, no matter what color or sex they are. Native-tongue/black/feminist insanity is the only distinction left in the world. Nowadays, women's got rights. They still need a lot of protection, though from reactionaries, don't they? Restraining orders or something. My bizarre behavior keeps my family and friends free and safe. And my family photos keeps us normal.

Wouldn't that make a good magazine title for feminism—*Intellectual Times*. School Marm, Belinda Adams. Ha, ha. A lot to be said for the mind, but I need that medication or I'd go nuts. That's the honest Jimmy-Carter truth. I used to eat my ejaculate thinking it would keep me young. But I had dark dreams from the medication last night. I'm not giving those things out, you know. None of them. Someone's scheduling me to live up here at Harmony Family Christian Center and own the property and land. No hassle. I'd like to build electric wires, steel wall around it. Build my castle dream, not a castle, an architect's design shaped like an Indian Tee Pee and a plastic metal. I think the *Newburgh Daily* has got copies of it. And I wish they'd cooperate with me here.

This is crucial, Mom. Psychiatry, now you created them from our RNA and DNA, look after our experimental humans like Berkowitz and animals and animal people.

EXPERIMENTAL HUMANS NEED A LOT OF PROTEC<u>SHUN</u>, CAKE, AND ATTEN<u>SHUN</u>. I wish the CIA would run these parts and wires all through me right. Those are hooked up to satellites, though no one believes me, or they do now and they're deliberately hurting me through them. They keep the heart and lungs going though, but I wish I could breathe through my nose, and feel my emotions, and poop. It's pretty liquid actually. It just won't come out. Coalissa might knock it out of me. Could be the cigarettes. Been hitting the vegetables lately. Seems to be helping. I just wish someone would run these parts and wires in me right.

Do you know someone who can do that?

No.

I don't either.

Mom, before we go any further, could I get this down. Let's back church efforts, faith based services to get aid. I been doing that a long damn time. I consider myself a member of the church, but I don't think they want me. Minister's son, though, up here at the Chinese restaurant said I could still drop in once in a while even though I keep sneaking out for smokes. And I don't want to plague the church or contaminate it. About the only thing the world's got going for it these days. In Capitalist countries, anyway. I'm involved in a lot of cults, Harmony Academy was one.

Why do you call it a cult?

Well, it's a Pentecostal church; and down south they handle snakes and take poison. That's pretty much cultish, ain't it? AA is a right wing cult. I been contributing a lot to that movement, getting them customers. We could take this thing right out of the cults, could build a real Protestant monk community as well as live in it. Take the cult aspect out of these aberrant religions—violence, suicide, bizarre stuff. I already did that on my radio. Mom, I was born in 1956, September 18th. We lived in a little house up there in Greenville. I hope you're giving tours. I'm in the cult of Christ's personality. Jesus died for me and rose again in the body of Christ. The collective body of Christ on Earth and New Heaven. The New Earth, the old Heaven, and the New Heaven. Hell. Purgatory. Paradise. The fundamentalists say there's just two worlds in the afterlife. The *Bible* contradicts it. I like this planet and every one in it.

Mom, the only reason I been staying out of AA lately, I'm just devoting time to art and our book. I got all that worked out, you know. Well, not the whole thing. I gave you some connections. Mom, there's a lot of cruelty these days and all through history, hunh?

All through human existence I suspect, not just through history.

All through history, and the cruelty comes from God. God doesn't stop it, does he?

Well, He tries to. He's perfecting his church for the rupture.

Rupture or rapture?

Rupture.

Ha, ha, ha.

It's not funny. It will be a rapture between Heaven and the universe created by God. After Hell finds its path to the universe I think Christ and Anti-Christ would coexist just so angels and demons could coexist.

I see what you mean. How can there be peace on earth until Christ and Satan reconcile.

William Blake, *Marriage of Heaven and Hell*. That's my favorite art work. I would like to get a copy of that.

I have *Blake's Illustrations of the Book of Job*. Do you want to see it? *The Book of Job* is my favorite book of the *Bible*, the one I have read, puzzled over, felt awed by the most. To think that, after all his suffering and questioning—Why me? — the response Job gets from God is a rhapsodic poem to Nature, his own creation, of which we are but a minute part.

Mom, did Armageddon, Heaven and Hell happen already?

What do you believe about it?

Well, I hope it's over with. I hope Israel isn't being encompassed with armies, the way it says in the Bible. I hope Armageddon, Heaven and Hell are over with. Well, not Heaven. Just Armageddon and Hell. I like my sorcery though, and wizard tapes, and occult. There's a lot of magic in tapes these days, and religion. After Uriah Heep and Ozzie

Osborne.

I've never listened to Uriah Heep and Ozzie Osborne. Magic and the occult are all about power, hunh?

Well, you don't have to listen to rock if you don't want to, Mom. Stick with your classical. I like my heavy metal rock, though. Both the environmental and internal, in reference to that painting I did that said, "By the lonely and cosmic whiskey" on a bottle I drew. Blended with 100% pure judgment fire.

Your beliefs are often vivid and colorful, Moonway. I see why they are so real to you. As real as memories or dreams. Odd, isn't it? That beliefs can have such power without any basis whatsoever in reality outside our own mind? That they are simultaneously so personal and so cultural. Hmmm.

"Admitted we were powerless" is the first of the Alcoholics Anonymous steps of recovery. This is an extraordinary admission for a human will to make. We desire to seize power rather than surrender it, and this personal desire is mirrored in the culture. Or maybe we get it from the culture. All fields of knowledge—history, philosophy, science, medicine, etc.—seek truths/beliefs that will give us the power we crave. All human relationships endure or fail by how we negotiate power among us.

I have a vivid memory of my pronouncement at twelve years old, "I am an atheist. I do not believe in God." I don't have any memory of who I said it to. Was it just to myself? At the same time that I don't believe in any institutional God I know about, all my life I have craved goodness. I want to know and do the right thing. Is God simply a contraction of Good which harmonizes nicely with "God is love?" A belief in God as love and goodness does not resolve the paradoxes, however, for there is as much diversity of opinion about what is good as there is about what is God. And then, what are we to do with the presence of hatred and evil. Meister Eckhart says I must continuously "give birth to God who is always needing to be born," labor pains and all. And I have always craved transcendent experience, whatever gives me the feeling of connection with something deeper and

243

beyond every day existence.

26. Recovery

This ghetto living sucks monkey cock. I don't want to drink, though, Mom. I get these cravings that are clearing up as I don't volunteer for these mental health places. Most of this babble should be getting better.

It's important to stay on the path of recovery, hunh? Do you think the past affects you in your recovery?

Just from conditioning from the environment, the mediatype, the stereotype. Putting me through hell. I feel like I been cloned. That comes from being in these concentration camps and being subject to all that psychiatric charting and stereotyping. I don't know if I am or not, Mom.

Stigma, hunh? It's hard to take; I have trouble with it, too. It's why I like you to clean up when we go out in public together. Do you feel like you are a clone, or like you have been cloned?

Both. And losing my art and writing still bothers me. That's crucial, a grudge of mine that won't quit. And my fractured arm. And my money, mail and phone calls. You know what George Warrick of AA said: "I keep a resentment just to stay sober." Keeps me going, believing in eternal life on earth in the body through medicine, science, religion, education. They keep me pitting myself against the world.

Does it help to talk about it?

Well, if it was a lawyer, that would be a different story, Mom. Some things I got to do to stay free. Then I got to do them. But I don't want to see a therapist because I don't want to be locked up any more. One way to stay free is to stay hygienic. I know that now. And I been working on it for a month and a week now. I'd mop the kitchen floor, but I got to save this arm for drawing. I'm gonna get my cleaning lady to do it. But I been cleaning everything else up. Shower. Changing my clothes. Taking my meds. I been doing good? I'd make amends financially, Mom, but no one will take my money.

Your continued recovery is the best amends I can

think of, for everyone, you too. If I ever get desperate for money I will take yours. Or if you ever get to the point that you have as much or more than me, I will take your money. Cleaning up is very good. Has anyone used this vacuum cleaner, yet?

I'll get the housekeeper using it.

On the steps, too, please.

Yes. You're not worrying about me, are you?

Yeah. I do.

I worry about you, too.

Yeah, you do, a lot. That's what it means to love, I guess. It isn't all there is to love, though. It wouldn't be worth it if it was all worry, would it?

No. Service is part of it. Sacrifice.

And the feeling of love is a good high.

Communication. Non-oppression. Terrorism resolution.

Hunh?

Ha, ha. I'm making a lot of progress in the last 20 years. Haven't been violent since '82 or '81. I feel happier, except I wish the CIA would unseal my nostrils and emotions.

Your nostrils might be sealed up from tobacco smoke.

Just a minute, Mom. All lawyers, all, and all advocates, all, and Madness Network News, all—I'm pre-pleading the 5th amendment.

How are the voices, now? Do they tell you to do things?

Not now. They're in the background. Now, they're all positive.

I've been thinking again about the serenity to accept the things I cannot change.

Courage to change the things I can.

And the wisdom to know the difference.

Mom, the only thing I can't change is the fact that I'm not God. I change all things through God. It's comforting to know that someone's looking out for me, someone supernatural.

I don't want that much responsibility, either, no way.

I don't think He does half the time. That's why I

advise Him to stay comfortable, room and environment temperature, security, luxuries, power, safety, money for Himself. My Higher Power.

You think He/She/It is interested in those things?

Yeah. God of the Bible ain't, but AA's a merger of all faiths.

Yes, it's worldwide. I was thinking about the things in my life I could change to get more of what I want.

Got to go out there and fish for what you want.

Yeah. Then I'd have to let go of whether or not the fish is attracted to my bait. I would like to get my books published. Like with a boyfriend, I have to get out there and fish for it, don't I?

I'm not taking any risks either, Mom. If they want me, they can come to me. I'm done taking risks, getting all embarrassed, depressed, suicidal, crazy.

Crazy making, isn't it? Fishing for attention, any kind.

You know what I thought of using Sex and Love Addicts Anonymous for? Writing kinky, perverted, and straight porno commercials. For money. For publicity.

I have problems with the wisdom to know the difference between what I can or should change and what I should let go of? Should I try, for instance, to be an influence for change in your adult life? And Shirley's and Martin's

Well, these cigarettes aren't helping me much, are they?

But you don't want me to control that, do you?

I don't want to control you, Mom.

You wouldn't try to stop me from smoking if I were still doing it?

I would. But you stick to your food. I'll stick to my cigarettes, and Dad can stick to his liquor. OK? We'll control those three industries. Don't get real fat though. That's not healthy. I shouldn't talk. I'm not going to preach. Have mental health start a Smokers' Anonymous. I'll attend. I probably try to do a lot of things for you I shouldn't. I wish God would help me get people back to work after these international strikes I'm leading. So the world situation would get back to normal except for war. Maybe I'd get back to normal, too. Eat more. Not be thinned down as fast by Republican OA. I'm losing a lot of damn weight. I can tell by looking in the mirror when I shower. I hope you never start smoking again, Mom. It's a curse. It ups the delusions, these damn cigarettes. I think there's a cure for cancer.

They're doing pretty good with cancer. Lung cancer is one of the toughest and hardest. But maybe someday.

They laughed at penicillin. How is the family, Mom?

Brett had a bit of a cold when I saw them over the week end. He didn't seem very sick. Shirley has migraine headaches every once in a while, bad ones.

Does she take anything for it?

Tylenol for Migraines, I think. And sleeping pills because getting too tired from not sleeping brings on migraines.

Does it help?

Sometimes, sometimes not. She says if she gets it early enough it helps.

Damn. I wonder what would help. Milk? Herbal tea? I know little Jeffrey needs vitamins. Damn rays from the military in my head.

Did you have anything to eat today?

Had hot dogs and fruit cocktail and milk. V8 and fruit juice. Bought a big giant jug of fruit juice, had a little handle on it. Do you drink your V8 juice, berry juice, and milk, Mom?

I eat lots of fruit and vegetables. I get lots of dairy for protein and calcium. I make a rich milk out of soy milk and skim dairy milk.

Those soy products don't settle with my stomach, or I'd change. I love regular milk. I worked a lot, too, Mom, growing up. That's being hidden, all the work I did. Pink Lloyd in Boston. Burger King in Florida when I split from ULK. Sweeping chimneys here in PI. Picking up trash in Woodland. Job at ULN , side job there, cleaning the art department there. What else? Picking up bottles and cans.

Delivering newspapers when you were a kid.

Newspapers. I'd like that emphasized a lot, my work

thing we're going through right now. Emphasize. Point in red. I forgot the harvests. Picking potatoes and working on potato harvesters was the earliest. In the early 70s, I was at Northridge Shoe six months. That's how I got my disability check. Thanks to good old Jim Walker. Remember him? They called him a fairy on E3, but he did me right. I'll do him right. I'll keep looking out for him through the years. He's in Newburgh somewhere, now. I don't hear from him anymore. I worked at cleaning chimneys for a guy out here Northridge. But I didn't enjoy it, my physical labors, I mean. I can't work now, Mom. Fractured arm, fractured wrist. mental illness. Now that I'm not watching so much TV and radio, I'm not being duped as much. They get you buying things, subscribing to programs you don't need.

I need more money. I could sue the court. $250,000 was involved in putting me behind bars, Mom. I read that on a document I have in my file. That was the fine. I was fined and put in there both, which is illegal. You know a slogan I originated: "I did the time. I pay no fine."

Wasn't that bail money? You never paid a fine. No one ever paid it.

No, I didn't pay it. Yes, someone paid it. Was it Dad? He ought to be reimbursed if he did. I need private property, a house and land, too. I'll get it doing just what I'm doing, now. And imprisoning the Postmaster General. But I shouldn't be ripping rockers off! Broadcasting on my CB. Keeps my SSI money coming. And it will get me a house and land on my own designs that I sent to the *Newburgh Daily News.* I'm keeping it under wraps. Private. That's the way I want it. If I had my own house, there would be less harassment. I'd have an electric fence and a wall all around it, so the police and riff raff couldn't get in. I like working on my terms, forming labor unions. I wish those lawyers would do something more for me. Get me more money. Money I've earned, honestly. Mom, could I borrow $5? I was supposed to get my check, but it didn't come in. I'll pay you back. I was counting on that check though, so food stamps wouldn't have to pick up.

I've talked to Victor and Cliff about the possibility of you getting a little extra money from your account for every meeting of Psycho Social Group or the day program that you go to. Would you like that?

Yeah. My commitment lately is to keep attending AA no matter what. And I need all the help I can get doing that. Sometimes the only friend I had in those courtrooms was my attorneys, and they've done a lot for me. You get filled in on a lot of things through the Anonymous Associations. I know that. The striking against them is just for more money. I struck the past two nights. People turn me against the program when they want to use or force you to use so they can use. Enablers.

But I don't buy that enabling thing anyway. The issue for me is alcohol and drug addiction, not cigarettes, Mom. These keep me off the pot and alcohol. And I'd like to get a cost investment from the Pepsi and nicotine and caffeine industries to do so. Keep me off dope and alcohol. I shouldn't throw my matches around. I'm going to phone in a call right now to the Help Line, have them help me with that. Leave the tape on.

Moonway Michael here. Listen, could you guys get me blowing my matches out before I put them in the ash tray. That's probably the whole problem. I don't always blow them out. I just throw them. Bye, bye.

They should help me out with that. That's the whole problem, probably. People see me throwing them matches. Ha, ha, ha. I don't want a fire in here. That's for sure. Been hitting the vegetables lately.

I'm glad you're doing that. And I like seeing art work you are doing up around your apartment.

Mom, you doing any art work?

Not any visual art work, except photos, for a long time.

How come?

Limitations, Moonway. Time. Energy. Commitments. I already have too many projects and commitments that I don't have time for. That's why. But

249

sometimes I really long to do it. And I might someday. Ah ha, here's your cat. Hi, Scandal.

Put her down, Mom if she bothers you.

I don't mind her being in my lap as long as she doesn't sink her claws into my legs.

She shouldn't do that. I don't treat her very good. Sometimes I just get pissed at her and push her right off the edge of my lap. I try to do it gently, but sometimes I snap at her when I'm busy and she wants to come up and be petted. I'm sorry Kiddo. I'm sorry, Babe. I'm sorry Little One. You gotta be fleet on your feet with me around. You know that, don't ya? I'm sorry, Kid.

She seems to like me, now. She used to be scared of me.

She's your grandmother, Kid. Grandmother Belinda Adams. I love that little cat.

It's good to live with something to love.

I like these talk sessions, Mom.

Me too.

V
He Wore this World like a Loose Garment

The sense of humor overcomes tragedy.

27. This Book Work is Fun

Mom, I'd like to bring up something else for the record here. All my theater and singing and acting is to back this collaborative book of ours. To put backbone into it. Financially. Protection wise. Including my CB broadcasts. This street theater's mean stuff, but you sure get an audience. Signs, costumes, get-up, makeup. And I want to keep doing that. I'm not sure about the signs where it's such a burden. Maybe ON STRIKE sign or something.

Mom, all of the legal and advocacy work I've done is to back this book. My Nicholson portrait is the seller in this, and underline the word Manson all through. Let's put Brett's, Jeffrey's and Marcus's art in, too. This book is turning into something, hunh, Mom?

We'll find out. We have to be patient.

I'm more a big military-underworld-underground-robot Ron Reagan than anything else. Don't quote me there. Left-wing robot. But this book-work is fun.

Yes, it is. Do you want me to erase everything you say that refers to your "Don't quote me?"

No, don't erase anything, Mom. That sounds so Nazi. No, anything goes. Anything you want to put in.

Writing a book is a personal act, Moonway, but publishing it is a public act. We have to think about artistic and social values as well as personal ones.

Well, I think most artists do focus on the money or the sale aspect of it. There's a lot of money in crime if you can collect it and stay sane.

I don't mean financial gain when I say artistic values.

Business, Mom. You got to quote statistics in the book, financial statistics. Revenues. Royalties. Don't you want to make money off it?

Oh, sure. But I don't count on that. If we don't make any money, it is still worth doing anyway just for the review, the adventure and discovery of selecting and organizing. What we are enjoying together right now.

Picking apart things, diagnosing things, prognosing

some things.

Analyzing. Trying to see the whole picture.

Everyone's perspective, including Dad's and yours and us kids. The ancestry.

The context: social, economic, political.

Mental illness is a good defense in court. Makes a lot of people leery of you. Keeps you safe. They think you're mentally ill, they don't blame you and they leave you alone, just like having cancer. These days it's all physiological with the behaviorists.

On the other hand, you pay a big price for being known as mentally ill?

Yeah.

Ever think about how your art and writing helps you?

It gives me a feeling of power.

Ahh. We keep coming back to power, hunh? Me too. Maybe that feeling is just the wishful anticipation of a happy ending. Those fairy-tales are forever a part of me because I read them so much in childhood, and then read them to you kids. But writing is also adventure and exploration. Even in this review we are doing, I often have a sense of seeing things I have not seen before.

My art and writing keeps the disability checks coming in. Helps me stay free and have an enriched fantasy life. That Jack Nicholson portrait could be the ultimate seller. Exposes what the CIA did to Jimmy Jones. 'Course they gave him the machine guns, so there could be some compromise here and there. He probably blamed them all, too. Look into the summary. It's got all kinds of publishers from my street propaganda. All kinds of media are waiting for a piece of the action 'cause of my CB broadcasting. All kinds of silent flick people waiting for me because of my street theater. But I don't want to broadcast these poems of yours you gave me, Mom. I want to sit there and listen to them. Thought of going modern through Moonway Ginsberg. The constitution says PURSUIT OF HAPPINESS. I'm protecting the Statue of Liberty from terrorists and oppressors, graffiti, and being torn down. I'm not selling out to the wealthy at all, the shag watcher, the Smoky Witness Club. Just a minute, just a minute, just a minute, folks. Just a minute. What's this? Finance the book, you guys, Libertarian Party, Moonway Michael, Membership Card, 2000/2001. That might get you into places. Financial ideas for the design of money of mine. My only camp. International Capitalism. Heil Hitler.

Other things, Mom. Interrogate me, if you want to. But I wish you wouldn't side with them. I wish you would go through Cliff Worth or the American Civil Liberties, the Communist Party, or NAMI, or *Madness Network News*, or . . . . I'm not holding the attorneys or supportive underground or underworld and liberals accountable for me, but I wish they'd keep defending me in courts. I'd like to dip and pry and get my money through small claims courts nationally. In the free world, leaving the reds to their world. There's a lot of money in crime, Mom, but I've never been involved, and it's been one big domestic dispute right down the line. We should keep ironing out coexistence, too.

With me, it's art and writing. That's what I want to do. I don't like being forced into singing by Dad. Of course he might need the money, but I'm done with acting and singing, Mom. I am. And that whole thing is to boost this book and the sale of it. My art, my acting, singing, theater, campaigns, protests. That's all to back our book.

I wish you wouldn't do that publicly.

What? Back the book? Why not?

I wish you wouldn't be that public about it at this point. It's not even done.

Well, it's not public, except for the bugs on this tape between you and me and the book.

Oh, all right. You're not broadcasting it?

No.

So you're talking about past stuff you have done that is backing the book? Even before we thought about doing it?

Yeah, and my propaganda on my windows, doors, walls. They tore one excellent wall down. Wal-Mart built an empire around it. I'd like photos of those. Got photos of the wall behind the movie theater on Main Street.

You're getting over-excited and loud, Moonway. Might disturb your neighbors?

Yeah. I'm just excited about this book. I won't get in trouble, Mom. They gotta bail me with anything they haven't charged me with already. They can't just save up charges like that, or I'll motion to legislate that you be charged immediately. Publicly, those signs I held up, those are all campaign materials, not protest. Privately, it's protest, a Protestant right and choice, and privilege. Protest-ant— original protest. And you churches who remain silent: publicly, I'm a doom prophet; privately, I'm a major religion. You getting family, friends, and offspring in the book, too, Mom, art and writing? I'm going to get my share of the profits if it makes it, ain't I?

50-50? Is that a good split?

Well, you're doing all the work. 60-40. 60 you. 40 me. It's both an underground and over ground publication, too. Uniting the Rubys and Oswalds in peace.

Peace would certainly be a social value. Don't count on it being published. I'd hate to go through all this and then think I'm the cause of your disappointment.

Don't worry, Mom. I mean it, World. You're not preventing this book. Heil Hitler. Where did that picture go? Here it is; I ripped it though.

Oh. That's too bad. It's good. Would make a good back cover for the book. You have a lot of pictures in that sketch pad. Be careful when ripping them out.

Mom, here's a song or poem or both, entry in the book. It's a golden one and could clear up a lot of things and get it started.

> Did Elvis's SWAMI think of all art,
> religion, politics, media, science, education,
> and music forming cliques
> and united, forming their own colleges?
> Or was it me or the Beatniks
> or the Beverly Hill Billies?
> Little matter we're a family.

This is a golden one. Could you put that in the book? Would ya? I got another one for the book called *New Terrorists*

Moore Bowen

Military or something, whatever we vote to call it.
Song-Poem

> With all of the fine and ignorant, saint and sinner,
> national and international breeding
> in the Michaels and Adams,
> we have quite the Red and Kap advantage
> over the world. The manager and producer
> contracts among us are all evidence
> against critics and media which ban us.

In the book, we're just bringing the psycho terrorist element into it. We also need to bring in square views, corporate views, and polit-bureau views. Incorporate all views. Let's dig up the Christian monkey thing. Scopes-Darrow. Both sides have their point. Neither side is total. It's too bad that we can't get our book here set to Uriah Heep and Randy Stonehill both with some of my public songs as the chorus.

You did good to hit the ashtray with your match that time.

Did I blow it out?

No. You shook it, but it hit the ash tray.

I gotta do something. I better get a lighter, a couple or 5 of them. I'm so inspired tonight is the thing. It takes interaction, Mom to bring it out of me.

Yeah, me too. I feel inspired when I cut and paste in organizing, when I compose to fill in gaps with family history.

My history's all lobotomized and shock treated out of me. Except for you here, and the book, I don't want to go through it again. And the area here fills me in on everything, living here, settling down, sticking with one place at a time. When will the book be done, Mom? September?

That's what I have in mind for the first draft. When it's finished? I don't have any predictions. Then, we might end up doing it just for the personal fun of it. If it doesn't sell.

Why not the money, Mom?

Just trying to avoid disappointment, Moonway.

That summary up there on the wall is crucial in this book, too. We could leach off it if we wanted to. Leach right to high blue heaven. Suck it dry. I didn't do much for you guys when I was growing up. Real punk Berkowitz type. Let's hold on to psyche, Mom. Psychiatry. I got a Christian theory here. It's in the blood. Real medicine should be in the blood. The psych texts are all involved with the mind. That'll go nowhere. Well, maybe they will. Skinner wants to start removing spirits and souls. You know I don't want that. You know what I'm . . . We better blip here. Blip. I'm not going to say it. I'm not going to prison again. I might be drinking souls and spirits in my jug here. Shall we put that in the book? Ha, ha. It gives me a jolly rush thinking about it. Makes me happy. Munkers should protect our freedom of speech, though.

Who is Munkers?

A congressman or something. Mom, you're not in any danger because of the book we're collaborating on, are you?

I can't see how.

Something violent should be done for you and me concerning the bans and media exploitations, VCR and computer rights. Mom, some dude printed his writings in original cursive written form which I've done by hand. Is McGraw-Hill interested? I think that's who published *Steal this Book*, by Abby Hoffman. But I want you publishers to pay for our book if you're going to use it. Or maybe this book is just for rent.

Moonway, keep in mind that if we can see more clearly what has happened, we will receive the gift of "taking, as Jesus did, this sinful world as it is" (Rheinhold Niebur). You know, the 11th step says to pray for the knowledge of God's will in all our affairs. I think God's will must be what happens, both the wonderful and the terrible. My greatest fear with this book is not that it will fail to be published, but that my vision will not be clear and brave enough.

28. The End

Stories in real life go on, Moonway, but this book has to end. What kind of ending should it have?

An eternal one. In the body, in the living body of each

257

individual—Belinda Adams, Richard Michael, Carl Daggett, Moonway Michael, Mahmud, and Chris Brice.

Any thoughts on the last lines?

Like this: Mahmud, if you keep protecting me from the terrorists, I wish you the best, and I don't care what you do. It's all up to you. Your fuse is up to you, Mahmud. And Chris Brice, too.

The terrorist issue raises the specter of tragedy. I argued one time with a literary friend that comedy is a greater, more encompassing vision than tragedy. Sometimes, I actually believe it. Other times, I think it's one of my delusions. Comedy is certainly much harder for me to write. But all it takes for a happy ending, a main component of comedy, is to stop the story in a happy place.

The sense of humor overcomes tragedy inflicted on a person. In my case, the criminal justice system almost murdered me.

But maybe tragedy and comedy are always in tension with each other, dynamic tension that keeps us alert and growing at the tips of our mental branches. Even so, every story has to stop somewhere, and every life surely has happiness in it. No book tells the whole story. Life is too rich and complicated. We can't tell this whole story, either, can we? But why not end it in a happy place?

I'm really into this BLT. When I get done eating, I can do better with this conversation.

I'm not sure how well I can do either with this cough.

You OK? Are you getting over that cold?

Yes, but I have been tired all week—thinking about the whole terrorist issue again with the awful terrorism going on in the Middle East, on both sides.

Now that I look at it in my own gluttonous way, that whole New York thing on 911 was a bummer, wasn't it?" You know what I was thinking at one point? I'd like one of those planes to nose dive right into the heart of Hollywood. A nuclear, military one.

I would be very sorry to see so many innocent people get killed who haven't done anything to deserve it.

Yeah. Boy George. *The Crying Game.* That was a

song in the movie, wasn't it? By Boy George. About the IRA? I went to the movie one time, and I left early. Something went wrong. They probably respect people's civil rights not to be forced to join. And it probably came through in the movie.

The movie was brutal. Shows how it makes people do cruel things. Feel and be cruel, too. I don't really buy the separation of being and doing. When I do mean things, I am mean. Even though it's neither all I am nor what I am all the time. All happy endings are mitigated, but how could anyone not want a happy ending?

I know I better keep going to AA, or it's just going to be a big bummer in my life, Mom.

The program helps to live life with more serenity and joy, hunh? And to endure the losses. I lost one side of the tape I made on my trip to the Dakotas. Battery went dead, I guess, and I didn't notice. I hate when that happens. I think I have lost something important. But then, think of all the losses of all the conversations that don't get recorded. Is this loss really more important than that? Speech is just sound waves riding on air, gone like wind as soon as uttered except for the lingering cool on the skin. Thoughts are even less substantial. All that talk and all that thought throughout human existence, utterly gone. More of *The Unbearable Lightness of Being*, Milan Kundera's novel. And I think it was Eudora Welty who said, "Oh this is the joy of a rose/ that it blows/ and goes."

All that doesn't get written down or VCRed of filmed, hunh, Mom? That's a commercial for the Cam Corder and VCR industry—"Imagine what you don't record that you should."

And still we burden our lives with the stuff we struggle to save. Am I talking myself into feeling OK about loss? With this book, we are recovering and saving some memories, trying to live the promise from *The Big Book*, "We will neither regret the past nor wish to shut the door on it."

I appreciate the Program, the last twenty years anyway. Except their anonymity traditions. And Bill Wilson's name is out there in the press, all the press.

We have some issues with anonymity in this book,

don't we? There's the show off in me wants to let it all hang out. And there's the shy, self conscious, stage frightened thirteen year-old forgetting her well-rehearsed lines at her first public performance in a new school. Social judgment is a real and cruel force in human life. Stigma. There are good reasons to respect the anonymity tradition. Have we talked about specific people in the program who were especially important to you? Without naming names

Not so much the people were so important, but the meetings, the principles. It got me something. Look around me here—three typewriters. I'd like to get one of them going. Everything I got, I got out of going to the anonymous meetings. I'm a real materialist lately. I hated school until I was converted. Then I liked the challenge of getting erudite, sagacious, wise. Real holy, monko Manson. Ha! I wouldn't hurt no one, though. And I gotta get these violent and suicidal feelings out of me to someone that won't snitch. That will help me with them. Rather than them erupting. No therapists though. No one from the Mental Health Center. You go through my advocate, Cliff.

Cliff, You, Dad, and Carl—consistent over-the-years relationships. What are your glad memories, Mom? Did you have pets?

I had a kitten once that I claimed as mine, though we weren't supposed to make pets of the farm cats, couldn't feed them because that would make them no good for keeping down the mice and other little varmints. So it was my private, even secret, pet. I think it was before I went to school. Holding and stroking it made me glad. It was a weak runt, not active like the rest of the kittens, and not wild like them. I tamed it, but it needed more than my love. Maybe my love, in taming it, weakened it. It died, and that made me leery of pets for a long time. I didn't want to get too attached to our dog, Skip, when you kids were little. But then, when he died, I cried anyway. It's hard not to get attached to a thing you care for, even when you consciously try not to.

I liked walking through the fields, reading fairy tales, and daydreaming about growing up and marrying someone who would fall in love with my ravishing beauty, awaken me, take me away from the misery of my fears, and take care of me and my family forever after. Though it embarrassed me to remember it, I never was quite comfortable ridiculing that daydreaming, even in my most avid feminist days. It sustained me.

Fiction—fantasy—is something we weave around ourselves to enshroud us in hope.

Yes, Moonway, I like that idea.

What else did you read?

I memorized the nursery rhymes, but I don't remember that happening. I only know I did because I remember them now. I read several times a gothic mystery called *Shadows on Cedar Crest* about a hidden lover. Mama loved the Science Fiction in *Fate*, and other magazines like that, and I used to read those. I liked the sense of the exotic I found in them, other worlds and other possibilities. But I don't remember many details. I read lots of *True Confessions* type magazines which I am comfortable ridiculing now. Fairy tales and nursery rhymes are much better as literature. Mama did get, for a time, a magazine called *Sexology* which I read every chance I could sneak it away.

I used to go into Marston's, stand there and read the most perverted porno.

We never had any access to porno, but, as I recall those *True Confessions*, they got pretty close. I think there was a heavy moral undertone, too, about what to avoid because the women, not the men, always seemed to be doing something they shouldn't that led to their downfall. I don't think I paid much attention to the morality at the time though.

We got no strip joints or anything up here. All we got is porno, hunh?

I don't know. I don't go out looking for raw porno. A friend one time gave me copies of Anais Nin's porno books because she said she couldn't stand to have them around. I read them, was titillated. Then when I left Cincinnati, I threw them away. They weren't worth carrying around, and I didn't think I ought to give them to the Salvation Army. I have also seen some of the more raunchy girlie magazines as well as *Playboy*. I don't remember where, have never bought them. I saw a couple of short soft porno films once with curious friends seeing their first porno movie. All of that was bereft of literary quality and boring, even when titillating.

On the other hand, I enjoy Henry Miller's books and the Movie *June* about Miller and his lovers, and *Lady Chatterly's Lover*, and many other books and movies that put pornographic elements into a larger social context; they teach me about the range of human sexual experience, the light and dark of it. I seek out those books. And there is a very dark side in the union of sex and violence. I have been fascinated by some of those movies I have seen that I can't remember the name of now. I'm off on a tangent here.

What other happy highlights in your life, Mom?

They're all connected to relationships—moments of deep affection with loved ones, even with my education and spiritual life—with other minds, with nature, with the mysterious eternal and infinite—God as some call it. Sometimes all of that in one simple unexpected moment that could easily go unnoticed. One time an otter swam out from under the ice when I was walking around Mill Pond, and we stared at each other. Too quickly, it plunged back down into the darkness under the ice. Perhaps I received the grace of that moment because it was too young to be as wary as otters usually are in this area. I go hunting for that kind of experience sometimes, but it always strikes me unawares.

Christ had relationships with his disciples. I think he was gay, though? No, just kidding. I don't want to be no fruit.

Yes, Christ had relationships with the multitudes.

They were quick relationships, though. He wore this world like a loose garment, like AA says. I'm wearing the whole world. Pursuit of happiness. I like the world and everyone in it. I like staying this side of the grave.

Nice phrase, Moonway—I like the world.

I like material. Materialism. Money. Cigarettes and Coffee. You, Dad, Cliff, and Carl. Mom, there's something important here. I've got to work on not volunteering anymore—We've gotta work on not being so fanatical by volunteering for those psyche and corrections places. I insisted on getting myself in there. I probably muscled my way in. I'm much happier in freedom. I know I am an exmate. But that limits me, too. I swore to Christ I was going to abandon all that. Go out and be videotyped as an artist and writer. Except it's *our* health, Mom—mental health is. Globally.

Right on, Moonway. All the problems in the world come down to problems of relationships and mental health, the failure of the love command. I can't believe those who blow themselves up, mail Anthrax, and crash planes into the most potent symbols of what they hate are acting from a mentally healthy state. And what about the actions of those who retaliate with bombing? US. We all have mental health problems trying to understand and respond to these events. We all get caught up in craziness.

I think thought, soul, and spirit are all separate from the body. If they could be linked somehow, held together. Maybe they are in cigarettes and drugs I used to do. Christ doesn't put down alcohol. He drank himself. Probably got drunk once in a while. Mercerum tannum—let live and let live.

Live and let live?

Let live and let live, I say. Between the Kaps and Reds. Between all colors and sexes. I think there's gotta be a "let live and let live" language of behavior on the earth In some cases, though, it's self defense like the ghettoes. That's my opinion. I'm not imposing it. Someone's gotta sass these people while we're living on the outside here where I wanna be eternally. Sass these people. Because that's all being ironed out through fists, knives, guns and fights in those places. I don't want to iron it out that way. We need better treatment. Boy did that Karesh stir up the shit, though, hunh?

Those people do stir up shit.

Those poor bastards. Do you feel for them?

Yeah, I do, especially when I understand the inner life and the outer context. But I haven't yet grown spiritually enough to love whole heartedly the sinner I do not know, as Christ wanted. I think about them. I wonder what motivates the violence. I want to understand them.

Oppression motivates that, Mom. A man's got to react. And women, kids and the elderly, too.

Hmm. Yeah, the feeling of being oppressed makes me feel violent. I do believe the world needs to find a way to love all we most hate.

Bill Wilson says, "Spiritual energy is broad and all inclusive."

That's a nice thought, Moonway, a happy moment to end on?

All right now, all: Vote for us, vote for us Adams, Michaels right now, right now. Put your XQ at the polls. Put Mahmud's name on the ballot at the polls, sky jacker down there at MCFP. This is Rocket Daddy, Hammer Daddy, and One, the Old Rocket Jacky Boy signing off.

Epilogue

Yes, real life does go on. In the time since we first drafted this book, wars began, ended, and go on. And there have been important changes in Moonway's life that need to be recorded here.

In the summer of 2002, I talked to Moonway's psychiatrist about the difficulty of finding effective medication. I also explained the family history of bipolar disorder and my sense that he was often rapid cycling between manic and depressed states. At the time, he was receiving Zoloft for depression as well as Risperdol and long-acting injections of Haldol for the schizophrenia. Dr. Long said she would like to try some new medication but was reluctant to do it outside the hospital. In the spring of 2003, she was provided this opportunity. Moonway's mental health "decompensated" again to such a point that he was involuntarily hospitalized at SMHI. I talked to the psychiatrist there and asked her to please consult with Dr. Long.

That hospitalization resulted in a change of medication from Risperdol to Zyprexa and Depacote, a drug originally used to treat seizure disorder, but found to be effective for many with bipolar disorder. The intramuscular injections of Haldol were at last discontinued. Very often diagnoses of mental illness depend as much on what medication is found effective for improved functioning as on symptoms in the *Diagnostic and Statistical Manual*. So in this case, because Moonway's functioning improved, his diagnosis was changed to schizoaffective disorder; he has symptoms of both schizophrenia and bipolar disorder.

With this change, I saw the first significant improvement in Moonway's quality of life that could be attributed to medication that I have ever seen in all the years of his treatment. For a long time, I saw no improvement in his schizophrenic symptoms; his delusions, paranoia, and obsessive behavior remained active. However, with his moods more stabilized, the schizophrenic symptoms have less power over his actions.

The second big change in his life was another move. The house he was living in would not pass the subsidy inspection because of needed repairs the landlord refused to do. I had been thinking for at least two years about buying a house to rent to him. I could see no other way to get him stable housing, and his frequent moves had become increasingly stressful for him and for me. So in June, 2004, I bought a small one-bedroom house where he now lives. He considers it his for life because I have promised that I will never evict him.

One day in 2005 we went to Mac Donald's for coffee and then to a convenience store for him to get matches to smoke. I sat on the curb with him while he smoked, and we talked about the heat, nearly 90°, very hot for Northern Lincoln before July. I was drinking iced coffee; he was drinking his hot. He said at first that he didn't feel the heat, but as we talked further about it, he took off 2 of his 3 T-shirts. Throughout this entire visit, he was switching between talking to me and talking to his voices about what he is doing to practice oppression. Once, after animated talk about suing the forces who refuse to get him his money, mail and phone calls, he said, "Maybe that's not real, hunh, Mom? Sometimes I don't know." When I dropped him off at his house, he said, "Mom, all it takes to have a good day is a little talk with someone you love who also loves you. It's all really as simple as that, hunh?"

Then, in the winter of 2009-2010 he stopped taking medication, decompensated badly, and was hospitalized again. The Depakote and Zyprexa were increased. A plan was put in place to monitor his medication daily. Now, July, 2012, the kind of speech that typifies so much of the rest of this book has become muted. He rarely talks to me as compulsively or frequently about losing his art and writing, about his fractured arm, and about regaining his money, mail and phone calls dating back to birth. He is much more cooperative and agreeable. He allows a house-keeper to clean at least the kitchen and bathroom regularly. Most importantly, he is happier and much less depressed most of the time. All of this not only improves his life a great deal, it also improves the lives of all who care for him. One day recently while I was visiting him, he said, "Can I fix you a meal, Mom?"

Acknowledgements

Poems from this novel have been published in *Cincinnati Poetry Review*; redriverreview.com; *Passager*; and *Awakenings*.

Many thanks to Harold Jaffee, *Journal of Experimental Fiction* Books, and Eckhard Gerdes for making the publication of this book a reality.

It would be hard to overstate the gratitude I owe to family, many friends, writers, and teachers for a lifetime of inspiration and encouragement. They are too many to list in this space, but some teachers deserve special recognition: Burt deFrees, my high school English teacher in the 1950s; Virginia Nees Hatlen, my Master's thesis advisor; and Gordon Weaver who taught me to write fiction. These teachers have been faithful friends and sources of encouragement for my writing through all the years since their initial teaching.

Thank you, all.

About the Author

see http://moorebowen.wordpress.com/

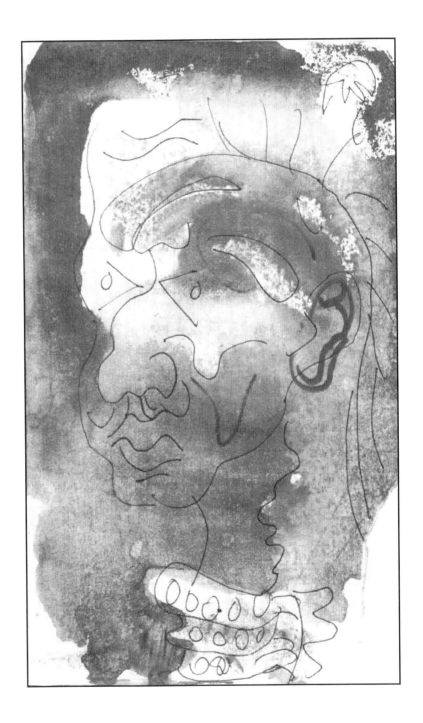

Great Works of Innovative Fiction Published by JEF Books

Collected Stort Shories by Erik Belgum
Oppression for the Heaven of It by Moore Bowen [2013 Patchen
    Award!]
Don't Sing Aloha When I Go by Robert Casella
How to Break Article Noun by Carolyn Chun [2012 Patchen
    Award!]
What Is Art? by Norman Conquest
Elder Physics by James R. Hugunin
Something Is Crook in Middlebrook by James R. Hugunin [2012 *Zoom
    Street* Experimental Fiction Book of the Year!]
OD: Docufictions by Harold Jaffe
Paris 60 by Harold Jaffe
Apostrophe/Parenthesis by Frederick Mark Kramer
Ambiguity by Frederick Mark Kramer
Minnows by Jønathan Lyons
You Are Make Very Important Bathtime by David Moscovich
Xanthous Mermaid Mechanics by Brion Poloncic
Short Tails by Yuriy Tarnawsky
The Placebo Effect Trilogy by Yuriy Tarnawsky
Prism and Graded Monotony by Dominic Ward

For a complete listing of all our titles
please visit us at experimentalfiction.com

22391122R00151

Made in the USA
Charleston, SC
20 September 2013